PRAISE FOR LAURA BRODIE

All the Truth

"Brodie writes with haunting insight about that moment when the world batters down the family door, breaking into the chambers of the heart, fracturing each person's tenuous hold on love and connection—leaving all in ruins until they find ways to recover each other . . . Her elegant prose sings with tautly rendered emotion and characters you'll never forget."   —Jonis Agee, author of *The River Wife*

The Widow's Season

"Brodie expertly walks the line between reality and fantasy, life and death, heartache and love, leaving readers hoping for the best and prepared for the worst—without ever really knowing the truth—until the final five pages."   —*Publishers Weekly*

"In *The Widow's Season*, Brodie draws on literary traditions, but hides the academic stuff under the flow of smart dialogue and sharp detail. This is a work of craft and imagination."   —*The Roanoke Times*

"In *The Widow's Season*, Laura Brodie confronts all the twists and turns of grief and loss, love and marriage, and the human heart with honesty, humor, and great intelligence. This novel is spellbinding, right up to its surprising and poignant final page."   —Ann Hood,
author of *The Knitting Circle*

"*The Widow's Season* is far more than what it seems to be at first—a straightforward story of a woman getting used to a crushing loss. It's smarter, slyer, and more unconventional than that. It's haunting—and haunted too."   —Elizabeth Benedict,
author of *Almost* and *The Practice of Deceit*

One Good Year:
A Mother and Daughter's Educational Adventure

"Brodie's contribution to the field is full of honest revelations that make it vital for anyone considering homeschooling; happily, her gift for good storytelling and keen observation (of herself and others) make this an absorbing read for everyone else."   —*Publishers Weekly* (starred review)

"Engaging, unpredictable. . . . No rosy manifesto to homeschooling, nor a condemnation, but a real-life encounter, full of stormy battles, power struggles and, most of all, passion. There are moments of pedagogic beauty. . . . Graceful and charming."   —*Kirkus Reviews*

"In a world where homeschooling is so often misunderstood, discounted, and even ridiculed, Laura Brodie offers a clear-eyed view and makes a valuable contribution to the literature on the subject. This is necessary reading for anyone with an interest not just in homeschooling but in education generally."   —David Guterson, author of *The Other* and *Family Matters: Why Homeschooling Makes Sense*

"A touching glimpse into a mother-daughter relationship . . . Will inspire you to foster a love of learning no matter what your schooling choice may be."   —Richard Louv, author of *Last Child in the Woods: Saving Our Children from Nature-Deficit Disorder*

"Funny, heart-cracking, and ultimately profoundly educational. I recommend this book to all parents and educators who have ever thought—I wish things could be different."   —Mary Pipher, author of *Seeking Peace: Chronicles of the Worst Buddhist in the World*

"Laura Brodie shines a spotlight on love as an essential ingredient [in homeschooling], creating a well-earned space on all homeschoolers' bookshelves and, optimistically, on the bookshelves of all parents."
—Linda Dobson, author of *The Ultimate Book of Homeschooling Ideas*

"The only thing worse than sending your child off on a bus each morning might be keeping that child at home. But Brodie manages the feat with wit, wisdom, love, and some hard knocks along the way. Her story gives hope that there is more to life than long division."
—Cameron Stracher, author of *Dinner with Dad*

"As a parent involved in homeschooling, I highly recommend this book. It's timely, beautifully written, and must reading for anyone who has ever wondered what homeschooling is all about."
—James Grippando, author of *Money to Burn*

Breaking Out:
VMI and the Coming of Women

"Brodie is an excellent guide. Once you open it, her book is hard to put down."
—Jane Tompkins, author of *A Life in School*

"Brodie tells her story with a light touch and an eye for telling detail."
—Jill Ker Conway, author of *The Road from Coorain*

"A fascinating and highly readable story filled with striking insights into American gender roles and revolutions at the end of the twentieth century. Brodie's book does a wonderful job of demonstrating the pressures for both continuity and change."
—Drew Gilpin Faust, author of *Mothers of Invention*

Titles by Laura Brodie

ALL THE TRUTH

THE WIDOW'S SEASON

ONE GOOD YEAR:
A MOTHER AND DAUGHTER'S EDUCATIONAL ADVENTURE

BREAKING OUT:
VMI AND THE COMING OF WOMEN

ALL THE TRUTH

· Laura Brodie ·

BERKLEY BOOKS, NEW YORK

BERKLEY BOOKS
Published by the Penguin Group
Penguin Group (USA) Inc.
375 Hudson Street, New York, New York 10014, USA

Penguin Group (Canada), 90 Eglinton Avenue East, Suite 700, Toronto, Ontario M4P 2Y3, Canada
(a division of Pearson Penguin Canada Inc.) • Penguin Books Ltd., 80 Strand, London WC2R 0RL,
England • Penguin Group Ireland, 25 St. Stephen's Green, Dublin 2, Ireland (a division of Penguin
Books Ltd.) • Penguin Group (Australia), 250 Camberwell Road, Camberwell, Victoria 3124, Australia
(a division of Pearson Australia Group Pty. Ltd.) • Penguin Books India Pvt. Ltd., 11 Community
Centre, Panchsheel Park, New Delhi—110 017, India • Penguin Group (NZ), 67 Apollo Drive,
Rosedale, Auckland 0632, New Zealand (a division of Pearson New Zealand Ltd.) • Penguin Books
(South Africa) (Pty.) Ltd., 24 Sturdee Avenue, Rosebank, Johannesburg 2196, South Africa

Penguin Books Ltd., Registered Offices: 80 Strand, London WC2R 0RL, England

This book is an original publication of The Berkley Publishing Group.

This is a work of fiction. Names, characters, places, and incidents either are the product of the author's
imagination or are used fictitiously, and any resemblance to actual persons, living or dead, business
establishments, events, or locales is entirely coincidental. The publisher does not have any control over
and does not assume any responsibility for author or third-party websites or their content.

PUBLISHING HISTORY
Berkley trade paperback edition / July 2012

Library of Congress Cataloging-in-Publication Data

Brodie, Laura Fairchild.
All the truth / Laura Brodie.—Berkley trade paperback ed.
p. cm.
ISBN 978-0-425-24763-1 (pbk.)
1. Young women—Fiction.   2. Virginia—Fiction.   3. Domestic fiction.   I. Title.
PS3602.R63486A79 2012
813'.6—dc23
2012001648

PRINTED IN THE UNITED STATES OF AMERICA

10 9 8 7 6 5 4 3 2 1

ALWAYS LEARNING   PEARSON

For Rachel

Tell all the Truth but tell it slant—
Success in Circuit lies
Too bright for our infirm Delight
The Truth's superb surprise
As Light'ning to the Children eased
With explanation kind
The Truth must dazzle gradually
Or every man be blind—

EMILY DICKINSON

PROLOGUE

EMMA was smoothing a blanket across her daughter's shoulders when she first heard the voices. They rose in quiet syllables from the open window, long vowel sounds combined with the rolling consonance of her backyard creek. Occasionally a girl's high laugh punctuated the lower tones, then all fell silent.

She stood and walked to the glass, her eyes wandering downhill past the sandbox and swing set and lightning-warped maple, to where the moon stretched its thin fingers in the water. There she saw them— three college students with silver beer cans glinting. They often appeared this time of year, like ladybugs or garden spiders. Nomadic partygoers, in the last week before graduation, who abandoned their fraternities to drink in the rural Virginia moonlight.

One mile west, old T. A. Hillyer had designated a corner of his farmland as an annual campground for the undergraduates. It was a tradition he had inaugurated when his son was at the college; Hillyer donated Porta-Potties, while the students brought tents and kegs and guitars and hired bluegrass bands to accompany their starlit debaucheries. Earlier that evening, Emma had heard strains of "Soldier's Joy" sifting through her poplar leaves. She had listened on her front porch while the chords, in delicate bubbles of sound, floated east toward the Blue Ridge. Usually the students stayed close to the source of that music. This trio now wandering her yard were probably some of the strays, the loners who preferred to hook up in private pastures.

She blamed herself. Each spring Emma invited senior English majors to an end-of-the-year picnic, circulating detailed maps, so that the location of this peaceful meadow, with its mallards and blue herons and foggy mountains in the distance, was common knowledge among crowds of young strangers.

Her daughter's bedside clock glowed: 10:45. Emma had let Maggie stay up late since it wasn't a school night, and now the child curled on her side, murmuring, "What's that noise?"

"Students." Emma kissed her forehead. "Sleep now while I chase them away."

Downstairs, she lifted a sweater off the hook beside the door and stepped onto the cold slate porch. Rob was visiting his mother in West Virginia; otherwise he would have handled this, tromping in heavy boots and wielding the baseball bat that leaned against their coatrack. "They take advantage of you," he always said. "You're too nice to them."

"Yes," she invariably replied. "I'm way too nice." Now Emma walked barefoot down the yard, wet clover seeping between her toes.

Across the creek the sycamores glittered with lightning bugs. They had risen from the grass just after sunset, dozens ascending in silent flashes while Maggie chased them, darting around the yard with hands cupped in half-moons. She liked to watch the captured bugs crawl through the crevices between her fingers, then spread their wings and relaunch, unfazed by her brief interference in their nightly routine. The insects now hovered high among the tree limbs, and Emma sup-

posed it was the sparkling branches that had attracted the students—
all those lights blinking like hundreds of cameras at a rock concert.

"Hello," she called as she approached the flat creekside, and the
students' conversation stopped as they turned to face her. She recognized them—middling young scholars who had struggled through her
British survey last fall. Perhaps this was a Wordsworthian act, this
impulse to roam the countryside and linger by moonlit streams. Perhaps these kids' beer-sotted brains would finally grasp the concept of
the sublime.

Be patient, Emma chided herself. When she was the students' age,
she too had carried six-packs of beer in brown paper bags, searching
woods and riverbanks for the best midnight party settings. Sometimes
she and her friends had gathered beside a local pond; once they had
played a drunken truth or dare inside a cemetery. But Emma would
never have had the gall to trespass on a professor's property, and that
seemed to be the difference between this generation and her own—
their sense of entitlement, as if all adults existed to serve them.

She liked one of the students, a tall brown-haired boy named Jacob.
All fall he had been a talker, the sort who always had an opinion
about Coleridge or Keats. Whenever the discussion lagged, Jacob could
be counted on to liven things up, although his papers had been disappointing, full of provocative statements but lacking the careful thought
needed to support a thesis. In the end she feared he was all flash
and no substance, and yet, on a dull afternoon, flash counted for something.

Beside him stood a girl whose name Emma never could remember.
She was thoroughly unremarkable, in faded jeans and year-round flip-
flops, her face thin, her flat hair neither brown nor blond. In class, she
had seemed to desire nothing more than to merge with the surrounding walls, which was why Emma had tried to draw her out, coaxing
her with open questions: "What does it mean to *you*, 'Beauty is truth,

truth beauty?'" Invariably the girl would shrug and smile, apparently assuming that any gesture of submission would suffice.

When the third student turned to face her, Emma flinched. She knew him all too well, this sluggish, drawling blond—Kyle Caldwell—the son of an alumnus with deep pockets. Kyle had a way of looking into her face much too intently, as if each of their encounters was a staring contest that Emma would eventually lose. Now she dropped her eyes and saw that the boy had pale, fleshy legs, fluorescent in the moonlight, which reminded her of his paragraphs—flabby and riddled with platitudes.

Still, she had given Kyle a B, in her cowardly generosity. Rarely did she add the dreaded minus to her B's, that infinitesimal sign that a student's work had slipped below Holford College's inflated average. She supposed she didn't want to face the students' nagging protests, or the indignation of helicopter parents. Avoidance of confrontation was Emma's specialty; she imagined herself as a kind of intellectual harbor pilot, steering away from the red buoys, constantly feeling for the main channel. But if anyone deserved her wrath, it was Kyle Caldwell, not because of his flaccid intellect—that was common enough—but because of her suspicion that Kyle was a thief.

He had come to her office once, to talk about a paper that was due the next morning. He hadn't chosen a topic and wanted to be fed one; Emma envisioned him as a gaping maw, always ready to ingest. She had wanted to throw him out, to condemn his aura of privileged sloth, but instead she had offered the usual admonitions against leaving papers to the last minute. He would have no time for revision, no time to *digest,* and Kyle had borne the lecture like a fixated poodle, locked in unblinking attention and confident that the bone would be given at the end.

After he was gone, Emma had stared at her bulletin board with the strange conviction that something was missing. Was it her heart, or her courage? Was it the intellectual standards that she had compromised years ago? She couldn't quantify the absence until the next afternoon, when she saw the item on Kyle's backpack—a blue-and-white button that said *War Is Not the Answer.* He must have taken it off her board when she left the office to xerox a poem for him. She didn't mind his having the button—they were meant to be distributed. What rankled was the feeling that he was subtly mocking her. Beside the old Bush-Cheney buttons that pockmarked his pack, her little circle of peace looked small and harassed.

Emma had done nothing except to counsel her seething brain. *Let it go, let it go.* That was her mantra these days—*Let it all go.* She needed a mantra, anything to lessen the irritation that had been festering in her mind. Over the past few years she had felt a persistent crankiness seeping into her thoughts, and she couldn't tell whether it was a symptom of her stress about getting tenure or an attitude contagious in American popular culture. Anger seemed to be the nation's latest pastime, with all the road rage and Mommy rage, bridezillas and bitches and chefs-from-hell. Anger was marketable.

Emma could never pinpoint the cause of her own frustrations. Was it merely the most difficult students, with their shameless expectations? Or was it her department chair, who always inquired about her day-care arrangements and never about her research? Or was she bothered most of all by the anonymous strangers who left beer bottles and McDonald's cups in the tall grass along the side of her road? Every afternoon when she drove home, plastic grocery bags waved from the branches of redbud trees.

Kyle Caldwell, now teetering from foot to foot in a tipsy dance, seemed to embody all three of her grievances. Throughout the semester he had expected rewards for his most mediocre efforts, and on top of that he had kept calling her "Mrs. Greene," no matter how often she corrected him with "Professor" or "Dr." And that beer can in his hand—that was liable to end up tossed into her neighbors' Queen Anne's lace.

She felt more antagonistic toward this boy than toward any student she had ever encountered, and it wasn't only the missing button—that small crime might easily have been forgiven. But then had come the occasion, shortly before exams, when she realized that her bracelet was missing from her office desk. It was a loose, silver charm bracelet, a good-luck memento from adolescence that she often stretched beside her keyboard. She had noticed its disappearance after a department meeting. Her office door had been standing open, and when she returned, she had immediately sensed the change. After searching through stacks of papers and books, Emma remembered that Kyle had passed her in the hall on the way back from the meeting, coming from the direction of her office.

In a fit of petulance she had telephoned the student president of the honor committee. He was an English major, a former student of hers with a sharp mind that she respected, but when she described her suspicions about Kyle the Kleptomaniac, the young man was skeptical.

"You didn't see him take the bracelet?"

"No, but I told you he has my button."

"Those buttons are everywhere. How do you know that one is yours?"

"I guess I can't prove it."

"Look, we can keep an eye on this guy in case there are other complaints. But in the meantime, why don't you wait awhile and see if the bracelet turns up?"

He was right. Emma hadn't seen Kyle take it; she had no concrete evidence, and to be honest, she was prone to losing things. It would be humiliating to make an accusation, then find the bracelet a month later, fallen behind her desk. *Let it go*, she had told herself. *Don't make a fuss.*

But now, seeing Kyle in her yard with his can of Budweiser, probably pissing on her flowers, she felt the months of simmering tension start to boil.

"Hello, Professor," Jacob said. "We're sorry to intrude." He came forward with a broad smile. "It's such a beautiful night. We were driving by and saw the full moon on your creek, and we had to stop and absorb the view."

Jacob always spoke with a veneer of politeness that Emma suspected was pure affectation, but she appreciated it anyway. His pronunciation was so clear, she wondered if Jacob didn't drink, or maybe he was the type of kid whose tongue was clarified by booze, whose thoughts gained a sharper edge at a certain blood alcohol content.

"I didn't hear your car," she said, and he pointed uphill to where a Range Rover was parked at the side of the road. She nodded. The students were always driving enormous vehicles, oblivious to the rape of Mother Nature.

Emma glanced at the moon, now disappearing behind a cloud. "I'm afraid I have to hurry you along. My daughter is trying to sleep."

"Of course." Jacob kept smiling.

"Do you mind if I use your bathroom before we go?" The invisible girl had spoken.

"Sure." Emma pointed up toward the house. "It's on the ground floor, next to the playroom with all the toys."

Kyle accompanied the girl, staggering uphill toward the lit porch, and as Emma watched she saw him place his arm around the girl's shoulders, both of them breaking into laughter once they had moved beyond their teacher's radius. Emma moved to follow them, not wanting Kyle unsupervised in her house, but Jacob was still talking.

"You can see the Big Dipper, it's upside down." He pointed directly overhead. "And Mars, and maybe Venus."

Emma wasn't in the mood for an astronomy lesson. "If my husband were here, he'd be chasing you off with his baseball bat."

"Sorry again, Professor. But this *is* a gorgeous spot."

Emma's eyes followed the creek downstream, across her neighbors' pasture, where a skeletal barn stood sentinel at the foot of Sleeping Elephant Mountain. The beauty of the mountain's black silhouette, rising from trunk to forehead, to the bony pachyderm spine, softened her mind. This young man, after all, was not the problem. Jacob appreciated Shelley.

"What are you doing after graduation?" she asked.

"Kyle and I"—Emma cringed at the sound of the thief's name spoken aloud—"are going to spend the summer at his parents' beach house. Then we're starting work on Wall Street. His dad is a big-shot banker."

"How lucky for you." Emma turned abruptly and began to walk uphill with Jacob hurrying at her side. What a shame that he was planning to follow his friend's lesser star. She felt as if Kyle had stolen one more thing.

"You and your friend seem inseparable."

"Yes." Jacob nodded. "We went to prep school together. He probably wouldn't have gotten through without me. I was always getting him out of trouble."

And now his father is paying you back, Emma mused, but not aloud. Never aloud.

When they stepped inside the house, they discovered Kyle and the girl coming down from upstairs. What were they doing up there? Emma wondered. Searching her bedroom? Laughing at her dirty laundry? Keeping Maggie awake? There was no limit to these kids' rudeness.

At least the girl seemed embarrassed. "Thanks for the bathroom," she mumbled, heading for the door. Kyle began to follow silently, until Emma glimpsed something purple sticking out of his pocket.

"Wait a second." She blocked his exit. Face-to-face with the boy's burgeoning double chin, Emma reached toward his hip pocket and pulled out a three-inch plastic mermaid with sparkling lavender hair. Behind her Jacob emitted a slow, hissing "Chriiiisssst."

"Empty your pockets," she said. Kyle stood there, dull as a plate.

"Empty your goddamn pockets." Emma's voice had dropped half an octave, into the low animal growl she usually reserved for those evenings when Rob was more than an hour late and hadn't bothered to call.

Kyle reacted instantly. He pulled his pockets inside out, and across the floor tumbled half a dozen Polly Pockets, rubbery clothes shed around tiny naked limbs.

"You are fucking pathetic," Jacob spoke, trying to gain control. "I'm sorry, Professor. Kyle's an idiot."

"What were you going to do with them?" Emma leaned her face within inches of Kyle's nose. "Have a party? Use them for some perverted drinking game? You know Holford has an honor code. I could have you expelled."

"You sure could." Jacob had taken his friend by the elbow and was negotiating him in a wide arc around Emma. "But he isn't worth the trouble, is he?"

She followed them to the door, where the girl was waiting.

"Get out of my house," Emma hissed.

"Yes, ma'am. I'm sorry, Professor." Jacob shoved Kyle out onto the porch, down to the brick walkway. Last of all went the girl, who reached up to push the screen door out of her way.

In that instant Emma saw it. The flash of jangling silver.

"My bracelet!" She ran onto the porch and grabbed the girl's wrist, then turned toward Kyle, holding up the girl's arm as if she had won a prizefight. "You gave my bracelet to your girlfriend!"

The girl wrenched her arm free and hurried to Kyle's side, rubbing her wrist and glaring back at Emma. For once Jacob had nothing to say, his mouth gaping at the offending jewelry.

Only Kyle managed to speak, muttering under his breath, "Crazy bitch."

"*What* did you call me?" For a moment Emma felt dizzy, overwhelmed by the rush of a thousand angry words erupting into her brain, flying from her mouth like molten rock.

"You fat, fucking little thief! I'm turning you in to the honor committee! You can kiss your diploma good-bye!" She spun around and yanked the screen door open.

"Now wait a minute." Jacob hopped up the stairs and approached with palms out, conciliatory. "You don't want to do that. Seven more days and Kyle will be gone. You'll never have to see him again. Why bother with all that trouble?" He smiled into her eyes, and Emma realized that she had misjudged this boy. He wasn't a promising young man; he was an operator, a wheel greaser, the slick facilitator of his criminal sidekick.

She returned his smile with a sarcastic smirk: "What? Afraid you'll lose your meal ticket?"

Jacob's smile disappeared.

Emma pulled the screen door back and stepped inside. Never again would she take this crap. Never again would she be the nice professor, the easy B-plus, the woman who gave unlimited extensions and hosted annual picnics. "Kyle will be hearing from the honor committee tomorrow morning."

"You can't do that," Jacob murmured.

"Watch me." Emma swung the main door shut.

Except that it didn't shut. Not all the way. Jacob had wedged his foot inside and was now inching the door forward with his shoulder.

"I just want to talk to you," he said.

Emma heaved her weight against the wooden door, trying to crush the intruding toes even as she felt them slowly advance.

"C'mon," Jacob said, his voice oily smooth. "Let's work this out."

And suddenly Emma recognized how dark were the surrounding trees, and how far she lived from her nearest neighbor. Her mind flew to her kitchen knives, German blades propped in their wooden block, handles spread in invitation, and she almost laughed out loud. All those years of mute acceptance, all the anger she had suppressed, to culminate in a student's foot, and now his knee, his leg, pushing into her home.

"I just want a word," Jacob said. Through the opening door Emma glimpsed Kyle walking back up the porch stairs, his expression—what was it?—almost smiling.

"One word," Jacob repeated as Emma's fingers groped toward the handle of Rob's wooden bat. Upstairs, she heard a stifled whimper from Maggie, watching through the open inches of her bedroom door.

Witness

Chapter 1

Blood was everywhere—on the floor, the runner, the hall table. So red I thought of fire climbing the walls, and the idea of fire made me want to escape. That's what my mom had taught me, in case of fire. Get out of the house.

From underneath my bed I pulled a folded rope ladder, anchored around the thick wooden bedpost. Mom had put it there a year earlier, always anticipating the worst. She was a woman with a mania for safety, constantly pushing bike helmets and life jackets and water filters. We had smoke alarms in every room. Carbon-dioxide monitors. Three times in the past two years she had talked to me about how to get out of my room in case of fire, and each time I was too short to reach the metal clasps that unlocked the windows. I was only five.

That night the window was already open, letting in the breezes and strange voices. All I had to do was open the screen, and I remembered my mother's instructions: "See these metal rectangles? See how my fingers pinch them in?" I was surprised at how lightly the screen lifted when I pressed the magic buttons.

When I threw the rope ladder out the window, it smacked against our house's aluminum siding, and I was worried that the students might run to this side of the house, see me trying to escape, and wait for me at the bottom rung. But after two minutes, when no one came, I climbed onto the window ledge. Mom had never demonstrated this; she had never tested whether the ladder would hold. Her fire drills were entirely verbal: "Crawl onto the window ledge, holding the ladder tight. Then ease yourself outside slowly and climb down the rungs, just like you've done at preschool, on the rope ladder."

But it wasn't like school. There, my toes could step through the ladder, so that the arches of my feet settled on each wooden cylinder. Here, with the ladder hanging against the side of the house, my toes could barely enter each rung before they hit aluminum. I had to tiptoe down the ladder, which was especially hard, since I was carrying a polar bear. I couldn't leave without Sophie, tucked under my right elbow. So I went down slowly and my toes slipped twice, but each time I held tight. Down, down I climbed into our rhododendron, crouching behind those big leaves until I was sure that the students weren't coming.

Mom had taught me to wait for her beneath the biggest poplar tree; that was our meeting place, in case of fire. But not this time. This time I needed to hide, far from the house. The woods stood thirty yards to my left, black and scary, but not so scary as that stranger who had pushed his way into the hall. To reach the trees I'd have to cross the open yard, and the students, if they turned, might see my white nightgown. But I couldn't stay long beneath the rhododendron; here, they would find me.

Pressing Sophie to my chest, I inched forward in the house's shadow, to the front corner, where, when I glanced around the edge, I could see the porch light shining on the two students still outside, who were too preoccupied to look my way. The boy was standing at our doorway, his eyes fixed on the interior, and the girl—the girl was on her knees, vomiting in the grass. At first I thought it was the sight of all that blood that made her sick. Now I think it was the beer—beer and blood and fear.

With both of them distracted, I bolted for the trees, hoping they wouldn't notice a white streak racing across the dark. The grass was wet and cold and sometimes sharp, but I didn't cry. I was a silent comet disappearing into the night.

CHAPTER 2

"So what happened next?"

Maggie opened her eyes and sat upright, startled by the deep male voice. Normally the doctor was so quiet she could lean back, shut her eyes, and disappear into her thoughts, rambling on and on, "white streak . . . black woods . . . bloody walls." The doctor seemed to like blood—he was always asking about it—so Maggie emphasized the gore.

She must have begun to fall asleep; otherwise he wouldn't have interrupted. Maggie often got drowsy in the afternoons, and this couch was so comfortable, with its soft suede upholstery and all the cushy pillows. She ran her fingers across the fabric, leaving four brown stripes running against the grain, then relaxed back into her habitual slouch, thinking how she would love to stretch her legs across this suede, to curl on her side and nap for hours. That would be the best therapy of all, to retreat to the doctor's office each afternoon and sleep. She had read somewhere that teenagers needed extra hours of dozing; they were like pregnant women, with a new life growing inside them.

Maggie hadn't been sleeping well for the past few weeks. Her dreams were back; she thought she had left them behind years ago, but now they were recurring nightly, full of twisted fragments of the students and her mother, and the darkness of the woods. When she was five years old, her dreams had been steady, nightly terrors, replaying scenes and words and colors. Her father's first response had been to buy a dreamcatcher that he hung from the top of her pink canopy bed, saying, "This will catch the bad ones, and leave the good." Maggie had liked the concept so much that even now she wore dreamcatcher earrings with tiny feathers that matched her long reddish-brown hair; they stroked her jawbone whenever she shook her head.

The pink canopy had been jettisoned by middle school, replaced by a collection of Johnny Depp posters, so that these days Edward Scissorhands stared down at Maggie from the ceiling above her bed.

"*That* would give me nightmares." Her dad had shuddered when she hung the poster. He had been lounging beside Maggie on her covers, assessing the young man with frazzled hair and dark lipstick whose moping eyes were destined to gaze at his daughter all night. Across the room, Sweeney Todd leered beneath his Bride of Frankenstein hairdo while Jack Sparrow held a heavily jeweled finger to his lips. Rob had sighed. What was it about these drag-queen images that enticed his child? Strange that a girl who never wore makeup could tolerate so much eyeliner on a middle-aged man.

"Johnny Depp is cool," Maggie had explained. "If he showed up in my sleep, that would be a *wonderful* dream."

While her father watched, she had stood on her mattress and Scotch-taped the dreamcatcher to Edward Scissorhands' chest, so that the string dangling toward her bed might connect her heart to Johnny's. Every night since then, the dreamcatcher's circle had slowly rotated right then left, a weather vane tuned to the barometric pressure of her desires.

Of course those bits of string and feather had never stopped a nightmare from invading her sleep, which was why her dad had introduced Maggie to the doctor nine years ago, saying, "He's a living dreamcatcher." Supposedly the doctor would filter her memories by daylight so that they would not haunt her sleep, and Maggie had to admit, the man seemed to know his business. By first grade her dreams had faded, until her weekly therapy dwindled to monthly sessions, then quarterly. She hadn't seen the doctor at all for the past five years.

But now the nightmares had returned, so Maggie was back on the couch, sifting through the past while the doctor's voice murmured quietly, as if he were speaking to her through a soft veil.

"Tell me what happens next."

"You've heard this dream a hundred times."

"Tell me again."

He reminded Maggie of the kids she babysat for, always wanting to hear their bedtime stories again and again. Especially the violent ones—witches and wolves and bloodsucking monsters, all wild for children's flesh.

"Tell me one more time."

But Maggie didn't feel like telling. Instead, she inspected her fingernails, bitten down to bleeding stubs. Last week she had painted them red with black-and-white yin/yang symbols, but now they were so chipped they looked like bits of Nazi confetti. She balled her fingers into fists and crossed her arms, glancing around at the creamy-white walls and pausing at the same diplomas she had sounded out, letter by letter, as a young child. Kenneth David Riley. Swarthmore, Columbia, UVA. Bachelor, Master, Doctor. The academic titles sounded like roles in a sex game, and Maggie supposed it was her part to play the bachelorette, the slave, the patient laid bare.

She didn't mind. Last week, when Maggie returned to the doctor after their years of separation, she had noticed something that hadn't struck her in elementary school—that Dr. Riley was a handsome man, dark-haired, with deep blue eyes and muscles in his forearms that tightened whenever he rolled his cuffs back from his wrists—his signal that they were getting down to some serious therapy. He was precisely Maggie's type—or so she liked to imagine—quiet and intellectual, with a brooding attractiveness. Twenty years younger and he might have been part of the *Twilight* cast, right down to his pale throat, chiseled chin, and well-defined cheekbones.

Come sit beside me, she wanted to say to the good doctor. *Lay your head in my lap and I will whisper my dreams into your ears.* Her eyes settled on the gray hairs multiplying at his temples and she sighed. Mortality was a terrible thing.

The doctor waited until Maggie's gaze had moved across his face, then he spoke directly into her eyes: "It helps to describe the whole dream."

Maggie smiled grimly. The whole dream, the whole truth, and nothing but the truth. That's what everyone wanted from her—a pile of violent words—because she was the girl with the story, witness to a murder that came back to her in strange, distorted dreams, so that it was hard to say how much was real and how much was nightmare.

Maggie had never told anyone the whole truth. In fact, when she was five, she had refused to say anything at all. She didn't have a single word to spare for the police, or even for her father, and at nine years' distance it was hard to say what had been going on inside her preschool brain, except some vague notion that the adult world had betrayed her, and her silence was a cleansing vow.

Part of Dr. Riley's task had been to excavate her story, to uncover all the broken shards that she was trying to bury. The doctor specialized in messed-up kids, mostly girls abused by their families—beaten, raped, locked in closets—their bodies starved down to the spindly texture of harpsichord keys. His office contained a wooden chest full

of stuffed animals that smelled like cedar, and on his shelves, inter-
spersed with books and ferns, stood a Lite-Brite and a tea set and boxes
of Play-Doh, as if the psychologist had never quite abandoned his own
childhood.

His method in their early days had involved toys and crayons and
lots of seemingly innocent questions: "Why is the house on fire?"
"What is the polar bear thinking?" For months Dr. Riley had collected
each fragment of Maggie's speech, each splinter of memory, as if it
were a tiny fossil, something to be dusted and inspected and pieced
with all the other bits until he could reconstruct the entire skeleton
of one night. Over the course of two years he had fitted her words
together until he had a complete rib cage, a skull, and a spine. Everything that is left behind when the soul has fled.

But as with all reconstructions, the doctor could only gather a
limited amount of evidence—a jawbone here, a vertebra there—the
rest was educated guesswork, and Maggie felt proud that she hadn't
revealed everything. She knew that the doctor was working under
some false assumptions, and she felt no hurry to enlighten him. There
was power in withholding key pieces of her puzzle—something to keep
this handsome man interested. And there was also the fundamental
matter of her privacy; even as a preschooler, Maggie had known that
some memories weren't meant to be shared.

"STAY with me, Maggie." Doctor Riley's voice had slipped into its low
coaxing tone. "Is this when the students come looking for you?"

Yes. From her spot twenty feet into the woods, Maggie could see
them walking across the grass, and the fat boy was calling, "Hey little
girl . . . Come on out. We won't hurt you."

His voice was sickly sweet, as if he couldn't even fake being nice.

Then the girl spoke, her face white and voice quivering. "I want to go . . . Let's get out of here. Please."

Fat Boy ignored her. He peered again into the woods and teased: "Come out, come out, wherever you are." When he advanced to the edge of the trees, Maggie realized that her nightgown was going to give her away. Enough flecks of moonlight shone through the branches, catching the white cotton, that he was likely to spot bits and pieces glowing beyond the leaves. He reached up with his fleshy arm and pushed a branch out of the way, then stared right in her direction with a slight smile and murmured, very quietly, "I spy with my little eye . . . "

It felt like one of those moments when a person sees a deer in the woods, and both human and animal freeze, assessing each other's eyes. Then the deer leaps and bolts, offering a glimpse of its white tail. That was Maggie, running off through the trees, leaving only the flash of her pale nightgown.

"And does he chase you?" the doctor asked.

"I don't know. That's when I woke up."

"But in real life he never chased you?"

Maggie shrugged, looking out the window at a maple nodding in the October wind. She didn't care much for real life, which was why so many books she consumed at home were filled with dragons and wizards and demons. Tolkien, Rowling, Pullman—they understood that fantasy wasn't an escape so much as a better lens for viewing the world.

"In *real life*, the students didn't come looking for me at all. I don't know if they ever saw me running across the yard. They just got into their car and drove off."

"And you stayed in the woods?"

Yes. She stayed in the woods.

"How did that feel?"

Stupid question, how did he think it felt? How would it feel for a terrified five-year-old to hide alone in the dark woods? Not even alone—surrounded by possums and foxes and skunks, prowling and staring and baring their teeth. But it wasn't the animals that had worried Maggie on that May night; she was more afraid of the shadow demons, the shapeless monsters she had often imagined seeping through her bedroom walls and standing at the foot of her bed, mimicking a dresser or a coat on a chair. Alone in the woods, she had felt them closing in, crawling down from the treetops, the air heavy with their breath, so she had sat on the ground with her back to a thirty-foot ash, pulling her knees to her chest with Sophie squished between, putting her forehead down on the tops of her kneecaps.

How did it feel? Like every inch of her body was screaming but she didn't dare make a sound.

"Scary," Maggie said aloud, looking into the doctor's eyes. "It felt scary."

Bland adjectives provided the best defense whenever the conversation grew too painful. They cued the doctor to back off, and today Maggie found him as obliging as ever.

"You had a birthday last Friday."

"Yes," said Maggie. "I'm fifteen now."

"Did you do anything special to celebrate?"

Maggie smiled. "My dad let me take the day off from school and we went to Jump Mountain Lodge. We spent two days hiking and canoeing."

"Was it nice?"

"Yeah, really nice. Especially getting to miss school."

The doctor paused. "How is school going?"

Maggie shrugged. "School is school; it never changes much."

"High school is a big step, don't you think?"

She sighed. "The building is big, and there are a lot more people.

But it still comes down to classrooms and tests, a cafeteria, and PE. Same routine as elementary school, just more homework and a lot of moving from room to room."

"What do you think of your teachers?"

Maggie stared into her right palm, wondering whether the branches at the bottom of her lifeline represented children, or husbands, or multiple deaths. "You've been talking to my dad."

"Yes."

Maggie smiled without lifting her eyes. One thing about Dr. Riley—he was always forthright when confronted. She never would have agreed to these sessions if she didn't feel that he was being absolutely straight with her.

"Your dad's a little concerned. He says you've been having problems with your geometry teacher."

"Not exactly problems. It's not like I even talk to her much."

"But you don't like her?"

No, Maggie didn't like Mrs. Murdock, and it was hard to say why. The woman wasn't strict, or angry, or unfair. She wasn't fake or hypocritical—Maggie's chief complaints against the adult world. Nor was she trying to impress anyone with her looks. Maggie hated it when teachers wore too much makeup, or high heels, or blouses unbuttoned down to the lacy edges of their bras, as if they, like all the other females in the building, wanted to impress the boys.

Maggie didn't care much about boys. She didn't wear mascara or perfume or part her bangs at the side. Her only nod to fashion came in seven pairs of Converse Hi Tops, arranged in a rainbow on her closet floor, red fading to pink fading to white with black checks. Beyond that, she stuck to ripped blue jeans and crewneck T-shirts— which was why she thought she should have liked Mrs. Murdock, because the math teacher didn't seem to care about clothing either. Every day, the woman wore solid-colored knee-length skirts, long-sleeved white blouses, and a well-worn pair of flat brown sandals. She stood at the blackboard, rarely facing the class, offering the students a continual view of her blond-streaked bun, with half a dozen bobby pins sticking out every which way like an abandoned game of KerPlunk.

Maggie assumed that Mrs. Murdock was shy, and she usually liked shy people. She figured they must have more going on inside their heads than all the usual blatherers. Most people let their thoughts spill like leaky faucets, but Maggie imagined that shy people had thousands of untapped ideas they might share with a patient listener. That's why she enjoyed sitting with the quiet girls in the cafeteria. Her dad told her that shy children often had the best minds; they would accomplish great things as adults.

Admittedly, he had said it because Maggie was painfully shy throughout the first half of elementary school. Up until the third grade she had kept quiet in class, sensing that she was different from the other children—the only grade schooler with a therapist. By age nine Maggie had begun to open herself to the world, reaching out to the kindred girls who seemed shy and smart and disenchanted—the one social circle where she could play queen of the hill. Adolescence had prompted a brief return to her shell, but she still could muster enough confidence to start a conversation at lunch.

"Do you think the problem is math anxiety?" the doctor interjected.

"What do you mean?"

"Are you good at math?"

"It's my worst subject."

"So could you be transferring your feelings about the subject onto the teacher?"

Maggie doubted it. "Mrs. Murdock is just weird. She gives me the creeps. I mean, she won't look me in the eye, and when people won't look at you, it makes them seem guilty."

"Eye contact is important," the doctor agreed. "But I'm sure you know Anna Kennedy, who owns the ice cream shop. She never looks into her customers' eyes."

"Mrs. Kennedy has Asperger's; she talks about it openly. Are you saying my math teacher has some kind of autism?"

"Not at all. I'm just suggesting that people have all kinds of reasons for their behaviors. In some cultures, direct eye contact is considered rude."

Maggie shook her head and felt the feathers on her earrings brush across her cheeks. "That's mostly for looking at the opposite sex."

Dr. Riley smiled. "You're a smart girl, Maggie. But you don't know your teacher's background, so you can't understand her motives. Mrs. Murdock is brand-new, and she's probably just as nervous as all of you ninth graders. Maybe you could try being nice to her."

There it was, thought Maggie. The social burden assigned to all quiet girls—*niceness*. At school, no one instructed the male athletes to be nice. No one pressured them to befriend new, nervous teachers, or include outcasts at their lunch tables. Maybe their moms suggested a little compassion now and then, realizing all the while that consideration of other people's feelings was their own, gendered chore, especially if they were the quiet type—because kindness wasn't even expected of all females. On reality TV the producers rewarded women's viciousness with tens of thousands of dollars, and at school the popular girls were too busy checking their hair in reflective surfaces to worry about other people's feelings. A teacher might tell them not to be mean, but rarely did the adults expect genuine empathy. And yet, Maggie could remember numerous occasions throughout her life when adults had encouraged her to be nice to the other children, be sweet with the little ones, be amiable toward the senior citizens. Was it something in her face that seemed to guarantee kindness to strangers? Was it written in the constellation of her freckles?

Ninety percent of the time she was willing to oblige, but lately she'd been experiencing that other ten percent, rolling her eyes at all the usual injunctions for female altruism. She supposed it was teenage hormones that made her feel ungenerous, but whatever the cause, she figured it was someone else's turn to befriend the new teacher. Maybe some boy who fancied Euclid could entice the geometry teacher to look him in the eye.

"Well," said Maggie. "We'll see how it goes."

CHAPTER 3

"WHY do you think the dream's are back?"

Maggie's dad always asked questions on the way home from therapy. When she was five, he had attended her sessions, sitting in the adjacent study with the door cracked so that he could listen without being seen. But now she was too old to tolerate spies, and he had to pry her for information, just like Dr. Riley. Men were always prying.

"I don't know." She turned away from him to stare out the car window, her nose almost touching the glass. They were passing through the four-block radius of Jackson, Virginia's downtown, where the streets were lined with brick shops nearly two hundred years old. Here was a knickknack store inviting passersby with pine-scented candles, and here was a cooking shop with three varieties of hot sauce displayed in a pyramid: Scorned Woman, Sudden Death, and Maggie's favorite: Ass in the Tub. Next came the bookstore, its pair of gray Persians curled in the window, fur pressed against glass, followed by the courthouse with its sparrow-strewn cannons and sunken Veterans' Memorial, where the garden club maintained patriotic annuals: red geraniums, white pansies, and purplish-blue lupines.

When they stopped at a red light, a carriage pulled up beside Maggie, drawn by two dark brown horses. The carriage didn't resemble those fancy Cinderella coaches she had seen in Central Park, with open tops and red velvet seats and newlyweds touching under fleece blankets. This plain rectangle, shaded by a canvas roof, held three wooden benches where handfuls of aging tourists fidgeted on long leather cushions. At the moment, the tourists were squinting skyward while a guide in a Confederate uniform pointed out the copper steeple of an Episcopal church where Robert E. Lee had served as senior warden.

Maggie supposed that these strangers found her town picturesque. They probably envisioned life in Jackson as charming and safe and full of conservative family values, and if this had been one of her ninety percent days, she might have smiled at them. At a minimum she would have granted that the area was pretty, with its narrow streets rolling west through tree-filled neighborhoods, before giving way to pasture and woods at the foot of the Alleghenies. These days, however, the complacency of it all made her want to drop a hydrogen bomb.

"The doctor says times of stress can trigger bad dreams." Maggie was surprised to hear her own voice, uttering the longest sentence she had offered to her dad in weeks.

"Have you been feeling stressed?" he asked.

She sighed and leaned her forehead against the glass. This was why she didn't talk to her dad much lately—he was sweet, but utterly clueless. Of course she was stressed, trying to survive the first few months of high school. Two weeks before the opening day she had started to feel sick to her stomach, which meant that she had been nauseous for seventy days. She had dropped five pounds from her already stick-thin body, and not intentionally. Maggie was not like the skinny girls at school who jabbered on about how fat they were, devouring brownie sundaes at the local ice cream shop, then puking their guts out as soon as they got home. She would have gladly gained weight, if she could have mustered an appetite, but Maggie hadn't been hungry for the past two months—another reason why her dad had suggested a new round of therapy. He said she was too thin and pale.

Look in the mirror, Daddy, she had wanted to reply. *Check out the scarecrow.* But Maggie could never bring herself to be cruel to her father. In middle school she had listened to other kids insult their parents, laughing at their fathers' frumpy bellies and their mothers' doublewide rear ends. It had shocked her, how crudely dismissive the children could be, so biting in their judgments and convinced of their own superiority.

She suspected that the other kids mocked her dad too, when she wasn't around, although not for his weight. Her dad had never been fat, and his body, once lean and strong, now seemed to be aging before its time, all bony and concave. In a crowd of middle-aged dads, he looked like Gilligan on an island of Skippers. He even had Gilligan's face— those wide brown eyes and froggy mouth with the lower lip protruding slightly. Most of the local men his age suffered from bulging stomachs, with wives at home cooking pot roast and mashed potatoes and peach pie, but Maggie and her father resembled two skeletons, performing a nightly *danse macabre* over their Kraft macaroni and cheese.

"Sure I'm stressed." She spoke without lifting her forehead from the window. These days the only kids who weren't stressed were the ones who didn't care about college, or whose parents didn't care, because it was the parents who caused the tension; the weight of their expectations hovered like an extra layer of gravity. Most of the girls Maggie knew had been biting their nails since fifth grade, sensing that they were being tested, sifted, and tracked, monitored by parents who were anxious for their children to stand out above the crowd.

Maggie's dad was better than most. If anything, he had wanted her to lighten up in middle school, and not stay up so late doing homework. "Grades don't really matter," he said, "until you get to high school."

Now everything mattered. Every bad grade could be used against her. Her report cards would be part of a permanent record viewed by dozens of strangers who would evaluate her based on scraps of the alphabet: A, B, C. Not that Maggie had ever made a C, or even a B, more than once. For her, grades weren't the issue. Maggie fretted that she wasn't involved in enough extracurricular activities, and those faceless admissions officers would be looking for that too. A passion for reading wouldn't be enough to attract them; she must be able to present herself as a well-rounded person, and Maggie was nothing but a collection of sharp angles.

Most smart kids were good at music; they could shine on a violin or a trombone, and she had tried to fit that mold, struggling at the piano for seven years. But she didn't have much to show for it besides a choppy rendition of the *Moonlight* Sonata. She would never win any contests or accompany the school choir, and that's what they would care about, those hypercritical admissions teams. Seven years of piano and no blue ribbons? No recording contract? Nothing to make her extraordinary—every college applicant must be extraordinary.

Athletics were worse. In elementary school Maggie had performed the PE dance common among nerdy girls, shuffling her feet in the outfield during kickball and softball, praying that pop flies wouldn't come her way. She could run with the crowd on a soccer field, but avoided all contact with the ball. Ultimately, she was grateful to the male teachers in middle school who seemed to have given up on the girls, letting them stroll the edges of the gym with pedometers strapped to their belt loops, chatting about Saturday plans while the boys played basketball.

So what should she write on a college entrance essay? That she was a member of the chess club? Which was true, she had been the club secretary in middle school, not that she especially liked the game. The more she played it, the more she realized that she didn't care about most of the pieces. It was okay with her if someone ate her bishop, the stodgy prick—or her pompous knights, always rearing their horses. She pitied the pawns, trapped in their small, forward steps, only capable of moving in a new direction if they were going to kill someone.

But the queen—Maggie cared about her. She chafed when some boy's idiot knight hemmed her in. The female should be all-powerful, but the masculine world conspired against her. The military, the Catholic Church, they were all bent on crushing female power. *Kill my king,* Maggie thought, *but let the queen survive.*

The one time Maggie confessed all these worries to her dad, one week before high school began, he told her that ninth grade was way too early to panic about college. She should get her feet on the ground at the new school, make friends, and try to have fun. A lot could happen in four years—her life might take on new directions; she might develop unexpected interests.

"And if you want an activity, why don't you join the school newspaper? You're one of the best writers in your class."

She knew he was thinking of her mother, the English professor with the flair for polished paragraphs, and a part of Maggie wanted to be like her mom, to look like her, write like her, echo her voice on a page. But most of the time Maggie couldn't bear to envision her mother, and regardless, she had cringed at the thought of writing silly high school stories about lame events: football scores and pep rallies and prom decorations.

"You could be the editor eventually, if you worked your way up."

At that, Maggie had paused. She enjoyed the idea of a weekly forum for blasting school lunches and standardized tests and sex-ed curriculums that preached abstinence and never mentioned contraception. Editorials could channel her ten percent days, transforming disaffection into a résumé builder. If she could rally the other smart, quiet girls at school, they might form a team of prefeminist rabble-rousers.

But then Maggie had contemplated the brunt of an editor's job—managerial chores, staff assignments, and worst of all, proofreading other writers' submissions. She didn't want to correct the puerile writing of careless classmates. Maggie would be happy to check her own work and the writing of a few special friends, but she had no desire to make all the other kids look good. She would rather publish their paragraphs in all their grotesque deformity: infantile subject-verb sentence patterns, misplaced commas, and absent apostrophes. Why should someone always clean up after the laziest students? Their syntactical messes. Their lunchroom messes. Their bloody messes. Students always left a mess.

Maggie lifted her forehead from the car window, leaned back into her seat, and closed her eyes. Her thoughts had come full circle to the core problem plaguing her mind over the past few weeks—the real cause, she supposed, of her dreams' return, and something she couldn't tell her dad. She had felt the problem sharply on the first day of school, in the hallways and at the lockers, surrounded by all those other kids who were laughing and flirting, the tangibility of their bodies striking her like a pungent odor. They resembled miniature college students—the girls all chesty enough, the boys asshole enough—and Maggie hated college students. She saw them all over town, sunbathing on sorority lawns and playing volleyball at frat houses; tutoring at her middle school in Spanish, French, and algebra; shopping at the Safeway—the freshmen pushing cartfuls of soda and the seniors buying beer. Maggie didn't want to go to a university and be one of them. In fact, she had never wanted to go to college at all, but try telling *that* to a parent. How could she explain to her father that all of her school days had been preparation for a goal she despised?

"You want to get some pizza?"

Maggie opened her eyes as her dad gestured toward the upcoming Domino's on the right—their third pizza in seven days.

"No," she murmured. "How about Mexican?"

CHAPTER 4

MAGGIE'S dream came quickly that night. She'd been asleep for less than an hour when she heard voices outside her window—distant, almost indistinguishable, except as male and female, and as she waited in silence, they approached her house.

Staring up from her pillow, Maggie noticed the pink canopy. She turned on her side, rising to her elbow to examine a dollhouse on the floor, full of Calico Critters: tiny cats and pandas and rodents dressed like 1950s schoolchildren. Her eyes turned to the open window as the voices grew more distinct, uttering words like *wasted* and *completely shit-faced*.

The couple had reached the porch stairs; Maggie could hear flip-flops slapping against slate. Next came the high-pitched sound of the screen door, whining open and smacking shut, followed by the dull creak of wood as the students stepped into the downstairs hallway. "Nice place," the female voice spoke, and from the direction of their steps Maggie knew that the pair were entering the playroom at the far end of the house.

She felt a flicker of shame, remembering how her mother had yelled at her earlier that evening for never picking up the room. Her naked Barbies and Polly Pockets still lay sprawled across chairs and tables, while a ruined landscape of miniature LEGOs crisscrossed the carpet, remnants of a zoo that once housed three-inch plastic dinosaurs.

Maggie listened to the students' giggles, wondering if they were laughing at the way she cut her Barbies' hair into bristling crew cuts, or the preschool paintings on her wall: lollipop trees and blue skies straight as rulers. She heard a few notes plunked on her alligator xylophone, initially tuneless, then shaped into an idle "Mary Had a Little Lamb." A toilet flushed, and the voices migrated back into the hallway, toward the front door, before stopping.

"No," the female said.

"It will only take a minute."

"I don't want to."

"*I don't want to.*" The male voice mimicked the female in a high sarcastic tone. "Just for a second. C'mon."

The creaking of a step told Maggie that the students were coming upstairs. Instinctively she drew back toward the wall, pulling her covers over her nose and across her cheekbones, so that only her eyes peered out. Footsteps paused at the top of the stairs, then moved across the hall into her parents' bedroom. Drawers scraped open and shut and Maggie recognized the tinny chords of her mother's jeweled music box, a tiny grand piano that played *Für Elise*.

Box springs groaned.

"We shouldn't," the female voice protested.

"Just for a second," the male replied. Another complaint from the springs was followed by chuckles, then the footsteps drifted back into the hall as the students began wandering from room to room, opening drawers, inspecting closets, gradually approaching her door. Maggie pressed Sophie against her chest, wishing her hardest, most solemn wish that these strangers would go away.

"Shhhhh," her door whispered across the carpet and the overhead light switched on. Squinting in the glare, Maggie saw a large boy in khaki knee-length shorts and black strap sandals, his fat white legs scribbled with strawberry-blond hair. The T-shirt that hung over his distended belly pictured a cartoon drawing of a shark about to swallow an unsuspecting diver. Even with her limited preschool literacy, Maggie could read the words: *Life Is Crap.* The student didn't seem to notice Maggie; he walked to the dresser, where he opened her purple box full of ribbons and barrettes, then he lifted her puppy-shaped piggy bank and jingled the coins. Finally he took her purple brush and looked into the mirror, styling his blond hair and smiling at himself, until his hand stopped abruptly. Within the mirror's image, over his right shoulder, he had seen the pink canopy and the wide, dark eyes, staring. For a moment he stared back into the mirror, looking directly into Maggie's eyes as if challenging her: What was she going to do about it? Maggie didn't blink; her eyes grew larger until the student dropped his gaze, staggered one step back, then hurried to the door without ever turning to face her. The room fell dark again as he switched off the light and pulled the door shut.

In the hall, the female voice asked, "What is it?" as the door opened again, and a girl's giggling face peered inside. When she saw Maggie, the student fell silent while they looked into each other's eyes. The stranger's features were dark, with the hall light outlining her intrusive silhouette, but Maggie thought she could discern the words *I'm sorry* form across the girl's lips as she pulled the door shut quietly, slowly, until only a thin stripe of light remained on Maggie's face.

New sounds rose outside the window, until Maggie could distinguish her mother's voice, uttering the word *inseparable.*

"Shit." The fat boy hurried to the stairs, and Maggie heard the couple's steps descending.

She woke just as the screen door creaked open.

AT lunch the next day Maggie nibbled a peanut-butter-and-jelly sandwich and a few carrot sticks before folding her arms on the cafeteria table and putting her head down. She needed to tell her dad to stop packing these lunches. PB&J was too ghetto and juvenile; did he think she was eight years old? Usually the jelly soaked through the bread or squished out from the sides, smearing the inside of the Ziploc bags that her dad recycled every day, washing them out and inserting another soggy sandwich. Most of the high schoolers bought lunch, even if the food was terrible—Wheatzza and Salisbury steak and stale tortilla salads.

"Are you okay?" Kate McConnell, Maggie's best friend, sat down beside her, pushing an orange plastic tray with a plate covered in fish nuggets and french fries. "Corpulent Kate," the other kids called her, or, in their cruelest moods, "Kate the Cow," due to the extra inches of flesh distributed across her body. Normally Kate had straight brown hair that hung to the middle of her back, but lately she'd been experimenting with curlers, so that now, as she scooched her chair toward the table, dozens of cylindrical ringlets bobbed around her ears.

"Nice hair," Maggie murmured, turning her face sideways to watch Kate dip an anchor-shaped nugget into ketchup.

Kate rolled her eyes. "Yeah, right." Pausing to look straight at Maggie, she pinched two curls between her thumbs and index fingers and pulled them down to the left and right of her face, touching her shoulders. When she let go, they bounced back up, veering back and forth. "I have a head full of Slinkies. I'm hoping they'll settle down if I keep brushing . . . Anyway"—she shrugged—"you look worse than me."

"Thanks."

"More nightmares?" Kate asked, and Maggie nodded.

Kate knew all about Maggie's dreams. Their friendship dated back to early preschool, which gave Kate special standing in Maggie's world. Maggie divided her life into before and after "the night," and since Kate straddled both sides of the calendar, B.N. and A.N., she served as Maggie's most trusted companion. Kate knew, for instance, about her friend's sessions with Dr. Riley. In fact, she was the first person to suggest that the doctor was handsome. She referred to him as Maggie's "beau"; every session was a date.

"Did you tell Dr. Hottie about your dreams?"

"Yep." Maggie nodded.

"What did he say?"

"He told me to be nice to Mrs. Murdock."

Kate bit into three french fries at one time. "What has that got to do with anything?"

Maggie sighed. "He thinks I'm stressed out about school."

"Well, duhhhh." Kate rolled her eyes again. "Did you tell him he's a genius? You gonna eat those Oreos?"

Maggie slid a small stack of cookies, folded in Saran Wrap, toward Kate. Every day Kate acquired part of Maggie's lunch—the apple slices that had turned slightly brown, or a banana with too many dark spots, or a nectarine with one bruise that had dripped juice into the bottom of her lunch bag. Maggie had hundreds of reasons for rejecting food, but Kate appreciated every bite. A few more years, Maggie thought, and she and Kate could pass for Laurel and Hardy.

"Dr. Riley thinks I might be suffering from math anxiety."

Kate shook her head, curls bouncing. "You always make A's in math, just like everything else."

"Not this year." Maggie sat up and unzipped the backpack that hung on the back of her chair. She pulled out two sheets of stapled white paper, and slid them in front of Kate, who glanced at the red writing circled at the top: 78—C.

"Wow. Sorry about that. But I guess one C won't kill you."

"I got a C on the last test too," Maggie replied. "You know what two C's stand for?"

"No, what?"

"Community college."

"Ouch." Kate pulled apart an Oreo and scraped the white filling with her teeth. "Will your dad freak out?"

"My dad always claims that he just wants me to be happy—but that's easier to say when your kid is making A's."

"Do you think you messed up your tests because you're not sleeping?"

Maggie shrugged. "I'm doing fine in my other classes. I just can't concentrate in math because Mrs. Murdock is so weird. It's like, sometimes I think she's watching me when I'm taking a test, so I keep glancing up to try and catch her in the act, but then her eyes are always shifted down, like I just barely missed her."

"That's what you get for taking honors geometry." Kate twisted open another Oreo. "If you were average like the rest of us, you could sign up for algebra with Mr. Wheeler. He takes us outside to play kickball, and passes out jelly beans whenever you get a question right."

"I suck at kickball even worse than math." Maggie sighed. "Anyway, you want to know the worst part? Yesterday after class Mrs. Murdock asked me if I could stick around after school today. She says she wants to talk to me about my work . . . I was thinking maybe I should call my dad and go home sick—say I've got bad cramps or something."

Kate shook her head. "Better to get it over with."

Maggie slouched low in her chair and stared across the room at the cafeteria's far wall. The pep club had painted *Go Lions!* in red and gold, and the art club had begrudgingly added basketballs, soccer balls, and footballs. The club president, however, was a Dalí fan, so the balls were melting or half folded, providing a droopy commentary on the teams' losing streaks.

Kate eyed Maggie while sipping her chocolate milk. "You want me to meet you at her room after school? For, like, moral support?"

"Sure," said Maggie. "You probably shouldn't come in the door, but it would be great if you could wait for me right outside."

AT three o'clock Kate negotiated the cinder-block labyrinth that led to Mrs. Murdock's classroom. Jackson High School was a dismal Habitrail, with low ceilings, fluorescent lights, and red and gold stripes on every wall, locker, and linoleum floor. Scotch-taped posters extolling the evils of drugs and alcohol marked the entries to stairwells and bathrooms, and slivers of graffiti scratched into orange-painted columns announced the names of girls who had recently lost their virginity.

When Kate reached Mrs. Murdock's door, she waved to Maggie, gave her a thumbs-up, then glanced around to make sure no teachers were visible before she extracted her cell phone from her purse and started texting. Maggie was sitting quietly in the classroom's back row. Mrs. Murdock's geometry was her last class of the day, so she hadn't risen from her chair for the past hour. She had hoped there might be a crowd of C-makers huddled in a group, prepared to endure the same lecture, but all the other students had filed out after the bell, until she and the teacher were alone. Mrs. Murdock was absorbed in the papers on her desk, and she did not raise her eyes as she said, "Come on up here, Maggie."

The desk stood at the opposite end of the room, and as Maggie crossed the gold-specked linoleum, she realized that this classroom troubled her just as much as the teacher. Because Mrs. Murdock was new, she had been assigned one of the school's thin windowed hovels, scarcely brightened by the ficus trees and posters of Greece (the birthplace of geometry!) that Mrs. Murdock had spread over the walls. Maggie suspected that this depressing space had begun to affect the woman's mind, the dearth of sunlight and air producing the same deadly malaise as carbon monoxide.

She paused before her teacher's desk, thinking that the woman would now have to lift her face and look into a student's eyes.

Or not. "Stand over here beside me." Mrs. Murdock spoke without glancing up.

Maggie moved to her teacher's right shoulder and was surprised to see that Mrs. Murdock wasn't grading tests or quizzes. She was doing sudoku puzzles—three at a time—puzzle books propped open with large quartz paperweights.

"Isn't it confusing, to do more than one puzzle?" Maggie asked.

Mrs. Murdock's pencil hesitated over a blank square. "Do you ever read more than one book at a time?"

Good point, thought Maggie, envisioning the stack of novels waiting on her bedside table.

"If I find a really good book," Maggie replied, "I'll read it straight through, not stopping for anything else. But most of the time I have two or three books going at once."

"It's like that with my sudoku," Mrs. Murdock explained. "If I'm absorbed in one puzzle and making progress, I'll keep at it. But usually I get stuck halfway through, and I find that if I try a different puzzle for a while, when I return to the old one I can see it with new eyes . . . Do you like sudoku?"

"Sometimes," Maggie said. "I like to read before bed, but if I can't fall asleep, sudoku helps to calm me down."

"Exactly." Mrs. Murdock tapped her pencil on the empty puzzle square. "Numbers soothe the mind. They have patterns and logic and order, and they don't fill your head with disturbing images. That's why I majored in math in college. All my history and English and science classes were centered around bad news—too many people dying, or animals losing their habitats . . . There are no tragedies in equations."

Strange, Maggie had always viewed math as a source of misery— the dark blot on her school schedule. But now that she considered it, her history and science books contained the real suffering of the world: global warming and genocide and mass extinctions. At least in math, the problems had solutions.

"What level of sudoku are you at?" Mrs. Murdock asked.

"I was doing some pretty advanced puzzles the last time I got into it."

"Here, then, take this." The teacher handed Maggie a red paperback with the words *Extreme Sudoku* spread across the front.

Maggie rolled her eyes at the flames spurting from the capital *E* and *S*; *Extreme Sudoku* sounded like an oxymoron. Sudoku wasn't bungee jumping or free climbing. Like Mrs. Murdock said, people didn't die in math.

"Should I bring it back soon?"

"You can have it." The teacher kept tapping her pencil on the empty box.

"Thanks." Maggie waited in silence, examining the framed pictures on the desk. These were the faces that Mrs. Murdock addressed when talking to her class—the woman's eyes rarely connected with students; instead she tended to settle on one of these photos, and Maggie saw, in the left-hand picture, a little girl, maybe four or five years old, with light brown pigtails, sitting on a swing and smiling tentatively.

"Cute kid," she said, causing Mrs. Murdock's pencil to pause.

"What's that?"

Maggie pointed toward the photo.

"Oh yes . . . That's my daughter, Lily."

The picture on the desk's opposite corner surprised Maggie. It was a framed painting of Jesus, the sort you could buy for five dollars at the local truck stop, with Christ posing all handsome and blond and dressed in white robes, arms spread wide as if he were welcoming Mrs. Murdock into a bear hug. Maggie usually ignored the paraphernalia of small-town southern religion: summer tent revivals and winter Christmas pageants, giant crosses looming in pastures along the interstate. She classified herself as a Buddhist-in-training, born to agnostic parents and bred to nature worship. From what she'd read in the Bible, Jesus was okay by her, but she had never seen a teacher bring Christ into the classroom. She wondered if the principal knew.

"Big fan of Jesus?" she asked.

Mrs. Murdock's face turned toward the painting. "I guess you could say that."

"You can sign up for one of his fan clubs on Facebook."

"Oh really?" The woman's attention went back to her puzzle.

Maggie saw no picture of a husband on this desk, no sign of Lily's father. She glanced at Mrs. Murdock's ringless fingers and wondered if Lily was an accident or an immaculate conception. More likely the math teacher was divorced and hadn't kept the ring, which made the woman a little more human in Maggie's eyes.

"It's a nine," she said, and Mrs. Murdock stopped tapping her pencil.

"What's that?"

"The number you need for that box. It's a nine."

"Well, look at that. You are absolutely right." Mrs. Murdock filled in the nine then closed the book.

"Do you know why I asked you here, Maggie?"

Maggie shrugged. "I've got a good guess."

"What did you think of your last test?"

Maggie thrust her fingers into the front pockets of her jeans. "Pretty lousy."

"I wouldn't say *lousy.*" Mrs. Murdock hesitated. "More like careless. I've looked at your eighth-grade math records, which are all excellent, and our tests haven't gotten far beyond a review of last year's materials. Any idea what the problem is?"

You, thought Maggie. *You and your weirdness are freaking me out.* But instead she just sighed. "I guess I've been distracted, new school and all."

"We'd like you to keep up your great work here at the high school." Maggie hated how teachers were always using the "royal we," like they were all a bunch of Marie Antoinettes.

"I think you can do much better work," Mrs. Murdock continued, "so I'd like you to stay one afternoon next week for a makeup test. If your new score is better, we'll throw out your last grade."

There was that "we" again, as if a handful of teachers would collectively drop her previous test into the trash.

"Thanks," said Maggie, although she didn't feel grateful. A C might be preferable to an extra hour in this depressing cave, imprisoned with a nutcase who referred to herself in the plural. And yet, it seemed that Mrs. Murdock was trying to be nice, as if she was one of those quiet females who had been trained since preschool to be instinctively accommodating. Perhaps Mrs. Murdock recognized Maggie as a distant cousin.

"I'm free next Thursday," Maggie said.

"Fine—you should plan on staying for an hour. Will you need a ride home?"

"I won't need a ride. My dad will come for me."

"Great. I'll see you then."

"So what happened?" Kate put away her phone as Maggie exited the classroom.

"She gave me this." Maggie held out the red sudoku book and Kate turned it over in her hands.

"What's suhdockoo?"

"Japanese logic puzzles."

"Okayyy . . . " Kate handed the book back and the two of them walked down the hall. "Is that all she wanted? To give you a present?"

"She wants me to come and take a makeup test next week . . . She says she'll throw out my last C if I do better the second time."

"So that's a good thing, right?"

Maggie shook her head. "It's still too weird. I mean, most times when a math teacher has a makeup test, they announce the date and everybody comes at the same time. But Mrs. Murdock asked me when I wanted to take it, like it's a private test just for me, and I know there are other kids in the class who made C's. Arthur Smith *failed*, and I don't think he's getting a retest."

"Arthur Smith is an asshole." Kate shrugged. "Mrs. Murdock probably knows that."

"Asshole or not, he'd be pissed if he knew I was getting a do-over."

"I wouldn't tell anyone if I were you. Just take it as a lucky break."

"That's what I'm planning." Maggie pushed open the metal door that led to a stairwell. "But it's still kind of creepy. I mean, why has she singled me out as her special project?"

"Do you think she likes you?"

"In what way?"

"Well, you say you think she watches you when you're not looking, and she gave you that present"—Kate nodded toward the book—"and now she's offering to help you out with a test. So maybe this lady's got some kind of special feeling for you?"

"Like she's gay or something?"

"Stranger things have happened."

Maggie shook her head. "I seriously doubt it . . . She's got a picture of her daughter on her desk, and she's also got a little shrine to Jesus."

"So do you think she's an über-Christian, and you're her good deed for the week?"

By now they had reached the front hallway, passing the entrance to the school's auditorium to their right.

"What's more likely," said Maggie, "is that she needs the smart kids to make A's and ace their standardized tests so she can get a good job review. I figure most of these teachers start the year knowing who's smart and who's not. Mrs. Murdock said she's seen my grades from middle school, and she's probably counting on me to lift up the class average."

They stepped outside the building, into the bright light of a fall afternoon. Maggie's dad was waiting on one of the red metal benches in front of the school, and when he stood, Maggie flinched at the chunky brown plaid of his flannel shirt. His wardrobe needed a woman's eye, but she wasn't about to volunteer. She and Kate had been talking for months about trying to hook him up with some local divorcée, a woman who could choose his ties, cook him a few decent meals, and divert his attention away from Maggie. He'd only tried a handful of dates in the past several years, never making a strong connection, and Maggie worried about how he'd fare once she moved away after high school.

"Hi, girls."

"Hello, Mr. Greene." Kate smiled. "How are you?"

"I'm fine. Did you get held up for a while?" He lifted Maggie's backpack from her shoulder as they walked across the parking lot toward his old gray Toyota.

"I had to go to a meeting after school," Maggie answered without looking at him.

"What kind of meeting?"

"Math club."

"That's great." He opened the car's back door. "I think you should join some clubs. When are they meeting again?"

"Next Thursday afternoon. I probably won't get out of school until four thirty."

"I'll be here."

"I'm sure you will."

Maggie's dad always picked her up after school. From kindergarten forward he had insisted upon it with such regularity, it had become a point of contention. In middle school, when the other girls were strolling five blocks into town to buy ice cream and coffee and hang out in the park, Maggie's dad had never let her walk with them. He picked her up and drove her to the ice cream shop, or coffee shop, or library, apparently fearful that she would disappear somewhere between points A and B. She understood his motives—her father had been absent on the one night when his wife and daughter really needed him, and ever since then he'd been trying to compensate by being the most visible dad in town, present at every school concert and play, every cakewalk and potluck, every three o'clock pickup. It embarrassed Maggie to have a stalker dad. She suggested that his boss might not appreciate an employee who left work every afternoon for forty minutes, but her father was a computer technician at Holford, where hours were flexible and everyone sympathized. If the office's single dad wanted to shadow his daughter, no one would object.

Once, when he was ten minutes late, Maggie had walked to the library with the other girls, leaving her dad a text message only after she arrived. By then he had spent a panicked half hour driving through town, searching in all the preteen hangouts. When he reached the library, his eyes were so red and his expression so wounded, Maggie had felt both guilty and ashamed of him. He gathered her into a tight hug right in front of the other kids, who had gawked at this over-the-top father-daughter love. Since then Maggie had known that it was better to hide in the car than to risk public humiliation, which was why she and Kate now sat chauffeur-style in the backseat, listening to their separate iPods and nodding at Mr. Greene as he glanced at them in the rearview mirror, saying, "Would you like to stop for ice cream?"

CHAPTER 5

A few nights later Maggie was back in the woods, propped with her spine against the ash tree. Her knees were pulled toward her chin and her nightgown stretched over her kneecaps with the fabric tucked under her toes so that her bare feet did not touch the dirt. She had pulled her arms out of the sleeves, inside the gown's white tent, and she was pressing Sophie's plush softness against her naked skin. With eyes closed and body folded to the smallest size possible, Maggie was prepared to endure the darkness.

Around her the Virginia woods throbbed with the rasping of cicadas, while occasionally a screech owl wailed, high and mournful. Maggie heard a screen door slap, and she pulled her arms out of their sleeves, stood, and walked to edge of the trees, peering through the lacework of branches and leaves. A woman was crossing the grass, long hair brushing past her shoulders—probably the female student, the one who had looked Maggie in the eye and mouthed an apology. Porch light framed her figure, shading her face just as the hall light had done before, so that Maggie could only discern a vague outline of cheeks and chin and eyes, and the darkness of the woman's shadowy mouth, slowly opening.

"Honey? Where are you?"

Maggie froze. This wasn't the voice of a stranger. These were her mother's frightened tones, calling toward the woods: "It's all right, baby. Tell me where you are."

Her mother was entirely white—white hands, white robe, white face. Her hair, normally a shining red, had a pale metallic glow, transformed from copper to silver in some mysterious alchemy. Maggie took several steps backward, retreating behind the leaves without the slightest whisper of reply. *This is my mother's ghost,* she thought, *glowing like the moon,* except for a few dark splotches of blood on her bare feet. Maggie looked down at her own white nightgown, her pale hands and elbows, and realized that she too was becoming ghostly. She and her mother were a pair of phosphorescent stones.

"You can come out, Maggie. No need to be scared."

But Maggie knew better. Despite her instinctive desire to cling to her mother, she understood that there were plenty of reasons to be afraid. Beneath that fluorescent exterior lay something sinister, some vague potential for violence. She watched as her mother's spirit pressed back a tree limb, and when the first bloodstained foot stepped into the woods, Maggie willed herself to wake up.

This is a dream, she told herself. *Wake up, Maggie.* Wake up *now.*

"WHAT do you think it means?" Maggie pressed Dr. Riley at their next meeting. "Why is my mother showing up in my head right now?"

"You'll have to answer that for yourself."

"I don't see why you can't take a guess. Freud interpreted dreams."

"Have you read any of those interpretations?"

"A couple, for a class."

"Do you think he got the dreams right?"

Maggie shrugged. "I think Freud had a lot of warped ideas about women."

"So what is the value in having someone else interpret your dreams?"

Value? Maggie loathed the word. "Isn't my dad paying you something like two hundred dollars an hour? What *value* is in that?"

"It's for you and your father to decide whether these sessions are valuable. All the answers lie inside your own head, Maggie. You just have to be willing to let them out."

"Haven't you ever heard of Pandora's box?" she responded.

The doctor smiled. "I don't think you have all the evils of the world inside you."

Maggie looked outside at the October maples, peaking in a brilliant orange. *Just a few particular evils.*

Dr. Riley rolled up his sleeves, folding the cuffs back. "Why don't you tell me what is really bothering you?"

Maggie wondered how long she'd been wringing her hands. She must learn to control these unconscious gestures that always gave her feelings away. "Tomorrow I have to stay after school for a makeup test in math, because my grades have been so bad."

"And your teacher still disturbs you?"

Maggie nodded. "I noticed something strange yesterday . . . A guy went up to her desk to ask her a question, and she lifted her face and looked him right in the eye. I was shocked. She never does that with me. So I went up to her desk to ask her a fake question, and you know what? She kept shuffling her papers the entire time she answered me, as if she was too busy getting organized to ever look up. Don't you think that's strange?"

"I think you're letting one person's habits interfere with your learning. You should concentrate on the subject matter, not on the teacher. Try to focus on the math."

Fair enough, thought Maggie, so she resolved to give it a try when she got home.

That night in bed, when she took out her geometry homework, Maggie attempted to lose herself in the numbers, concentrating on the relations between line segments rather than the relations between human beings. Despite all her oddities, Mrs. Murdock had been right about one thing: there was no murder in these symbols. Mathematics might have helped to build the atom bomb, the Nazis might have recorded their genocide in numeric tables, but the abuses of math differed from the numbers themselves. These black marks remained innocent as the white paper they rested upon.

Maggie fell asleep with the geometry book open in her lap, and once again found herself standing in the woods, watching a silhouetted female approach slowly across the lawn. This time the woman didn't call her name. She was just as quiet as Maggie, her feet gliding noiseless along the grass, and when Maggie glanced down at those silent toes, she saw that they weren't bare or bloodstained. They were shod in sensible sandals beneath a knee-length skirt.

Wake up, Maggie told herself. *Get out of here*. But she couldn't wake. She was condemned to watch the movements of an oddly robotic Mrs. Murdock, babbling geometry: "Collinear . . . coplanar . . . exterior angle theorem." Strangely enough, the woman didn't walk straight toward Maggie. She approached the woods ten feet distant, never looking in the girl's direction, and when she reached the trees, she stepped into their shadows without hesitation, merging into the darkness as if she too needed a place to hide.

THE next morning Maggie felt too nervous to eat breakfast, and at noon she passed her entire lunch over to Kate.

"Worried about the test?" Kate asked, but Maggie shook her head.

"Not the test, just the teacher." She didn't tell Kate about her dream—how she had already spent an hour alone in the woods with Mrs. Murdock, the teacher sitting against a tree, hugging her legs to her chest and planting her forehead on her kneecaps. Maggie's sleeping brain had processed Mrs. Murdock as an echo of herself.

Later, when the three o'clock bell rang, students flooded through the hallways and out the building—Kate among them, off to her weekly choir practice. Maggie rose from her desk with grim resolve, allowing herself a few minutes to visit her locker, sip some water, and take a few deep breaths before returning to the math teacher's space.

"Your work is on the table." Mrs. Murdock pointed when Maggie returned, and she saw that the test had been placed at the back of the room, far from the teacher's desk. Did Mrs. Murdock also want to avoid close contact? Did she applaud Maggie's decision to sit in the back row?

"Put all your books away. You have an hour."

Concentrate on the subject matter, Maggie thought as she situated her backpack on the floor. *Don't look at the teacher, and for God's sake, don't think about your stupid dreams. Just focus on the math.*

The problems seemed easy enough, and yet Maggie's mind was littered with so many broken images she could barely read the instructions. The red and gold stripes running along the classroom walls looked like horizontal flames, and the entire school was a fiery death trap, with its high, narrow windows that could never be opened, its maze of halls never pointing to an exit. Maggie needed an escape route, a chance to climb out and run away from the threes on her test, which were now morphing into eights, the fours that were curving into nines while the zeros opened their wide black mouths, shouting. *You're not going to make it. You can't stay here.*

But then Mrs. Murdock did a strange thing. She rose from her desk, straightened the papers in her hands, and announced: "I'm going to the library. Just leave the test on my desk when you are done." She lifted her purse and manila file and walked out of the room, passing Maggie's shoulder without looking down.

Her exit was so abrupt, Maggie needed a moment to absorb the reverberations. Had Mrs. Murdock sensed the tension in the room? Did Maggie's proximity make the woman's skin crawl?

Maggie had never taken a test without a teacher present; there was nothing to keep her from cheating, except her own unwavering conscience. She supposed Mrs. Murdock trusted her, or else the woman was testing her in more ways than one. Maggie looked at the open door, half expecting to see her teacher, watching to discover whether Maggie was honest, but the doorway stood empty. She was alone, with only the electric buzz of fluorescent bulbs to trouble her mind. After a while she could sense her heartbeat slowing, her breath coming easier. The strange woman was gone; the math was simple; she had nothing to worry about.

She completed the test in half an hour and walked it up to Mrs. Murdock's desk, pausing to consider the picture of the girl on the swing, whose thin, nondescript face wore an anxious expression, as if she were asking permission to smile. Maggie returned to her desk, hoisted her backpack to her shoulder, and hurried out into the hall, planning to stop by the bathroom two doors down before calling her dad to say that math club had ended early. As she reached for the metal handle on the restroom door, it opened and Mrs. Murdock stepped out, almost running into Maggie. The woman didn't have time to drop her eyes, and instead looked directly into Maggie's face and said, "I'm sorry." For one brief moment the two of them stared at each other, then the teacher stepped aside and walked away, not toward her classroom but down the hall and into the stairwell.

Maggie didn't move. She stood before the closed door with her breath suspended, thinking, *Oh my God.* Walking inside the bathroom, she let her backpack slide to the floor, then bent over double as if kicked in the stomach. "Oh my God."

After a few seconds she rose, pulled two paper towels from their metal container, and soaked them with cold water. Pressing them to her face, Maggie felt the liquid on her lips, forehead, and eyelids, then threw them away and examined her dripping reflection in the mirror.

What now? she thought. What should she do? Pulling her cell phone from her front pocket, she called her dad.

"I need you to come now, okay? Can you come right away?" For once Maggie was glad to have a driver on call.

"What's wrong?" Rob sounded alarmed.

"I'm feeling sick, and I need to get home."

When she exited the bathroom, Maggie glanced right and left, making sure Mrs. Murdock was nowhere in sight. She hesitated in the hallway, knowing that the stairwell her teacher had entered was the shortest route to the front door. Maggie decided to take the back exit, which led past the band room, toward the school buses. She was about to hurry in that direction when, for a brief moment, she paused and pressed her lips together. Fast as she could, she returned to Mrs. Murdock's empty classroom and ran to the teacher's desk, where her test lay waiting. Dropping her backpack to the floor, she unzipped it, opened a spiral notebook, and wrote one sentence. Then she tore out the sheet of lined paper, leaving the messy scraps dangling at the sides, and laid it on top of her test. Zipping her backpack, she raced out of the classroom and hurried down the hall.

Twenty minutes later, when Mrs. Murdock returned to her room, she lifted the sheet of paper from her desk and read five small words:

I know who you are.

Accomplice

CHAPTER 6

GRACE Murdock folded Maggie's note and tucked it into the side pocket of her handbag. Events were set in motion now, after months of suspension; the course she had initiated upon returning to Jackson had taken hold, and there was no going back.

Her only surprise was that the girl hadn't recognized her sooner. Grace had thought Maggie might expose her on the first day of school. Lying awake through the restless nights of August, with a window fan that blew stagnant heat across her body, she had envisioned the scene—how Maggie would enter the classroom and freeze. She would stare and point, maybe yell or curse, and Grace would bear it, focusing her eyes on the floor and allowing Maggie to accuse her, revile her. Tell everyone who she was, what she was. The accomplice. The liar.

She had thought there might be some value in public shame; a mortification of the spirit might allow her soul to emerge purified at the end. Not that Grace craved it; she had felt no masochistic glee in the tableau she envisioned on those sleepless August nights. In fact, she had accepted this job at Jackson High School under the assumption that Maggie Greene would not be attending. Nine and a half years ago Maggie's family had lived out on Wade's Creek, eight miles beyond the town limits, which meant that the girl should have been a freshman at Mount Wilson High School. Had Grace known that Maggie and her father had moved into Jackson's school district, she probably wouldn't have taken this job, for although she felt compelled to return to the scene of her crime, to go back to her old college town, that campus of two million bricks and a hundred white columns, those rural roads twisting through stony hills and riverfront meadows—she had never wanted to be Maggie Greene's math teacher, to face the girl every day and hold authority over her. It seemed grotesque, each time she wrote a grade on Maggie's work, especially if that grade was anything less than a capital A for *Apology*.

Grace had envisioned her ideal reunion with Maggie as a onetime encounter, a conversation in an empty restaurant or on an isolated park bench—any spot that might serve as a modern confessional. When she had seen Maggie's name on her class list in July, Grace had been tempted to resign from her new position immediately. *That's it*, she had told herself. *This charade is over.*

She had thought to plead a sudden illness, to claim that the hard fist of guilt growing inside her chest was a tumor, real and malignant, because that was how it felt, both tangible and terminal. But she hadn't followed through, and when Maggie failed to recognize her on the first day, Grace believed that she had been granted a reprieve, some time to gather her thoughts.

It made sense that Maggie hadn't immediately recognized her. Grace had changed since her college days, trading her blue jeans and Abercrombie flip-flops for a collection of skirts and blouses, cream, white, and gray, utterly "unobjectionable"—that was the word that had crossed her mind when she bought them at Target. As for her hair, she no longer had the flat, two-foot sweep of sandy-brown strands that had trailed her as an undergraduate. A few years earlier she had cut them to shoulder length in the name of professionalism, the shearing of hair being the sole rite of passage into adulthood that Grace felt she could control. Marriage had been another rite designed to settle her life into a mature routine, but her years with her husband had spiraled into a clumsy swamp of attacks and reprisals, leaving her with a married name that she didn't associate with herself, although she kept it, expecting no one in Jackson to recognize a Mrs. Murdock. Along with her new clothes, hair, and name, her soul was different too, or so she hoped. Looking at Maggie's scrawled claim of recognition— *I know who you are*—Grace felt inclined to write back on another slip of notebook paper: *You know an incomplete shell of a person from nine years ago—you don't know me.*

As she gathered the student quizzes from her desk, closing her books, lifting pencils, and shutting down her computer, Grace wondered how she could ever describe her circumstances to a fifteen-year-old girl. More than anything, she owed Maggie explanations, the full story of why she was here now, and why she had been at the girl's home nine years ago—but explanations were complicated, each moment in life being contingent on all that came before. For Maggie to understand the chain of events that linked the two of them, she would have to know something about Grace's past and present, family and friends, the whole web of relationships that caused the intersections in people's lives.

Above all she would have to know about Lily, Grace's four-year-old daughter. Lily was the main factor that had drawn Grace back to Jackson, the daily gravitational pull that determined the orbit of her mother's years. Grace remembered clearly that moment in the hospital when her obstetrician had placed the unwashed newborn onto her belly. She had expected a newborn to be a wriggling, floppy thing, but Lily had raised a steady head and looked into her mother's eyes with such intensity in her dark, infant gaze, in that moment Grace had known the terror of loss. Here was the most sacred charge of her life—a human being so precious, so willing to accept her mother's adoration and reciprocate with warm, soft-skinned affection, that Grace had been struck simultaneously with the amazement of life and the fear of death. She had spent the first two years of Lily's existence as a crib-side shadow, watching for the rise and fall of her baby's chest, listening for the almost imperceptible breath, sometimes placing her hand on the sleeping infant to feel the fluttering heartbeat and rest assured that this fragile wisp of life would not disappear overnight.

Only after Lily's second birthday had Grace begun to feel confident, partly because toddlers were so much sturdier than infants, but beyond that, she had convinced herself that there was a predestined reason for Lily's existence, a purpose that guaranteed the child would not be taken away anytime soon. Lily had come into this world not only to offer Grace some joy, but to serve as a constant reminder of the worst thing Grace had ever done: She had contributed to the separation of a mother and daughter.

Motherhood had caused Grace to fathom the impact of her past, and now that Lily was almost five years old, the age Maggie Greene had been nine and a half years ago, Grace had begun to link the two girls in her mind, and to nurture a superstition that if she didn't make amends to Maggie soon, she too might be separated from her daughter.

Grace placed the stack of quizzes into a large manila folder and stuffed it into her bag, then surveyed her desk one last time. The wooden-framed pictures of Jesus and Lily served as anchors at the desk's upper corners, Jesus on her right and Lily on her left, two points in the triangle that held her tenuous world together. She credited Jesus with bringing Lily into her life. Not God. The Father had never interested her as much as the Son, mostly because her own father had been a silencing presence in her childhood, a man with little patience for females, associating them with small concerns, all chatter and shopping.

"Your father loves you," Grace's mother had always insisted. "He just has trouble saying it, because he's so reserved."

Grace shut off her classroom lights, locked the door, then walked down the hallway past the rows of red and gold cinder blocks. She waved at Mr. Beaufort, the earth science teacher, still reading lab reports at his desk as she passed his door.

"Don't stay too late, Sam."

"No chance of that," he replied.

Sam looked to be in his early sixties, with the same graying temples, receding hairline, and wire-rimmed reading glasses as her father. She wondered if he had daughters, and if so, did he adore them? Did he hug them and say that they were beautiful? Love was not something that should be reserved; it should not remain unspoken for thirty years. Love should fall in a constant shower, helping the spirit bloom.

Grace stepped into the stairwell, wincing, as she always did, at its mural of Roman temples and toga-clad gods with Pegasus hovering in a cloudy sky. Something about Mercury in his winged cap and thin, muscular legs reminded her of Maggie's dad, the parent who appeared most out of place on freshman orientation night. Mr. Greene had sat at a desk in the back of Grace's classroom, with Maggie standing guard at his shoulder, as if the child and parent had reversed roles. A dozen other parents and ninth graders also occupied the room, listening to Grace's six-minute summary of honors geometry, but only Mr. Greene had been knowledgeable enough to raise a hand and ask: "Will you be spending much time on proofs and theorems?"

God bless any man who understood geometry. Most of the other parents had been ambitious mothers who cared more about grading policies than class content, trying to chart their children's courses to the Ivy League and questioning whether the new math teacher might get in their way. The two other dads in the room had seemed embarrassed, as if they had arrived at this orientation by mistake and were now destined to move from classroom to classroom in awkward exile. They were doughy men, softening with middle age, but Mr. Greene seemed more gaunt than Grace remembered from nine years ago. Maggie's dad looked as if he'd spent the past decade running a daily marathon.

When she answered his question, she did not look him in the eye. Grace knew they hadn't met before—only Maggie and her mother had seen Grace in person—but she didn't know what pictures might have made their way into newspapers, and she prayed that he wouldn't recognize her. With her hair pinned up and her face much older, she wouldn't resemble the black-and-white clippings from the past; still, she glanced at Maggie's father only briefly when he spoke, and answered his question with her eyes on other parents.

When the bell rang, ushering families to distant classrooms, she had noticed how Mr. Greene rose and placed his arm around Maggie's shoulder. No other parents touched their children—few teenagers would have tolerated parental affection in public—but this father and daughter appeared to be a team. Grace had lowered her eyes, sensing that it was intrusive to even look at them.

Now she emerged from the stairwell into the central hallway that extended past the high school's main office. To her left, beyond a glass wall partly obscured by venetian blinds, she could see two secretaries behind dark wooden desks, chatting with the head basketball coach. The ninth-grade counselor emerged from a back office and joined the trio, briefly looking up to wave at Grace, and Grace waved back, pushing through one set of metal doors into a vestibule that served as the students' cell-phone lounge, where half a dozen adolescents were exercising their thumbs.

"Good-bye, Mrs. Murdock," one boy spoke without looking up from his phone.

"Good-bye, Eddie," she replied, pressing through the next layer of doors and surfacing into bright October sunshine, a relief from the school's fluorescent lights that gave her the sense of being underwater all day. In front of her, a cluster of red metal benches framed a flower bed with a bronze sundial. The horticulture class changed the flowers each season—for autumn, yellow and red chrysanthemums.

The faculty and senior parking lot stretched right and left for fifty yards, rows of student pickups and teachers' sedans visible each day from Grace's classroom windows, where she had occasionally noticed Maggie's father leaning against the door of what looked to be an old gray Toyota Camry. Whenever his daughter arrived, Mr. Greene always hurried forward to lift the heavy backpack from her shoulders, carrying it to the car and opening the door for his child. Watching them, Grace had recalled her own father's awkward chivalry, how he opened doors with cold propriety, far from Mr. Greene's gestures of quiet affection. She couldn't say whether her dad had ever felt any real tenderness toward her. He might have treasured a son—an athlete or soldier who could return from a foreign war to fight his father's home-front battles, the daily struggle between Dad's True Value Hardware and the invading forces of Home Depot.

Grace had never been able to fake an enthusiasm for bolts and wrenches. She had always been her mother's child, eager to help with lemon bars and Christmas cookies, and the excess spaghetti sauces that her mom froze in Tupperware containers. Until age thirteen she had spent most weekday afternoons in her mother's kitchen, watching the neighbor women who gathered at the Formica-topped table to knit and chat and thumb through JCPenney catalogs while sipping Irish coffee. Mrs. Higgins, Sellers, and Stone shared an unflagging interest in the marriages, diseases, and bankruptcies of all their acquaintances. They had the good fortune to live in a small Virginia town full of personal sorrows, and the good sense to slip quietly out the back door whenever they heard Grace's father pull into the driveway at five forty-five.

There had been safety in that kitchen—safety and warmth and ease, for although Grace's mom was not an effusive woman, her love for her daughter had been unwavering, and it troubled Grace to think that Maggie Greene had been raised without a mother's daily care. A girl needed a mom to teach her how to bake pies, braid hair, and perform essential hygiene. Every time she saw Maggie Greene arrive at her classroom with oily skin, torn sneakers, and pseudo-Goth T-shirts, Grace knew she had much to atone for.

Atonement, however, was a fancy word, too grand for Grace's life. It hardly explained why she was here in a high school parking lot, unlocking a green Ford Taurus and dropping her bag onto a backseat spotted with stains from dozens of Happy Meals. *Atonement* didn't exist in a world where joy could be purchased with extra ketchup. If she was going to explain herself to Maggie, she would have to find words as mundane as her existence, beginning with an admission that her biggest reason for returning to Jackson was purely selfish and material; she had taken this job because she needed the money.

Maggie would understand that—she and her dad didn't seem to be rolling in cash. The Greenes would know how it felt for a family to live in a constant state of financial stress, and what compromises that daily pressure could inspire in a human heart.

Grace headed north out of the parking lot, driving past the football field, the baseball diamond and tennis courts, stopping at the light beside a hilltop Exxon with a built-in Dairy Queen. Taking a right on red, she counted the numbers aloud as she accelerated beyond the Five Guys burgers, the Motel 6, and the 7-Eleven. All this town needed was a Super 8. Next came the Applebee's, the Awful House, the Walmart, the half-empty shopping center featuring Homer's Antique Mall, with its front yard covered in naked Cupid lawn statues and Corinthian birdbaths. Another half mile and the town's struggling commercial strip narrowed to a two-lane country road, sending Grace on a forty-minute drive through pastures and wooded hills that would eventually carry her east over the Blue Ridge and down into the outer limits of Placid Springs, a town twice the size of Jackson, with a plastics factory, a medical center, and a train station, but still not big enough for Grace to call it a city.

Placid Springs was her parents' town, the site of her birth, her awkward childhood, her distraught adolescence, the place where she, a thirty-one-year-old mother, had returned eleven months ago when her marriage unraveled. Since then, her life had become an exercise in revisiting the past, living in the same house, the same kitchen, the same bedroom only slightly altered since high school, except that her parents had added a small cot for Lily, so that mother and daughter now lived as roommates. "Only temporary," she had assured her parents when she arrived with Lily's toy chest and boxes of clothes. Moving in with her parents would give her a chance to save money while she settled into a new job and searched for an affordable home. But honestly, she couldn't say how long she'd be stuck there.

Money had always been the chief problem in Grace's life, and it would continue to be a problem if she stayed with the public schools. She had hoped that marriage would fix that—that a husband with a steady job might free her life from the fear of economic collapse that had hung like an angel's sword over her childhood. But now, as her ten-year-old Ford Taurus groaned its way up the western side of Humpback Mountain, scenes from her marriage flashed through her mind in a grotesque pantomime.

She would have to tell Maggie about the embarrassing course of her love life, if she wanted the girl to understand why Grace had shown up at her house one night with two obnoxious college boys. All the trouble in Grace's life had centered around money and men, the fatal alliteration that kept repeating in her mind as she wound her way, layer by layer, through the Blue Ridge: *Money and men, money and men.* And now her brain added new alliterative twists: *Money and men and marriage. Maggie and money and men.* What was her life, thought Grace, except a string of cautionary tales?

CHAPTER 7

AT the top of Humpback Mountain the trees closest to the road resembled Dr. Seuss creations. They were draped in kudzu, without a trunk or branch visible, doomed to suffocation beneath a tangle of climbing leaves, and that struck Grace as a common fate—for one life to be strangled by a relentless crowd that stole all sunlight. Perhaps she should tell Maggie about the trees, or perhaps Maggie had already seen these puffy emerald giants, and knew that there were lives dying in shadow beneath the gowns of green lace.

Grace needed a metaphor to distance herself from the pain of her adolescence; otherwise how could she explain to Maggie how it felt to be the girl who never dated in high school, the girl no one asked to the prom, or to dinner, or on a picnic? Not because she was ugly. No—all throughout her agonizing years of high school, when she looked into the mirror and pondered her wispy, light brown hair, her hesitant eyes, her thin face with its slightly angular chin, the word *ugly* never came to mind. She was neither unattractive nor beautiful, neither striking nor repellent. She was the girl in the middle—the steady, prosaic norm. The sole physical feature on which she prided herself was her unblemished skin, apparently immune to acne, freckles, and birthmarks. And yet a blemish might have made her noticeable in high school—a mole at the corner of her lip, a scar that required explanation; those might have enticed a boy to pause. As it was, her face could be assessed and dismissed in five seconds, and she never had the guts to attract attention through artifice—bright makeup, a tattoo, purple highlights in her hair. To make matters worse, her personality was as bland as her face; she was not particularly smart, nor notably stupid—of moderate talent in a row of flutes and middling speed in a cross-country race. She was a reliable member of the crowd, the girl whose name people never could remember.

Sandra McCluskey—that had been her name throughout her childhood—the name of her father's mother and grandmother, a working-class, ordinary name, which, in its casual version, Sandy, sounded more appropriate for a golden retriever than a girl who desperately wanted someone special to notice her. Grace was her middle name, rarely spoken until two years after college, when she first turned to Christianity as an antidote to loneliness, suspecting that Jesus might be the only loving male figure in her life. She'd been singing "Amazing Grace" with a couple hundred southern Baptists underneath a vast white tent, thinking how the striped circus tents of her childhood had been replaced by this sanctified big top, when her voice suddenly choked, and she was surprised to find a few tears escaping down her cheeks. A woman to her left took her hand and squeezed it, and in that instant, sparked by the first physical gesture of kindness she had ever known from a stranger, she realized that "Grace" was the name of her true spirit. "Sandy" was a texture, an uncomfortable adjective, a pair of syllables that couldn't represent a heart newly christened in tears. Changing her name might be the first step toward changing her life.

Perhaps Maggie Greene would understand that desire for transformation, the emphatic wish to raise one's life to a higher plane, something more exciting, more popular, more beloved. From what Grace could tell, Maggie too was an unremarkable girl, a girl who might have remained unnoticed if not for the notoriety of one traumatic night. Maggie was not blessed with her mother's brilliant red hair, or her father's brooding eyes. She seemed very smart, but unlikely to reach the top five of her class. Neither a queen bee nor a loner. Grace had seen her speak to a few female friends but rarely to boys, and Maggie probably questioned whether one day she would be asked to a prom.

That had been the chief question of Grace's high school days, prom season being the annual blight that ruined all the weeks before. While other girls focused on who was going with whom, what dress to wear and what shoes would match, Grace had spent each spring watching from a lonely distance. No older boys had sought her out during her freshman or sophomore years—she hadn't expected it—but junior year she had tried, for an entire month before the dance, to smile at boys, say hello, make them aware of her existence and availability to anyone who might want some female companionship. She had felt like putting a sign across her chest, *Free Access in Exchange for a Prom Invitation*. Some of the other dateless girls invited their male cousins, or were escorted by friends of the family recruited by their parents. Grace spent prom night with Ben & Jerry.

Senior year promised nothing better—all fall and winter no boy asked her to a movie, or to a party, or out for a Coke, so why should anyone ask her to the prom? And so she devised a plan to avoid humiliation. Two months before the dance she told her small circle of friends that her uncle's family in North Carolina had invited her to go to the beach with them in May, and wasn't it a shame that it was right during prom weekend? She repeated her announcement regularly over the coming weeks, ensuring that no one would ask whether a boy had invited her to the dance, and when prom weekend came, she hid out at her house and begged her mom to tell anyone who called that she was out of town—not that anyone did call, or notice, or care.

Thus had begun Grace's career as a liar—the path that would ultimately tie her to Maggie Greene. She had found, after that painful night, that lies were easy, even pleasant, to relate. *The weather at the Outer Banks had been too cloudy for a tan, but the sand dunes at Kitty Hawk had been full of hang gliders.* Grace discovered that she had a gift for fiction. The lies came in vivid detail, creating a gregarious alternate world. In the coming months she told them with guiltless abandon, recounting her travel plans for the summer and describing the boy she met at an overnight math camp. Why should she have any allegiance to facts, when reality had never been kind to her?

Maggie Greene was the first person to whom she owed the truth, because Maggie's was the first life damaged by Grace's lies. Prior to the girl's appearance, Grace thought that her lies were helpful to the people around her, lessening their discomfort in her presence, removing their need for pity. Her fictions made her a palatable companion, and she thought that her friends believed every word of her stories, so sincere were their expressions of curiosity and envy. Only years later did she wonder if those girls, with their questions about the beach and the boy and the camp, were secretly embarrassed by her.

College was supposed to have ended Grace's misery. College—the promised land after the slow exodus from high school. The place where all middling girls could find their niche, and share it with a boy who would give them their first, long-overdue kiss. Or so Grace had dreamed when she left for Holford thirteen years ago—she had imagined that she was embarking on a youth long deferred. In college she would enjoy the pleasures that the popular girls had known since middle school.

And so it was disappointing to find that Holford's social circles were as exclusive as her high school cliques. Did she wear the right clothes? Did she know the right people? Was she a member of the right sorority? The answers were No, No, and Are you kidding? Grace did manage to carve out a small social life during freshman year, going out for coffee with a few guys and trying some coed movie nights. She also joined the outing club, which meant that she was alone in a canoe with a male junior for three hours, and she pretended that it counted as a date.

She would have been content with those meager scraps of socialization were it not for every April, when Holford held its big Spring Fling. Freshman year her mom called every other day in the two weeks before the dance, asking if Grace was going. Apparently Mrs. Higgins had a nephew who was really sweet (code for boys who were ugly but kind). Wouldn't Grace like to meet him?

She seemed so disappointed when Grace didn't attend, as if the dance was the biggest test of her daughter's future success, that Grace decided, during her sophomore year, to resort to her old habits. She informed her mother that she was going to the dance with a guy from her history class named Tom. He wasn't her boyfriend, but he was nice, and Grace was certain she would have a good time. Afterward, she told her mother about the great restaurant Tom chose for dinner, and the party they stopped by after the dance, and how Tom was a perfect gentleman, delivering her safely to her dorm by two a.m..

Junior year the lies got worse. Two weeks before the Spring Fling Grace told her mom that she had a date, just to ward off the annual maternal anxiety, but that was a big mistake, because her mother insisted on taking her shopping in Charlottesville for a new dress, and she spent two hundred dollars—a fortune for a hardware salesman's family. During the shopping trip Grace made up stories about her imaginary date: Ian Campbell, a tall senior history major with strawberry-blond hair, freckles, and a great sense of humor. Her mom wanted to come to Holford and meet Ian, since she lived only an hour from the college, but Grace said no; guys who asked a girl out for just one date didn't want to meet parents. Mrs. McCluskey asked her to take pictures, and Grace apologized after the dance for forgetting to do so.

At the end of her junior year Grace felt like transferring to another college, just to avoid the embarrassment of the next Spring Fling. College seemed like her best chance of ever meeting a man, and if she couldn't manage to attract even a short-term boyfriend within the next twelve months, she feared she would never get married. So why not try a new group of people at a larger university? Maybe she would have a better chance in a much bigger pond. But almost no one transferred before their senior year. All of Grace's credits wouldn't transfer with her, and she would need at least five years to graduate, piling up more student loans.

Then a miracle happened, right in the middle of fall term, in Professor Greene's British lit survey. The students had each written a one-page analysis of Keats's "Ode on Melancholy" and Professor Greene had divided them into pairs, telling them to comment on each other's work. She had matched Grace with Kyle Caldwell, a boy Grace had never spoken to, though she knew who he was, having lived in Caldwell Hall during her freshman year.

Grace had felt embarrassed about the page she'd written, because she thought the poem was full of sexual innuendos, and she had described them bluntly, expecting her thoughts to be for Professor Greene's eyes only. So here was this guy she hardly knew, taking ten minutes to read Grace's two paragraphs, as if he was absorbing every detail about female genitalia. She learned later that Kyle had a mild case of dyslexia, and reading was always a slow process for him, but when he finished, Kyle gave her a completely earnest look and said, "This is the most awesome analysis of a poem that I've ever read."

She thought he was mocking her, but Kyle swore sincerely: "The way you talk about the temple of delight, and the poet bursting joy's grape against his palate—I didn't notice any of that stuff." When Grace read Kyle's paragraphs, devoid of any original thought and plagued with grammatical mistakes, she understood how he could be so easily impressed. Kyle apologized, but she insisted that English wasn't her strong suit either. Numbers made a lot more sense to Grace than anything by Keats.

Kyle wasn't much better in math than in English. He confessed that he was making a C in accounting because of the math, and asked if Grace might stop by his fraternity that afternoon and help him with his homework. *Yeah, right.* Boys had asked her to "help them" with homework before, which usually meant they wanted her to do the whole assignment while they watched TV or went to a party. Still, she'd never been inside the SAE house—it was the wealthiest frat on campus—so she appeared at the designated hour, just to see the Persian rugs and leather armchairs. She and Kyle sat outside on a back porch that matched Grace's vision of a Moroccan café, full of brown wicker and gold satin pillows, surrounded by bromeliads, hanging ferns, and ceiling fans.

Kyle seemed genuinely interested in Grace's explanations of assets and liabilities. He finished most of the homework himself; she merely shared suggestions whenever he got stuck, and at the end he offered to pay her twenty dollars. *Like a nerd-prostitute*, she thought, refusing the cash. Instead, Kyle took her out for an ice cream cone.

From there, Grace had become Kyle's regular math tutor, meeting him twice a week at the rental house that he shared with two other guys. Apparently Kyle's parents had hired tutors all his life—in elementary school, to help with his reading, in middle school for math and Spanish, and during prep school to raise his SATs. As a result, he had developed the conviction that he was hopelessly stupid and would always need someone to hold his hand. Grace thought Kyle was a lot smarter than he gave himself credit for. He could complete all of the accounting problems on his own; he just needed her to check for careless mistakes.

In one month his accounting grade rose from C to B-plus, and he credited the success entirely to Grace. Kyle was the first person who encouraged her to become a math teacher. Grace loved geometry and calculus and could tolerate algebra, but she had always assumed that her people skills were too weak for teaching; the kids would eat her alive. Kyle Caldwell, however, made her feel likable, competent, and for the first time in her life—special. After a month the tutoring segued into steady dates.

Kyle wasn't brilliant or handsome, but the mere fact of his physical existence delighted Grace's mother. Every week she wanted to hear details of what Grace and Kyle had done. What restaurants had they visited? What parties had they attended? Once, before a dinner date, Grace let her mom visit for the afternoon, just so that Mrs. McCluskey could shake Kyle's hand when he arrived to pick Grace up. She lived in Holford's Green Forest Apartments, next to the new aquatic center, and when Kyle pulled up in his BMW convertible, Mrs. McCluskey had gawked at the window.

"I told you he was a Caldwell," Grace whispered. "Please don't stare." Kyle invited Mrs. McCluskey to join them for dinner, but she said no, she needed to get home to her husband, and Grace smiled to think of all the joyful news her mother would report. From that point forward, she was the golden daughter; her past failures faded beneath the cleansing reality of Kyle's existence.

Grace never told her mom that Kyle was a thief. That detail surfaced one afternoon when Grace and Kyle were buying beer at the Safeway self-checkout line. The attendant walked over to check Kyle's ID, and as soon as she turned her back, he took a pack of Trident from the candy rack. He didn't rush or glance around to see if anyone noticed; he just picked it up as if he owned the gum and put it in his pocket. Grace was shocked, but once she noticed that small act, she started to see how he often lifted merchandise from other stores. At Walmart, Kyle would fill a cart with a dozen items and run them all through the self-checkout line, except one. When the machine asked if he had anything left in his cart, he would press no, and pay for everything else. It was as if he felt entitled to one bonus gift each time they went shopping: a chocolate bar, some Life Savers, a box of tic tacs.

Grace suspected that this candy theft was tied to Kyle's weight problem; thirty pounds of extra flesh had given him the appearance of a chunky, overgrown toddler. Maybe he was compensating for some childhood deprivation? His mom had probably denied him sweets when he was a kid. But then Grace saw him take other things—CDs and ChapStick and iTunes cards—and he didn't seem to view these acts as stealing. According to Kyle, he spent so much money at the stores, he was entitled to a few freebies.

He displayed the same attitude toward Holford; supposedly the college owed him more than he was getting in exchange. Once, when he needed a stapler for an English paper, he strolled into the department secretary's office while she was at lunch and "borrowed" hers, never returning it. "My dad has given this school so many millions," he explained, "we deserve a lot more than a stapler."

Grace also watched him steal from people who owed him nothing. At a party in a house rented by three Holford girls, she and Kyle were walking through a bedroom to reach the master bath when Kyle stopped to examine the makeup, perfume, and jewelry on a dresser. After sniffing a few of the perfume bottles, he stuffed a small green vial into his jacket pocket. "A souvenir," he said, smiling at Grace. She had no idea what he did with that perfume—he never gave it to her—but what struck her most was how Kyle always got away with his theft; everywhere they went he lifted something.

She didn't want to be around when Kyle's luck ran out, so Grace started waiting in the car whenever he stepped inside a store. She even considered breaking up with him, theft being a worse sin than her own penchant for lying, but Grace's slim moral standards couldn't trump her desire for a date. The Spring Fling was approaching in April, and she was determined, once in her life, to attend a school dance. Besides, her mom was so excited. Mrs. McCluskey had visited at the end of March, taking Kyle and Grace out to dinner at Applebee's, which she obviously viewed as a special treat, but since Kyle's parents never ate at chain restaurants, he seemed surprised that a mother would choose a place with plastic-laminated menus. Her car had shocked him too—Grace could see it in his eyes. She supposed he'd never met anyone who drove a Buick.

When the Spring Fling arrived, Grace wore the dress her mom had bought the previous year, and asked a friend to take a few pictures of her and Kyle, imagining that she could erase all previous lies if her stories came true during her senior year of college. She and Kyle ate at a French restaurant, and enjoyed a few slow dances in Holford's Greco-Roman dining hall, where a dozen shipped-in palmetto trees were strewn with white Christmas lights to achieve the Caribbean theme. There was nothing for Kyle to steal, other than a few silk orchids from a table, which he stuck into his lapel like a boutonniere.

Had Grace been wise, she would have broken up with Kyle shortly after the dance. They had no future together; after graduation Kyle was heading for New York to work in banking, and the only time she had visited Manhattan, the noisy crowds had terrified her. She could never teach in a big-city public school—a nice middle-size suburban community seemed ideal.

Many times in the past few years, Grace had daydreamed of returning to those April days after the dance, ending her first love on a high note, and wishing Kyle well. Then she would never have set foot in Professor Greene's house, never watched Kyle steal dolls from a five-year-old girl, never witnessed the confrontation when he finally got caught. Who would have thought, after all that shoplifting, that Kyle wouldn't be nabbed by a Walmart clerk, but instead by a professor, at her home? And the ugliness that followed—the escalation from shouting, to threats, to bloody violence—it had all triggered the worst lies of her life. Lies to the police, lies to her family, lies that hurt Maggie Greene.

Winding down the eastern slope of Humpback Ridge, Grace felt sheltered by the mountain laurel and rhododendron, the miles of moss and soft pine needles and fiddlehead ferns. Sunlight flickered across the hood of her car, and as she watched it flash and disappear, she wondered if she should call Maggie when she got home. They needed to arrange a time when they could meet privately, but she didn't want Maggie's dad to answer the phone. Her obligation was to the daughter, not the father. Mr. Greene hadn't been present nine years ago; he hadn't stared at Grace from his bedcovers with terror in his eyes. If she called the house and asked for Maggie without explaining herself, Mr. Greene might assume that his daughter was in trouble—that her grades were bad, or there had been a problem in class; he might ask for a parent-teacher conference.

She could always send an e-mail, but if Maggie didn't reply, Grace would never know whether the girl had received her message. She often wondered if her words disintegrated into cyberspace the moment she pressed send, so many people never replied.

For a message so delicate, Grace needed to look into Maggie's eyes and search for comprehension, perhaps even a glimpse of sympathy. It was risky, to base her peace of mind on the goodwill of a child, especially a teenager who might not feel charitable toward any adults, but she had brought this fate upon herself. Tomorrow after class she would ask Maggie to stay for a few extra minutes to set a time and place for a long talk.

Another ten minutes and Grace had entered the Appalachian foothills, where woods bowed to meadows, cattle, and farmhouses, before the pastures gradually transformed into subdivisions—hayfields dotted with houses on every five or six acres, each one trying to grow a few maples and dogwoods too small, for the time being, to offer more than a handful of shade. Next came the subdivisions with two-acre lots, then one-acre lots, then rows of town houses with front-facing garages and postage-stamp lawns, followed by no garages and no lawns, and finally the road widened into a four-lane corridor packed with McDonald's and Wendy's and Burger King, Exxon and CITGO and Shell, the same dismal welcome offered by most towns across America.

Grace turned right, then left, entering a tree-lined neighborhood full of modest homes, mostly two-story frame houses with slim front porches, and a few brick ranchers whose awkward additions protruded like goiters from their sides and backs. She pulled into the driveway of a petite Cape Cod painted olive green with white trim—the same colors for the last thirty years, retouched but never reconsidered. Gathering up her bag of student work, Grace stepped out of the car and headed for the back door. Her father and his friends always entered through the front, moving straight to the coat closet and living room recliners. The back door was the women's entrance, leading past the laundry room into the beige-countered kitchen, where today's scene varied only slightly from her childhood memories. Mrs. Higgins was sipping coffee, reading the latest issue of *Redbook*, while Grace's mother, almost sixty, leaned over Lily at the counter, her veined hands cupped around the child's pink fingers as she helped the four-year-old hold an electric mixer steady over a large metal bowl.

"We're baking cookies!" Lily announced, turning to smile at her mom.

"I can see that." Grace walked over to give her mother and daughter quick kisses on their cheeks. "What kind are you making?"

"Snickerdoodles!" Lily's favorite word.

"Who gets to lick the beaters?"

"Me!"

"And you." Mrs. McCluskey ejected the beaters and handed them to Grace and Lily. "I'll get out the cookie sheets and you can grease them," she told her granddaughter, before turning to Grace. "How was work?"

"Fine."

"Anything interesting going on at the high school?" Celia Higgins asked.

"Nothing much." Grace shrugged. "The seniors are voting for a homecoming king and queen to be crowned at the game on Friday."

"I can't get over the idea of a homecoming king." Mrs. Higgins shook her head without glancing up. "What boy wants that?"

Who wouldn't want it? thought Grace. Although the homecoming king was essentially a king of fools, chosen from the school's most palatable nerds, the math-club boys who had been nominated told Grace they were delighted. Parody was their element, and they looked forward to escorting the queen's court onto the fifty-yard line at half-time. When else could they walk arm in arm with the school's crème de la crème, the girls with the clearest skin, the softest cashmere, and the heaviest orthodontic investment?

"Seems like girl stuff to me," Mrs. Higgins continued. "But I'm a dinosaur. Would you like a cup of coffee?"

Grace shook her head. "No thanks. I'm going to grade these quizzes before dinner."

Mrs. Higgins waved her off with a flick of her wrist and Grace gave Lily another squeeze before retreating to her room upstairs.

The house's second level contained two bedrooms, with a small full bath between. Grace and Lily occupied the east room and her parents shared the west, which was fitting, so her mother explained, because the younger generation should witness the sunrises while the older faced the sunsets. Not that you could glimpse either from these rooms, looking out on the neighbors' shingled roofs and into open windows where children sat alone, watching TV.

Both bedrooms had sloped ceilings, so that now, as Grace stretched out on her bed, the ceiling leaned southward toward her toes. Only Lily could walk upright at the far end of the room; she enjoyed standing on tiptoe and touching the ceiling, walking her fingers along its slope until she could no longer make contact, then climbing onto the bed and standing at its foot, following the ceiling until halfway toward the headboard, where the plaster escaped her fingertips again. Whenever Grace watched her daughter's bare feet tiptoeing across the pink-and-green stitched bedcovers, she felt a stab of irony. She had returned home from a dead marriage to find that her mother had covered her old bed in a wedding-ring quilt.

Now Grace's right index finger traced the pattern, following one band until it connected to the next, and the next—multiple marriages, she thought, not one monogamous lifetime union. Sighing, she reached toward her bedside table and lifted a puzzle book, *Black Belt Sudoku*, and she filled in all the eights and sevens before she heard Lily's footsteps, running up the stairs. The door swung open and the child stood there in her four-year-old perfection, dark hair in braided pigtails, red lips with bits of cookie dough at the corners. Lily ran over and hopped onto the bed, snuggling up beside her mom.

"I thought you were going to grease the pans and bake the cookies," said Grace.

"I'm tired," Lily moaned. "Grandma says she'll do it. Can we read a story?"

"*Madeline*, or *Curious George?*"

"Both."

THE next day Grace didn't eat breakfast, and the two cups of coffee in her empty stomach left her skittish and heavy-footed on the morning drive. She crossed the mountain in record time, absorbing news of suicide bombings and plane wrecks and economic woes until her imminent confrontation with Maggie seemed part of a vast, bleak tapestry—so much death and carelessness and heavy guilt.

Once the school day began, she felt distracted in all of her classes, writing the wrong numbers on her chalkboard, having to erase and apologize, and erase again. The sentences she had rehearsed the previous night—*I believe that Jesus plans these things. He wants us to be reconciled*—now seemed ridiculous. Maggie was probably an atheist who would scoff at any mention of Christ. Besides, the words came across as an excuse, as if she were an obedient servant acting against her will.

Grace tried to craft a secular version at lunch in the teachers' lounge. In a notebook of wide-ruled paper she drafted a sentence: *I think that fate arranges these things—our meeting is a form of destiny.* She liked the sound of "destiny," the way it was propelled by a hard consonant before trailing off into a lingering vowel, but the rest of her sentence sounded as if she was going to propose to the girl. Grace tore out the page and balled it up.

Maybe she could fit "destiny" into a better sentence, something about life's strange twists and turns. Grace swallowed a few bites from a tuna-fish sandwich, remembering how she had once taught a Hispanic girl named Destinee whose name had inspired jokes among the cruelest middle school students, since her plain face, poor family, and miserable grades seemed to destine her for nothing better than a job at Hardee's.

Now Grace penned the simplest, most straightforward message she could manage: *We need to talk about what happened nine years ago. I have a lot to tell you, things you might not know. When could we meet?* Grace tore out the sheet and folded it carefully, tucking it into her skirt pocket.

By seventh period, when the students trickled in for geometry, Grace could not hold her hand steady enough to write a number eight on the chalkboard. The loops emerged tremulous, like a wandering piece of yarn, so she sat at her desk and concentrated on her picture of Jesus. *Lord give me strength.* After the bell rang and the students began to whisper and giggle, she raised her eyes to Maggie's desk, but the chair was empty.

"Has anyone seen Maggie Greene?" Grace tried to sound non- chalant.

"I think she's out sick," one girl responded. "She wasn't in English or science."

Of course. Maggie would need a day to absorb the shock. Grace took a deep breath and walked to the board, relieved that she would have one more night to perfect a few words of contrition.

On Thursday, however, Maggie remained absent, and on Friday, when the geometry students filed in for their last class of the day, Grace stood looking out her window, rigid with dread.

Mr. Greene had pulled into the parking lot, and was now stepping out of his car.

It hadn't occurred to Grace that Maggie would send her dad—that Grace's story might have to be offered to the father, instead of the child. She had imagined that she and Maggie were linked together;

the girl would remember how their eyes had met nine years ago, and understand that the two of them must eventually speak.

She took a step back from the glass as Mr. Greene locked his car door. Grace didn't want him to glance up and see her watching. Instead, she observed from a safe distance as he disappeared into the building below. Soon the front office would buzz her room and call her downstairs, where there would be no private space to speak to Mr. Greene alone, and no way, in a brief encounter, to fully account for her presence at this school, or at his home. If he spoke to the principal first, she might have to explain herself to both of them at the same time, and those two men would never understand the distinctly female predicaments of her life, how it was that an unassuming girl could get mixed up with dangerous boys who showed up at people's houses in the middle of the night.

The crackling intercom interrupted her thoughts.

"Mrs. Murdock?"

Grace inhaled slowly. "Yes?"

"Can you have someone bring down Maggie Greene's homework assignments? Her father is here to pick them up."

Grace stared at her hands, silent.

"Mrs. Murdock?"

"Yes, I'll send someone right down."

How stupid of her, to have forgotten the school policy. If a student missed two consecutive days, a parent was supposed to come to the main office and pick up the child's makeup work. It was the principal's way of combating truancy—making sure that parents were aware of the absences, and of the amount of work that piled up every day. Parents who carried homework in their hands might take the time to look over it, and feel responsible for ensuring that it was completed and returned, or so the principal hoped.

Grace flipped through her manila folders, removing two work-sheets and paper-clipping a note card to the top: *Complete pages 56–7 in your textbook, then solve the even numbered problems on these sheets. Be prepared for a test on Tuesday. And please see me ASAP.* As a small gift to the father and daughter, she attached Maggie's makeup test to the back, with a big red A on top. *Excellent.*

"Melissa?" She summoned her most reliable student. "Take these down to the office."

Ten minutes later, when her class was absorbed in a quiz, Grace stood at the window and watched Mr. Greene drive away. It troubled her to think that Maggie had missed three days of school on her account. The ninth grade had taken its annual field trip to the college's Bozeman Theater that morning, to watch a production of *Much Ado About Nothing,* so Maggie was not just skipping geometry, she was missing important events in her other classes, and probably falling behind on all of her assignments. Once again, Grace's presence in the girl's life was causing damage.

When the final bell rang and the building began to settle into its weekend malaise, Grace stayed behind to write an e-mail.

Maggie,

I am concerned that your absences are going to affect your grades in all of your classes.

No, too official. She backspaced through the message and started again.

Maggie,

We need to talk. Please reply. Grace Murdock

She frowned at her bluntness. Numbers were the only vocabulary Grace had ever mastered; equations were her sentences, proofs were her short stories. By comparison, this little note appeared clipped and primitive.

She sighed. So much stress over a handful of syllables. Grace gave the picture of Jesus on her desk one last, imploring glance, then pressed send.

CHAPTER 8

"HEY Maggie, you just got an e-mail."

Kate was sitting at the desk in Maggie's bedroom, watching You-Tube videos on her friend's laptop. The desk, a white, wooden affair, decorated with gold trim and fake-crystal knobs, was too small for Kate's hefty legs, its compact ornateness perfect for an eight-year-old princess. Or maybe a deposed princess, thought Maggie as she looked at the chipped wooden roses carved into the back of the chair. On the opposite side of the room the matching dresser was missing half of its knobs, and the mirror had grown cloudy, so that whenever Maggie stared at herself, she sensed that she was fading into a flash-back.

For the past half hour she'd been reclining in bed, in a state of mock exhaustion. "I think I've got, like, swine flu—lots of chills and a fever in the afternoons, and I'm sick to my stomach half the time. I don't know if you should even be here. I mean, I'm glad you came by, but this is probably contagious."

"You missed the Shakespeare field trip," Kate replied, unconcerned about chills and fever. "Mrs. Blake told us how the 'Nothing' in the title refers to a hole, which really means a woman's hole, you know? So that got all the boys interested enough to shut up during the play, and they were snickering every time the actors used the word 'whore.' But then they felt ripped off afterward, because there were no sex scenes."

The e-mail arrived, announced by two high, tinny notes, which, to Maggie's ears, sounded like "Uh-oh."

"It's from your creeper math teacher."

"Don't open it!" Maggie sat upright.

"Too late . . . Don't worry—it's short and harmless. Just says she wants to talk with you . . . You'd think she could have told you that in person sometime. I mean, I've never gotten an e-mail from a teacher."

Maggie shrugged, pretending to be absorbed in the latest issue of *Vogue* that Kate had brought as a get-well present. "I told you she's weird."

"So can I delete this?"

"Sure."

Kate started to download a five-minute video. "Are you coming to the homecoming game tonight?"

"How can I come to the game if I've got swine flu?"

Kate turned to face Maggie. "Well, you *are* coming to the dance tomorrow, right? You've *got* to come to the dance."

Maggie slumped in bed, staring up at Johnny Depp. "Why should I come to the dance if I don't have a date?"

"Homecoming is like a group-date thing. Holly and Beth are eating dinner at my house, then we'll all be getting ready together. You've got to come too. That dress you bought two weeks ago is hot, and you know Mike will be there."

Maggie had zero interest in dances, but one of the senior nominees for homecoming king, Mike Hodges, lived three houses down the road, and she was hoping he might be crowned at the football game. All summer he had been nice to her, inviting her into his house to check out his science lab, something she suspected might be a pickup line—"Come into my basement, little girl, and I'll show you my volcano." Maggie had been disappointed, by summer's end, when Mike hadn't touched her. He hadn't even stepped close enough to smell her hair, which she had shampooed with coconut Suave, just for him. The most he had ever done was to hold open the basement door while she walked five steps down into the cool, musty air of a concrete space, where gardening tools leaned against cinder-block walls and shelves made of bricks and planks held dozens of half-empty paint cans. In the middle of the basement, plywood sheets propped on sawhorses held a range of experiments, from electrical circuits, to a gerbil maze, to Maggie's favorite—a landscape of crystals that Mike had been growing for four years. It reminded her of Bryce Canyon and the trip out west she'd taken with her dad when she was ten. Here was a world of two-inch hoodoos that sparkled red and gold when Mike flipped a switch, revealing a ceiling lit by hundreds of little Christmas bulbs, all rigged through one Eveready battery. The lights made Maggie think of Ralph Ellison's *Invisible Man*, 1,369 bulbs in the basement of a maniac, but she didn't say that aloud. She didn't want Mike to know that she had read many of the classics on her mother's old bookshelves— the Brontë sisters, and the Dickens and Austen volumes that said *Desk Copy, Not for Resale* in gold lettering across the back. She'd traced her finger across her mother's notes in the margins of *Pride and Prejudice*— scribbled thoughts on women's education and Mary Wollstonecraft and the French Revolution. She'd even tried a few chapters from Tolstoy and Dostoevsky, but why tell any of that to Mike? A science nerd might not like an English nerd.

"I'll try to go to the dance," Maggie told Kate. "If my dad's okay with it."

"Come to my house for dinner, all right? I'll help you with some makeup."

Maggie rolled her eyes as Kate shut down the computer, lifting the copy of *Vogue*. "So what do you think Mrs. Murdock wants to talk about?" Kate asked.

Maggie shrugged. "Probably all the work I've been missing. My grade must be tanking."

"Do you think you did okay on the makeup test?"

"No clue." Maggie hadn't told her friend about Tuesday afternoon—how she had run away after realizing Mrs. Murdock was the same college girl whose high laughter had drifted up from the creek nine years ago. Maggie didn't plan to tell anyone—at least, that was the decision she had reached on her first day home from school. "Get some rest," her dad had told her. "You work too hard." He had been worried, the previous afternoon, by her bloodless face and eagerness to hurry home. She hadn't breathed a syllable of explanation; the past nine years had brought her father enough trouble, so that all of Maggie's current impulses were tuned toward limiting the damage. These days she tried to bring her father only good news: excellent report cards and certificates of achievement, no cavities at the dentist's office, no cancer at the doctor's. She didn't ask him to spend much money on her clothes or technology, and she hadn't burdened him with the daily struggles of middle school, figuring that most of her problems would fade if she waited them out.

But Mrs. Murdock wasn't likely to fade. She seemed rooted at the high school, the seventh-period wall that Maggie would crash against every day. And what could her father do about that? Transfer her to another school? The two other public high schools within driving distance were drug-infested and academically weak, and private schools were too expensive and far away. Her dad might insist that Maggie be assigned to a different math teacher, or press for Mrs. Murdock to be fired, which would be embarrassing. Either way, the past would be stirred up, and everyone at the high school would be gossiping again about her family.

She had also decided, on her first day home from school, that she wouldn't tell Kate. Their friendship relied on an understanding that they did not discuss the past, which was one of the things that Maggie appreciated most. Other girls who had come to Maggie's house in previous years asked uncomfortable questions. Where is your mom? What happened when you were little? Why are you seeing a therapist? They had been too young, nine years ago, to absorb the Greene family's story as it unfolded. Preschoolers didn't read newspapers—those colorless adult mysteries—and their mothers turned off TVs and radios when the talk became violent. And so Maggie's earliest friends had been blessedly oblivious, caring more about bicycles, Barbies, and puppies than the sordid details of other people's lives.

Curiosity came later, by the middle of elementary school, when the children began to absorb fragments of adult knowledge. Their parents murmured distorted versions of the truth, bits and pieces they recalled from Jackson's weekly paper. Local professors remembered details from the *Washington Post*, vague scenes of reporters running a media carnival at Maggie's old house, parking vans with satellite dishes in the grass at the side of their country road, filming the mountains, the creek, and the porch, while her dad yelled curses from the screened windows. In a town of eight thousand people, most adults knew some version of the story, and for years Maggie had endured the scrutiny of shopkeepers and grocery-store clerks whose gossip crept into the vocabulary of their children, casting shadows at birthday parties and sleepovers.

Kate, however, had never contributed to the shade. She seemed to instinctively grasp that some parts of life were painful, and should be left alone. Maggie figured her friend's sensitivity came from Kate's own troubled childhood. Katerina Poroskova, daughter of an alcoholic, unmarried teenager, had been abandoned at age two in a Russian orphanage plagued by rowdy boys, until one day a childless American woman, searching for an infant, spotted her on a bench, silently enduring the pokes and pinches of a spiky-haired, skinny demon. Could she take that little girl for a walk?

Away from the tempest, the defensive toddler had blossomed into a garrulous girl, who arrived at Jackson's Montessori preschool two months later, still painfully shy but amazed to enter a classroom where boys and girls could read and paint and construct pink towers without kicking one another.

Maggie had known about Kate's background before the girl ever arrived in America, because Kate's adoptive mother taught English at Holford, with an office right across the hall from Maggie's mom. Professor McConnell was a widow who had spent two years trying to arrange an overseas adoption, and she had kept Emma informed of all the developments in Russia—the corruption and bribery, the promised infant who never materialized, the sweet toddler who needed a rescuer.

"Be nice to the girl, she doesn't speak English," Emma had instructed the first time she invited Kate and her mom over to the house. Three-year-old Maggie had wondered what a Russian girl might look like. Would she have steely blue eyes like a Siberian husky?

No, Kate had soft brown eyes, and it was easy to be nice to a girl who was delighted with everything. Kate had loved the creek at Maggie's house, stomping in purple Crocs and scooping up minnows with her bare hands. She had loved Maggie's Calico Critter dollhouse and Kapla blocks and blue Moon Sand, and she had been thankful for every cookie and apple. Within one year her bony frame had grown "pleasantly plump"; Maggie's mom jokingly referred to Kate as "Scarlett" because of the child's determination to never go hungry again.

Kate and Maggie had become best friends, but friends who didn't talk about deep subjects. In middle school their most serious conversation had centered around *Swan Lake,* and whether a human might be better off spending half her life as a bird. Kate's mom, in deference to her daughter's Russian heritage, was forever buying tickets to Tchaikovsky ballets, or renting *Doctor Zhivago,* or trying to get her daughter to read Chekhov or *Anna Karenina,* though Kate had never made it past the opening paragraph. *All happy families are alike,* Maggie thought as she looked now at her friend, tagging photos on Facebook. Then she looked across the room and saw her face in the mirror—*Each unhappy family is unhappy in its own way.*

No, Maggie would not tell Kate about Mrs. Murdock—not until she worked out her own plan. For now her only confidant would be Dr. Riley, the empty jar into which she poured thousands of penny thoughts. He could be trusted to keep the bizarre news from her dad until the time was right.

Dr. Riley, however, would press her to take some sort of action. "Speak to Mrs. Murdock," he would insist. "Hear what the woman has to say for herself, and decide how you want to respond." Right now Maggie couldn't stomach the idea. Her sole impulse was to avoid that face, that voice, that dark shadow mouthing "I'm sorry." Last night the teacher had resurfaced in her dreams, still muttering mathematical gibberish, causing Maggie to wake and pull her comforter over her head, curling into a fetal retreat.

But she couldn't hide for long. This morning she had overheard her dad, calling their family doctor and repeating her swine-flu story. He had scheduled an appointment for Monday at one o'clock, which meant that if Maggie didn't return to school that morning, her dad would have to shell out a thirty-five-dollar copayment only to hear the usual warnings about her low weight, and the risk of anemia.

"I better get home," Kate said, tossing the *Vogue* onto the foot of

Maggie's bed. "Mom wants me back for an early dinner before the game. Should I call tomorrow morning about the dance?"

"Sure," said Maggie. "My dad will probably offer to drive us home."

Kate paused at the bedroom door. "We'll miss you tonight."

"Yeah, right." Maggie waved her off.

Once Kate had left the house, Maggie heaved herself from her covers and padded downstairs in her extra-large T-shirt and Armadillo slippers. Her dad was on the living room couch, watching TV, so she gave him a kiss on the cheek and slouched down beside him.

"What's for dinner?" she asked, knowing he measured her well-being according to her appetite.

"I hadn't planned anything because I thought you wouldn't be hungry. Are you feeling better?"

"Yeah, I'm starving."

"How about if I get some Chinese takeout?"

"Sure. Shrimp lo mein for me, and steamed dumplings."

With her dad gone, Maggie lifted the remote and spent thirty minutes flipping through channels. *Law & Order, Bones, Forensic Files.* Murder, murder everywhere. She turned off the TV and picked up the phone beside the couch, planning to arrange a time to see Dr. Riley. She had missed her Thursday appointment because of her "illness" and wasn't scheduled again for two weeks—too long to hide such a big secret.

The doctor's home phone rang once before a woman said hello.

"Hi, Mrs. Riley, this is Maggie Greene."

"Hello, Maggie. How've you been doing?"

"Okay, I guess. I hope I didn't interrupt your dinner."

"Oh no, the boys are eating pizza in the basement."

Maggie shuffled her feet. So much for her elaborate visions of other families' meat-and-potato dinners. "Is the doctor in?"

"No, he flew out to San Francisco today for a conference. He'll be back on Wednesday. Is there anything I can help you with?"

Maggie hesitated. "No, I guess not."

"Ken's associate, Dr. Clark, will be in all week. She's really good if you need to talk to somebody right away."

"That's okay. It'll keep."

When she hung up, she heard a rustle of plastic behind her, and saw her dad emptying the take-out bags on the kitchen counter.

"Who was on the phone?"

"Just Kate. She forgot something." Maggie hated lying to her dad. For them, reticence was common, but deceit was uncharted territory. Still, if she told her dad that she wanted to schedule a special time to see the doctor, he would fret; she had never volunteered for an appointment.

Together they unfolded TV trays and peeled apart chopsticks, and Maggie feigned enthusiasm while they watched reruns of *The Office*. She guessed that four dumplings and half a box of lo mein, followed by a big breakfast the next morning, should buy her admission to Saturday's dance.

"How much work did the school send home?" Maggie reached over and took a bite of General Tso's chicken from her dad's tray.

He gestured toward a stack of papers on the hall table. "Latin, science, history, and geometry. But I don't think you should feel obligated to do it all. They shouldn't give sick kids a lot of homework."

"It's no problem. The stuff isn't hard. I'll get started after dinner."

That, too, was a ploy. If her dad saw her spending hours on homework on a Friday night, he'd be eager for Maggie to go out on Saturday. Good parents were predictable, and her dad was unfailingly good.

The next evening Maggie showed up for dinner at Kate's in a red satin spaghetti-strap dress that hung loose just above her knees. She refused to wear the tight, strapless, two-foot swathes of fabric that passed for elegance among most of the hooker-chic girls in her class, and the one-inch heels on the sandals provided by Kate were as high as she was willing to tower. She did give Kate free rein with her face, allowing eyeliner, rouge, burgundy lip gloss, and brown eye shadow with sparkles of gold.

"You look fantastic," said Kate. "You really should wear makeup more often. At least mascara and some lip color."

When Maggie looked into the mirror, a Goth princess stared back. "Whatever," she said, puckering her lips.

An hour later, inside the school gymnasium, piles of girls' high heels were discarded against the walls. The only decorations were white Christmas lights draped around doors, and clusters of red and gold balloons tied to the ends of the bleachers. Most of the smart kids were sitting in those bleachers, as if the dance were another sporting event where their role was to watch the athletes and cheerleaders moving their bodies.

Against the far wall, the refreshment table offered bowls of chips and bottles of water—anything that couldn't be baked with pot or spiked with alcohol. From her vantage in the bleachers' third row, Maggie could see Kate dancing in a circle of fist-pumping girls, while to her right Mike Hodges was standing near the Doritos. He was wearing a blue blazer and crimson tie that she guessed had been chosen by his mother, and he looked tall and gawky in an appealing, Jimmy Stewart way. He hadn't been crowned as king at the game. The students had chosen the heaviest boy on the court—Dave Huffner, who, despite his weight, had an impressive gift for tap dancing. Dave had managed to bring down the house at last spring's talent show with a tapping mash-up of "Singing in the Rain" and "It's Raining Men."

Maggie watched as a shock of brown hair drooped over Mike's right eye. He kept tossing it back as he talked to a friend at his side.

"He's cute," a girl in front of Maggie said.

"Yeah, but he's weird," another replied.

"I don't care. He's still cute. I'm going to ask him to dance."

Maggie sat up straight, watching the girl glide on stockinged feet over to Mike's corner, putting her hand on his shoulder as she approached from behind and running her fingers through her long blond hair as she spoke, right hip cocked to the side. Maggie wondered how her own thick hair would look if she ran her fingers through it so much; it would probably frizz up into a reddish-brown trapezoid.

To her surprise, the blonde came gliding back to her friend in the bleachers.

"Did you ask him?"

"Yes."

"What did he say?"

"He said he would dance with me if I could tell him Newton's first law of motion."

"Oh my God, I told you he was weird."

"*Beyond* weird." They started laughing.

Maggie smiled, then stood up and walked to the food table. She didn't want any chips, fearing Dorito breath and orange teeth, but she lifted one Tostito and nibbled at its edge until Mike turned her way.

"Sorry you didn't win homecoming king," she said.

"That's okay." He smiled, stepping toward her. "Dave looks better in the crown . . . I didn't see you at the game."

"I was sick."

"You didn't miss much." Mike stared at his feet. "I hear Dave is having a party at his house after this dance. Are you going?"

Maggie blushed. "That'll be mostly for seniors like you. Besides, my dad thinks I turn into a pumpkin if I'm not home by midnight."

Beside them, the fast music ended, and Maggie could see Kate's eyes, searching the bleachers for her.

"Let's slow things down," the DJ murmured, "with a ballad from Adele."

Maggie took a deep breath. "Hey Mike."

"Yeah?"

"A body at rest will remain at rest."

A broad smile lit up his face and he pressed both of his palms to his heart, left hand over right. "Unless acted on by an unbalanced force."

He reached forward and took her hand, and while the blondes in the bleacher stared, he walked Maggie to the middle of the gym, put one hand around her waist, and twined his other through her fingers for an old-fashioned slow dance. Maggie, who had only seen couples swaying together in tight, full-body hugs, stood flustered for a moment, awkward and unsure.

"Put your left hand on my shoulder," Mike said, smiling. "I'll lead."

CHAPTER 9

ON Sunday morning Maggie lingered in bed, trying to relive the tactile memory of Mike's hand on her waist. Last night, when the song ended and the room returned to a sea of grinding bodies, Maggie had blushed at the broken spell and said thanks, hurrying back to Kate. Now she regretted her haste. If she had stood there and tried to talk to him, would they have stepped outside and had a long, thoughtful conversation? Could one lovely moment have changed the course of her life?

Her right hand was already beginning to forget the temperature of his fingers, and by nighttime the image of Mrs. Murdock had replaced all visions of Mike. On Monday morning Maggie's only thought was to find a convenient cave where she could hibernate for the rest of the year. Not only would that save her from the geometry teacher, failing the ninth grade might cancel the college expectations that weighed so heavily on her mind.

"Don't you want your breakfast?" her dad asked as she stirred her soggy cornflakes.

"I'm not hungry."

"Feeling sick again?" He walked over and placed his palm on her forehead.

"Maybe a little queasy."

"I haven't canceled your doctor's appointment yet. He could still see you at one o'clock."

"It's all right." She brushed his hand away.

When her dad dropped her off at school, she entered the first row of doors, then stopped to peer through the second layer of glass. Mrs. Murdock might be lurking in the hallway, planning an ambush, but Maggie couldn't spot her. Stepping inside, she hurried to her locker unmolested. The routes to most of her classes passed through Mrs. Murdock's hall—she would have to loop around the building to avoid the woman's door, which meant arriving breathless and several seconds late to a few classes, but so be it.

She survived until lunch without laying eyes on the woman, and the cafeteria provided a Green Zone, deterring all teachers with its smell, noise, and crowd. Still, math waited at the end of the day, and although she might endure her other classes, Maggie couldn't bear to step inside Mrs. Murdock's room and see the woman grading quizzes as if she was just an average teacher, leading a normal life.

"You want those tater tots?" Kate reached for Maggie's plate.

"Take them all." Maggie slid the tray over.

She wanted to call her dad and say she felt sick again, but that would disrupt his workday, and he might be annoyed that he had already canceled the doctor's appointment. Instead she decided to spend seventh period in the "girls' lounge"—a low-traffic bathroom at the northwest corner of the school, near the vo-tech center. Girls with vague complaints of cramps and headaches routinely gathered there to sit on the sinks or lock themselves inside stalls where they texted for half an hour.

Every few days the assistant principal, Mrs. Walker, raided the place, sending girls back to class with a "yeah, yeah" to stories of PMS and bipolar breakdowns. First offenders received harsh warnings; second timers earned an hour in detention. Three offenses and a student could face an all-day in-school suspension. Mrs. Walker inspected the bathroom at different hours every week so that no one could predict her appearances, but according to the lunchroom gossip there had already been a raid that afternoon, so Maggie hoped that by seventh period the lounge would be safe.

She hadn't realized how ridiculous she would feel, sitting in a bathroom stall for forty-five minutes reading *The Toilet Paper*, a laminated sheet of cartoons and anecdotes taped to the stall door, warning students against smoking and drinking and date rape. Someone had scrawled *I love reefer!* across the top with a black ballpoint that dug into the plastic so deeply, a blind student could have deciphered the words with her fingers. In the handicapped stall next to Maggie, two girls were discussing the homecoming dance: who came drunk, who left drunk, who slow-danced with whom.

"Oh my God, did you see that Dave Huffner brought his crown to school this morning? Like, the joke is *over* and he's still clinging."

"It's pathetic."

"Ultrapathetic."

Maggie covered her ears and closed her eyes, wanting to block all five of her senses: deaf to the girls, blind to the stall, oblivious to the hard ceramic toilet seat. Worst of all was the stench, a potpourri of urine and Lysol, marijuana and clogged toilets, with a hint of vomit. She tried breathing from her mouth, but could taste the smoke. After ten minutes the odors had infested her hair and clothes, settling into the pores of her skin, and she abandoned the bathroom early, retreating to her locker to gather her books and sweater. When the bell rang, she hurried outside, hoping to air out her hair and clothes before her dad arrived.

Tomorrow she would need a better plan. Maggie wondered if she could get away with walking up the street to the Dairy Queen during seventh period. The seniors sometimes enjoyed afternoon ice cream breaks, exiting in twos and threes and returning to the school with dipped cones and Oreo Blizzards. Students in independent study courses exited as they pleased, and the newspaper staff was always strolling in and out the front door, scheduling interviews outside the school. Ninth graders, however, were confined to the school grounds, and Maggie feared she would look too young and delinquent, walking alone past the baseball field and tennis courts.

A better plan surfaced in the cafeteria the next day. With only two hours left before seventh period, she was performing a mental inventory of janitors' closets fit for hiding when she looked up from her raspberry Jell-O and saw, through the dirty windows, how the back of the school formed a wide U, with the vo-tech building to the right, the gym to the left, and straight ahead a green expanse with half a dozen picnic tables leading out to a soccer field, and beyond that, the woods.

Those woods weren't merely a thin property line of pines, or a two-acre buffer between the school and a new subdivision. They stretched for miles into the Jefferson National Forest, blurring the boundary between town and wilderness. *The woods are lovely, dark, and deep,* Maggie thought. She could disappear into them, just as she had done when she was small—avoid the college girl by blending into the trees.

Her only question was how to cross the soccer field unnoticed. But then again, who would see her from this side of the building? Neither the gym nor the vo-tech center had any windows, and no one would be in the cafeteria during seventh period. Besides, who would care about one girl taking a walk?

During the class change between sixth and seventh periods, Maggie snuck down to the ground floor near the gymnasium, loitering until the halls were almost empty. When the bell rang, she opened the back door, slipped outside, and let its metal thud shut while the clatter of the bell muffled the sound. Maggie didn't run; neither did she look back or glance right or left. She focused her eyes on the trees and approached them purposefully, as if her next class was meeting in the forest and she was two minutes late.

When she entered the woods, she sensed that she had crossed into an alternate, more authentic world, free from buzzing fluorescent bulbs and noisy, irreverent humans. The woods that had been dark and frightening when she was a child welcomed her with bright red arms, and she imagined herself as the first student to discover these trees, the only girl to disturb the finches as they hopped on fallen leaves—an illusion shattered ten yards farther when she stepped on a used condom. Another thirty feet and Maggie reached a circle of cigarette butts and beer bottles half buried in the dirt, where a fallen tree served as a makeshift bench: the legendary "smokers' club," a favorite hangout, years ago, for the school's most disaffected teens. These days they preferred hideouts with Wi-Fi access.

Turning left, she walked deeper into the woods, away from the discarded cylinders of Skoal, prepared to trek forty miles to West Virginia, then on to Kentucky and Illinois—so long as she was back at the parking lot to meet her dad at three-fifteen. One hundred yards more and Maggie stopped at a group of three boulders leaning inward against one another like a trio of exhausted women. They were typical of the rocks scattered across the county—glacial remains rumored to contain the hardened spirits of Indians. Two deer beside the farthest boulder paused to stare before bolting, and their startled eyes told

Maggie she had reached a spot that other students rarely visited. Dropping her backpack to the ground, she gripped the tallest boulder and wedged her foot into its nicked side, pulling her way to the top, then lying down on her back and staring up through the trees' canopy.

Sunlight fell across her skin in dozens of small flecks, reminding her of her Latin teacher's story about Zeus impregnating Danaë with a golden shower. Was that a shower of light or rain, or something else? And did the Virgin Mary experience God as a shower of light? She wondered if the word *rape* ever crossed those women's minds.

Maggie disliked pregnancy stories, preferring a bodiless narrative for herself. She imagined this entire forest lit by a purifying flame, and she was the phoenix poised to rise from the ashes. Why had she never thought to visit these woods before? This rock was much more peaceful than any hiding place at school. She could spend every seventh period on its back, forget geometry, and study botany instead—botany and geology and Transcendental Meditation.

A crunch of leaves drew Maggie's attention to the left, where she expected to see another deer assessing her with liquid eyes, but instead she met the face of a man in sunglasses—a black man in a blue shirt and charcoal pants, who stared at her, unsmiling, as he slowly crossed his arms.

CHAPTER 10

TEN minutes earlier Carver Petty had been standing at his office window, watching shadows from the soccer goals lengthen across the grass, and asking himself, *Where does that child think she's going?*

The girl was wearing torn jeans, flip-flops, and a dark purple T-shirt with a blue plaid backpack slung across her right shoulder. He couldn't see her face, only the reddish flecks that the sunlight caught in her wavy brown hair as she advanced toward the woods. She hurried as if late for an appointment, probably a tryst arranged by text message.

He sighed. Up until that moment Carver had been enjoying the day's blessed slowness. Every quiet day was a measure of his success, meaning no fights, no weapons to confiscate, no scent of marijuana drifting from a bathroom, no phone calls to harassed parents, explaining that their no-good kid was in trouble, again. When Carver had initially taken the job as high school cop, this place was supposedly on the brink, plagued not only with the usual alcohol, drugs, and tobacco, but with the first signs of gang graffiti and clothing. At least that was what Buddy Blair, the officer assigned to the school for the previous four years, had claimed. Supposedly the Mexican families who had opened up the new El Tequila café were troublemakers.

Carver hadn't trusted a single word that oozed from Buddy Blair's mouth. Sure, gang activity was something to monitor at any high school—Richmond and Roanoke had been reporting problems for the past decade—but Blair was the kind of guy who ranted about illegal immigration whenever any new Hispanic family moved to town, and if the Jackson Police Department was going to pretend to give a damn about gang activity, why not talk about the KKK? Nobody had cared about the high school graffiti when it said *Fuck the Niggers,* or when swastikas appeared on bathroom doors. Some migrant worker with a Mexican flag on his ball cap was threatening, but it was okay for white boys to flaunt the Stars and Bars on their belt buckles.

Carver glanced over at the two rows of desks in the back of his room, where a boy in a camouflage hunting jacket, jeans, and brogans was slumped over a sheet of math questions: Bobby Lee Grant, a sixteen-year-old with a third-grade reading level, who probably had a Confederate bumper sticker on his pickup. Carver wondered if the boy understood the irony in his name.

"Are you making progress on your math, Mr. Grant?"

The boy slumped farther. "Not much."

Carver looked back across the soccer field, where the girl was disappearing into the woods. He noted the exact spot where she disappeared, to the left of the withering blackberry bushes and to the right of the sumac tree.

Walking over to his desk, he locked his computer and lifted his keys. Seven years had passed since Buddy Blair had left the Jackson police force to become a guard at the county jail, prompting Chief Miller to offer Carver this job. Carver's first response had been silent indignation. *Yeah right.* If the department's resident dumb-ass had finished with a job, why not pass it along to the token black guy? He was the only sergeant darker than a saltine in a county 95 percent white, and for ten years he'd endured jokes about "petty crime" and "petty theft," as if "petty" was his specialty, so why not give him the pettiest job of all, babysitter to a bunch of juvenile delinquents?

"Before you say no I want you to think about it," Miller had said. "This isn't just some bullshit assignment. Fact is, in a town this size the high school sees more drug activity than any other location, and you've had more experience with students than anyone else in this department."

Which was true. Carver had spent half his nights for the previous ten years dealing with drunk college kids, responding to complaints about noisy parties, and escorting staggering girls back to their sororities. In the process he'd developed a reputation among the students as a decent man, an officer who didn't mind the young people as much as the other Jackson cops did. Most of his fellow cops viewed the college crowd as spoiled rich brats who deserved to be brought down a few notches.

"This town's college students are a whole different breed from the high school kids," Carver had told the chief.

"That's right." Miller nodded. "But you've got a daughter at the high school, so you know the place better than any of us right now."

At the time Carver's daughter, Jessie, had been finishing the ninth grade. He'd been raising Jessie on his own ever since she turned six, when her mother left for Atlanta with another man. Since then, she'd been the focal point of his life, and Chief Miller was right—the high school needed good policing. Every day Jessie came home with stories of kids selling joints in the back rows of English, drinking shots of Wild Turkey with their cafeteria lunches, and having oral sex in the bathrooms.

The high school job had originally been a half-time gig for semi-retired cops, which mostly involved delivering the freshman orientation lecture on drugs and alcohol, performing random inspections of student lockers, and monitoring the crowd at dances and football games. But then came the Virginia Tech massacre, followed six months later by a shooting in the school lobby, compliments of a hunter's son who, in his last act before dropping out, had brought his dad's rifle into the main hallway and aimed it, not at any person, but at the statue of the school mascot, a golden, snarling lion that faced the students every day when they entered the building. The boy had emptied five rounds into the lion's mouth before being tackled by the senior counselor.

After that the town's parents had insisted on greater security, which meant metal detectors, quarterly lockdown drills, drug-sniffing German shepherds, and a full-time position, community policing style, for any cop who could tolerate teenagers. Carver had initially agreed to a three-year commitment, promising to stay just long enough to see his daughter graduate and hopefully make a difference in a few kids' lives. College was too late—he'd seen too many freshmen arrive in town as confirmed alcoholics or drug users. With fourteen-year-olds he might have a chance to steer some high-risk kids in the right direction.

Now, as Carver picked up his sunglasses, he questioned whether this girl was part of his high-risk crowd. He didn't recognize that reddish-brown hair or the slouching walk, but it was early in the year, so he hadn't met all the freshmen. This kid headed for the trees was probably a ninth grader, going to meet an impatient boyfriend.

He hoped he could stop the girl before she took off any clothes— Carver hated interrupting teenage sex scenes. Buddy Blair might have gotten a thrill every time he caught kids in the act, but to Carver, the high schoolers resembled a bunch of giraffes, all knobby legs and long tongues and spotty skin, and he didn't even want to think about their sex lives. In fact, Carver's first priority when he arrived seven years ago had been to throw cold water on the school's promiscuous climate—all the kissing in the halls and gauntlets of groping couples in the stairwells. As a police officer, he could not tolerate illegal substances; as a father, his list of objectionable activities was more extensive, including profanity, disruptive behavior in the classroom, and public displays of affection beyond hand-holding. "No kissing or cursing" was Carver's motto, and with the principal's permission he had spent his first few weeks patrolling the hallways at class changes, using his most dramatic, booming voice to confront any couple who dared to make out in public. "Young man, keep your hands to yourself! . . . Young lady, this is a place of learning, not a brothel!"

Within two weeks Carver had recruited five other teachers to join his anti-PDA squad, explaining that if there was no discipline in the halls, there could be no discipline in the classrooms. Eventually most of the teachers had agreed to step outside their rooms at class-change time and police the areas immediately around their doors, since the mere presence of a visible adult within twenty feet was enough to eliminate most groping, bullying, and cursing.

That had left the bathrooms as the school's key trouble spots, but Carver was proud to have gotten most of them under control within one semester. He had recruited one of the assistant principals, Mrs. Walker, to help with the girls' rooms while he covered the boys', which were notoriously drug-ridden. The principal had had to swallow hard over all the suspensions during Carver's first two months—triple the usual total under Blair's tenure—but Carver explained that once you set the standard, the kids would start to toe the line.

Carver had walked into several sex scenes, gay and straight, during those early weeks of bathroom duty. The repeat offenders had responded by seeking out the school's remotest closets and empty classrooms, but eventually Carver had discovered every nook and cranny where kids, and occasionally teachers, might hook up, and he'd managed to chase most of the sex out of the building, which is why he assumed this girl heading for the trees had a boyfriend waiting. The woods were the last outpost for uninterrupted blow jobs.

Carver tucked his sunglasses into his pocket and lifted his stick, not because he needed it, but because good policing was theatrical, especially when it came to handling teenagers. The uniform, the stick, the booming voice—all were calculated for dramatic effect. He figured half of his authority relied on showmanship, although he almost never wore the hat—too many memories of white state troopers hassling him when he was young. Buddy Blair had worn his hat constantly, indoors and out, tipped low over his eyes when he watched the students file through the metal detector each morning. What a jackass.

As he headed for the door, Carver turned back briefly toward Bobby Lee.

"Mr. Grant?"

The boy barely lifted his eyes.

"You see those two security cameras?" Carver pointed to the room's front corners. "Those cameras will record everything you say and do while I am gone. If I come back and discover that you have spoken a word or stood up from your chair, you'll be in this room for the rest of the week, understand?"

Bobby Lee nodded.

In fact, the cameras didn't work at all. They were part of Carver's show, with red lights blinking every sixty seconds, giving enough illusion of surveillance to allow him a few opportunities each day to walk the halls, inspect bathrooms, and maintain a visible presence. He needed regular breaks from his detention duties—not that he minded overseeing kids like Bobby Lee. In fact, in the first days of his job, when he had sat at his desk pondering his enormous office—formerly a staff lounge—he had decided to volunteer his space as a detention hall, figuring that was the best way for him to meet the school's most troubled kids. In doing so, Carver had ingratiated himself with the principal and the beleaguered faculty. A teacher merely had to ring Carver's cell, give him the name of that day's troublemaker, then hand the phone to the student. "Mr. Harris?" Carver's loud voice would resonate across the line. "You have been expelled from your classroom. You have exactly sixty seconds to arrive at my office before I call your parents, starting from now. One . . . two . . . three . . . "

"Carver's classroom"—that's what the teachers called his office. The students brought their assignments and worked silently under Carver's gaze for the rest of the period, joined by the occasional hard-core delinquents who were serving all-day in-school suspensions. Before they returned to their regular class schedule, Carver required each student to write a five-sentence paragraph about what he or she planned to do in the future, and Carver was just as intolerant of spelling and grammatical errors as he was of drugs and tobacco. Between his insistence on absolute silence and perfect punctuation, most detainees never wanted to return.

Carver stepped into the hall, strolling past the cafeteria and gymnasium to the school's back door, which he pushed open with one hand, emerging into sunshine. He couldn't blame a girl for wanting to exit early on a day like today—seventy-five degrees, a clear autumn sky, and air that tasted clean. Carver appreciated the fresh air most of all, since his office was located right next to the cafeteria, and it reeked of decades of greasy hash browns and chicken nuggets. Open windows and plenty of Febreze only gave the greasy odor a slightly cinnamon tang; every day Carver had to take a shower the minute he got home, throwing his uniform into the wash with a cup of Tide.

After his first year on the job Carver had told Chief Miller he would need a special uniform allowance, since his shirts were fading from all the laundering. Amazingly Miller had agreed, knowing Carver to be strict about personal hygiene—the kind of man who insisted on a close shave, neatly trimmed hair, and clean nails. The greasy odor on his collar was especially offensive to Carver because it perpetuated the worst stereotypes about black men—that they were dirty and low class. He hated smelling like some kid who worked at McDonald's.

Now, as Carver crossed the far boundary of the soccer field, he could see the roof of the county jail, a quarter mile down the road to his right. The jail was another part of Carver's show. He used it for his "three strikes and you're out" policy with detention regulars: After three visits, a student and his parents were required to join Carver on a special afterschool field trip to the jail—"to reserve your room," Carver explained. After displaying the lovely accommodations, food, and exercise space, Carver would hand the parent a copy of the student's paragraphs about future plans and say, "This is what your child wants to do with his life. And this"—gesturing to the barbed wire—"is what he's headed for right now."

A few parents complained to the principal about the school's new police state, and some students were heard to mutter about the "nigger Nazi," but Carver got results. By the end of his first semester the number of students arriving for detention had dropped from one every fifteen minutes to one every three hours. Hallway fights and French-kissing were reduced to a minimum, and even the test scores improved slightly, which Carver attributed to better classroom discipline, although the teachers had other ideas.

After three years, when his contract ended, Carver decided to continue on a year-by-year basis. He had molded the school into an environment he could tolerate, and he knew that no other officer would exert half the effort. Besides, the kids had dedicated a yearbook page to him, which he had framed and hung on the wall behind his computer. These days Carver figured he owned this place, which was why he felt annoyed to see a girl disappear into the woods. She must be a ninth grader, too new to have heard about Officer Petty's eyes in the back of his head.

When Carver entered the woods, he stopped to take out his

handkerchief and wipe his brow. Seventy-five degrees was hot enough to produce a line of sweat across his forehead, and he liked to appear cool and collected when confronting a teen. As he ducked under the sumac branches, he removed his sunglasses and registered a silent wish that he wouldn't find the girl doing drugs. If she was giving some boy a blow job, the girl wouldn't be expelled, just humiliated. Carver insisted on parent-policeman conferences for any kids caught in the act. With the school nurse present as a legal buffer, he liked to ask the parents explicit questions. Is your child practicing safe sex? Have you counseled this kid about birth control? Did you know that 10 percent of teens have a sexually transmitted disease by the time they reach college? The nurse would then give the parents a packet of pamphlets on chlamydia, gonorrhea, and genital warts. Have a nice day.

By now Carver was standing in the middle of the old smokers' club, but smelled no smoke. The abandoned Skoal and half-buried cans of Coors looked to be a few years old, which he welcomed as another feather in his cap. The only footprints led eastward, away from the usual mossy rendezvous points where he had caught kids before, in flagrante delicto. If this girl wasn't headed for the usual delinquent hot spots, Carver wondered if it was worth trying to follow her. These woods stretched for miles, and she could turn in any direction, even double back and return to the school without him noticing. She was carrying her backpack, so maybe she was headed home; she might be a senior with permission to leave early, though Carver doubted it. If there was one thing he could recognize after twenty years as a cop, it was guilt. Nobody took the backwoods out of school unless they were hiding something.

He decided to follow the girl for at least a short distance, guided by a broken tree limb and some crushed leaves, but Carver was no tracker. He was about to give up and turn around when he spotted two deer, leaping away from a spot just north of him.

There, he thought. *Got her.*

CHAPTER 11

WHEN Carver reached the three boulders, he saw the girl's right hand lying casually, palm upward, at the top edge of one of the rocks. She wasn't holding a cigarette or a beer or a syringe. Instead her arms were spread as if prepared for crucifixion.

Carver glanced around for a boy and detected no one else. He took a few silent steps forward to see whether the kid was crying; sometimes girls ran away from class when other teens were vicious, or when a boyfriend dumped them. Maybe this girl had gotten a cruel text message. She seemed to be staring into the trees, so Carver looked up and saw that the leaves were definitely worth staring at—all yellow and red, with occasional patches of lime.

He debated whether to leave the child alone. From the side he couldn't identify her face, but he knew she wasn't one of the trouble-makers. Most of the problem kids were identified by the end of middle school—they arrived at Jackson High with extensive paper trails, and although Carver was willing to give every kid a fresh start, he knew which ones to watch.

From what he could tell, this girl was nowhere on his radar. Maybe she had a good personal reason to be here; maybe she needed some solitude. Most of the privileged white kids didn't get enough time alone. They spent their lives rushed from one activity to the next, from school to sports to hurried meals, to evening music rehearsals followed by three hours of homework overseen by ambitious mothers. Maybe this girl was part of that crowd, oversupervised and over-wrought.

But whatever her circumstances Carver couldn't walk away. There was always the chance that the girl might be wavering on the brink of trouble—planning to run away from home, or waiting for some hard-luck boyfriend who was late. Maybe she'd pull drugs from her pockets the moment Carver turned his back.

He put his sunglasses back on, pushed aside the branches that shielded him, and took a few steps forward. The girl turned her face, and when their eyes met, Carver crossed his arms. That small gesture usually sufficed to make a child run or curse or collapse into tears and pitiful excuses. But not this girl. She turned her face back upward and kept staring into the leaves.

"How long are you planning to stay up there?" Carver asked.

"I was thinking thirty minutes," she replied. "But right now thirty years looks pretty good."

She didn't speak with the heavy southern accent typical of most county kids. From the way she pronounced her full "ing"—*thinking*, not *thinkin'*—Carver guessed she was one of the town kids, maybe a professor's daughter.

"Well," he said, "I was about ready to head home for the day, but now I'm stuck here waiting on you."

The girl rose up on her elbow, assessed him again, and sighed. She pushed herself up to a seated position, then scooted over to the edge of the boulder, hung her legs down, and allowed herself to drop to the ground, falling briefly to her knees before standing to face him.

When he looked at her straight on, Carver was surprised. He knew this girl—every cop in town knew Maggie Greene. She was the little kid who had stonewalled the county sheriff's department nine years ago in what was probably the most famous killing in the past twenty years. The Jackson police hadn't handled the investigation, since it occurred outside town limits, so Carver had never been inside the Greenes' house, or seen this girl when she was small. He only knew the details shared by deputies, several of whom had taken a turn trying to get the five-year-old to talk. Apparently the only words she had uttered during multiple interviews were "I have the right to remain silent."

Carver respected that. From what he'd heard, Maggie Greene had turned out all right—one of the smart kids who made good grades and stayed out of trouble. So why was she here, hiding out in the woods?

Sometimes the trouble didn't start until high school. Children who were traumatized when young often managed to keep their heads above water until adolescence, when their worlds came crashing down.

"Where are you supposed to be?" he asked.

"Geometry."

"Who's your teacher?"

"Mrs. Murdock."

"Got a test today or something?"

Maggie shook her head.

"Feeling sick?"

She shook her head again.

"So why aren't you in class?"

Maggie lowered her eyes without answering, and Carver could see, in her physical stillness, a glimpse of what the deputies must have witnessed nine years ago—the ability to shut down, as if the girl had pulled a plug.

"You're not going to tell me, are you?"

Maggie did not move or speak.

"So what should we do about this situation?"

With her eyes still lowered, Maggie slowly held out her wrists, hands hanging down, ready for handcuffs.

Carver suspected that she was mocking him, but something about her limp resignation made him smile.

"I don't think we'll need the cuffs today. You just come along."

Maggie lifted her backpack then followed one step behind him through the woods, dodging the sticky spiderwebs that caught Carver in the face and maintaining absolute silence until, at the edge of the trees, he pushed a limb out of her way.

"Thank you," she murmured.

Someone had taught this girl her manners.

FIVE minutes later Maggie had settled into a desk in Carver's classroom. She wasn't exactly detention material, but he stuck with his usual routine. "Take out a sheet of paper and write me a paragraph, at least five sentences, about what you plan to do when you leave high school."

Now it was Maggie's turn to cross her arms. She raised her eyebrows and slouched down in her chair with a sullen, "you *must* be kidding" pose.

"You have five minutes." Carver walked to his desk and picked up the phone. "You said your teacher is Mrs. Murdock?" Maggie nodded. Carver looked up the teacher's extension on his bulletin board, then pressed a few buttons on his speakerphone.

"Mrs. Murdock?"

Background noise from the geometry class crackled over his speakerphone, with a student reciting the SSS inequality theorem: "If two sides of a triangle are congruent to two sides of another triangle . . . "

"Yes?" A woman's tentative voice emerged over the noise.

"This is Officer Petty. Could you call me back on my cell?"

The phone fell silent, and Maggie heard a ringtone that sounded like Stevie Wonder's "Overjoyed."

"Yes, I have one of your students in my office. Maggie Greene. That's right . . . I found her in the woods behind the school . . . No. She won't tell me what the problem is, but as soon as you get a chance, I think you should come and speak to her . . . Good. Thanks."

Carver put down his phone. "She'll be here in a few minutes. Keep writing."

Maggie didn't look up, but Carver could tell from the trembling of her pencil that she wasn't happy. If he had to guess, he'd say the girl was scared, which seemed odd. He'd only met Mrs. Murdock once, at the orientation for new faculty, but he recalled the math teacher as far from intimidating. He remembered thinking he might need to give the woman a few tips, to keep the students from walking all over her.

A few minutes more and he heard the shuffle of a woman's sandals in the hall. "Officer Petty?"

"Come in." He rose from his desk and walked over to shake Grace Murdock's hand. Christ, this woman looked scared too. Skittish as a squirrel, with a cold, sweaty palm. Sometimes Carver had this effect on new teachers; they responded to his uniform with a flinching discomfort. But when he saw Mrs. Murdock glance at Maggie, Carver knew that it wasn't his badge or baton, or even his black skin, that was causing the problem. Clearly there was something going on between these two females, but he couldn't figure it out until the woman turned away from Maggie and briefly looked into Carver's face.

Well I'll be damned, he thought. Sandra McCluskey. The college girl who was mixed up in the Greene family mess. A different haircut and a new name, but Sandra McCluskey nonetheless.

What had the county sheriff called her, nine years ago? *A bag full of lies.* Carver remembered the sheriff complaining in Chief Miller's office: "I've got a little kid who won't talk, and a college girl who won't tell the truth." And now both of those females were together at Jackson High.

Carver sat at his desk and pretended to be absorbed in paperwork, carefully monitoring every move that the pair made. Mrs. Murdock watched Maggie for a moment, while the girl kept her eyes fixed on her desk, writing her required sentences. Then the teacher approached Carver. "Can I have a piece of paper and something to write with?"

Carver tore a sheet from his yellow writing pad and handed her a pencil. She put the paper down on one of the desks, leaned over, and wrote something quickly. Not more than a sentence or two, from what Carver could tell. She folded the paper three times, small enough to fit in a thank-you card, and she returned his pencil. He watched as the woman approached Maggie, murmured a few words too quiet for him to discern, then placed the note on the girl's desk.

With that, Mrs. Murdock turned and left the room.

Carver opened his mouth to protest. Normally he expected teachers to take their students back to class. Maggie Greene belonged in geometry, not in detention, but she probably didn't belong in Sandra McCluskey's class.

Carver watched the girl as she stared at the yellow paper. Eventually Maggie lifted the note delicately, just as he had seen his daughter, Jessie, lift dead butterflies, pinching the wings between thumb and index finger. Maggie unfolded the note and read the contents, and to Carver's dismay her eyes welled up until two large tears slid down her cheeks.

Normally he had no sympathy for girls who cried in detention. As a fellow showman, he knew the manipulative power of tears, and for years he'd stood by stoically while women wept over speeding tickets, shoplifting charges, and school expulsions. Making females cry was part of his job.

But this girl's tears were different, because they obviously embarrassed her. Maggie was wiping them away fast as they came, until Carver walked over and placed a box of tissues on her desk.

"Maggie." He spoke her name for the first time. "I've got a pretty good idea of why you are skipping your math class, and if you need a schedule change, or some other accommodation, the school can arrange it."

Maggie folded the piece of paper, placed it in her front pocket, and shook her head. "Thanks, I think I'll be okay. Can I go now?"

Only five minutes remained before the final bell.

"Sure." Carver nodded.

When she was gone, he read the paragraph she'd left behind.

When I am done with high school I want to be free. Free from my imprisonment in this building. Free from the claustrophobia of a small town where everybody talks about their neighbors' business. Free from the eyes of teachers and parents and strangers who think they know what's going on inside your head, when they know nothing at all. I want to go someplace where I have no past, no name, and no expectations. I want to start over.

CHAPTER 12

OUTSIDE Carver's office, Maggie headed toward the school's front door, anxious to escape before the bell rang. She couldn't face a thousand students milling in the halls, staring at her flushed face and red eyes. She couldn't bear to have Kate grasp her shoulders and say, "Oh my God, what's *wrong*!"

Maggie took out her cell phone as she walked, glancing down the halls to make sure no teachers were nearby.

"Hey Dad? I'm glad I caught you. Kate's mom is going to take us over to her house, and then I'll walk to your office. Okay? I'll be there by five o'clock."

More lies, more guilt, but she couldn't face her father until she had thought things through. If he saw her now, with her short breath and racing pulse, he would assume that she was sick again, but this sensation flooding her veins was not illness. It was agitation and confusion, combined with a flash of hope, compelling her to rush down the halls and out the front door. She hurried through the parking lot as the final bell ended the school day behind her.

How bizarre, that the woman who'd been invading her dreams, causing her to hide in woods and school bathrooms, had been able to grant her this sense of release. She wondered if Mrs. Murdock understood what she'd done, just by placing a little slip of yellow paper on Maggie's desk and murmuring, "I read the note you left for me . . . Do me the favor of reading my note for you."

Maggie stopped at the road, uncertain which way to turn. To the right, her dad's office waited two miles away, past the motels and fast-food restaurants, down the hill and over the concrete bridge that crossed the Shannon River, then uphill toward Jackson's main street and the northern end of campus. Most of the school buses and cars followed that route, and they would pass her as she walked, with students shouting rude comments from the windows. Nobody walked home from high school—you either drove a car or caught a ride with a parent or friend, or took the bus to the middle of town and dispersed from there. Walking was weird.

If she turned left, she could avoid most of the stares and loop her way toward the college slowly, along back roads that led past woods and white farmhouses and decrepit gray barns. After a quarter mile she would pass Mawyer's Nursery, then the county fairgrounds and Vesper's Garage; beyond that, the route offered little more than a few old houses labeled as antique stores. A suspension footbridge crossed the Shannon three miles south, leading to the student hiking trails at the western side of the campus, where the athletic department had rope courses and climbing walls and a rappelling platform at the top of the Shannon's cliffs. That route would deliver her to her father's office in a little over ninety minutes.

Her dad's old Supertramp CD echoed in her head, *Take the long way home . . . take the long way home,* as Maggie turned left. Yellow oak leaves tripped across the road, and a few cars crushed them, heading toward rural intersections with village names like Brindleburg and

Possum Hollow and Tinkerville. Maggie hiked the first half mile in six minutes, nodding at a woman who was exiting the nursery with a tray of red and pink geraniums. Another half mile and Maggie was still flushed with adrenaline, although her backpack had started to dig deep into her shoulder. She hadn't considered the weight of Latin and biology and geometry when she decided to walk these three miles, and at a quiet stretch of road lined with blue chicory and goldenrod, she stopped to rest, slinging her pack onto the ground under a tree. From her front pocket Maggie retrieved the precious yellow note and unfolded it, checking to see if the contents had remained unchanged, or if some black magic had altered the words before anyone else could witness them.

The message was still there, in all its stark simplicity. Eight words to stir up Maggie's restless mind:

Your mother was right to kill Jacob Stewart.

Victim

CHAPTER 13

EMMA Greene leaned back in her office chair behind piles of over-stuffed manila files and closed her eyes.

So. The invisible girl had returned.

She had read Maggie's e-mail five times, and the words were still taking shape in her mind:

Hi Mom,

Something really weird has come up, and I have a favor to ask. I told you about my math teacher, Mrs. Murdock? I figured out why she bothers me. It turns out Murdock is her married name, and she's really Sandra McCluskey.

Yesterday we had a long talk. She told me all about nine years ago, and how you were right to protect us against Jacob Stewart. Apparently Jacob was really dangerous, and she's been wanting to apologize for all the lies she told.

Could you come down here this weekend so I could tell you about
it, and you could speak to her?

Maggie

Christ. Emma shook her head as she opened her eyes. How the hell
did Sandra McCluskey wind up as a math teacher at Jackson High
School?

She lifted her phone and called Rob's work number.

"Hello, computer services."

Emma could hear her ex-husband clicking at his keyboard much
too aggressively, the sign of a bad day.

"It's Emma," she said.

"Hi, Emma. What's up?"

"I just found out about this Sandra McCluskey stuff."

The clicking stopped. "What are you talking about?"

"I'm talking about Maggie's math teacher . . . hasn't she told you?"

"Maggie says that she doesn't like her math teacher, but what does
that have to do with Sandra?"

Emma sighed. "Look . . . I'm forwarding you an e-mail that I just
got from Maggie."

"Okay . . . got it."

Emma waited in silence until she heard the expected response—a
low groan. "You had no idea?" she asked.

"Of course I had no idea. Who would expect Sandra McCluskey
to come back here?"

"I thought you went to the school's open house and met Maggie's
teachers."

"I did, but—" Rob hesitated. "I mean, Mrs. Murdock doesn't look
anything like Sandra. She's got different hair, and different clothes."

Emma rolled her eyes. "Wow, Rob, you really are on the ball. What else is going on in Maggie's life that you have no clue about? Is she doing drugs or something?"

Wrong move. Her ex wasn't in the mood for sarcasm.

"Where the hell do you come off criticizing me?" Even two hundred miles away, she could sense him clenching the telephone receiver, the tops of his ears getting red the way they always did when he was angry. "If you hadn't moved three hours away, you might know more about your daughter's life."

He was right. She wasn't exactly Mom of the Year.

"So, are you coming down?" Rob asked.

"Of course I'm coming down. I'm going to tell Sandra McCluskey to stay the hell away from our daughter."

"Don't do anything stupid," Rob warned.

"What's that supposed to mean?"

"Don't come here planning to pick a fight."

"You mean, don't get angry and kill someone?"

"That's not what I said."

"Yeah, right."

"So now you're picking a fight with me?" Rob's voice was needle sharp. "It's not like everyone in the world is out to get you, Emma."

Why did this happen whenever she talked to Rob? These days they could never have a conversation without spitting insults. "We'll talk about it when I get to town. I'll come down on Friday after work."

After she hung up, Emma took two Advil from her purse, swallowed them with the cold remains of her afternoon coffee, then turned off the lights, leaned back in her swiveling chair, and closed her eyes again. She could feel the earliest twinges of a migraine, and the only way to avoid it was with silence and darkness. Pinching the bridge of her nose between her thumb and third finger, she let her hand spread open, her fingertips tracing the bones of her eye sockets until her palm touched the end of her nose. Emma repeated the massage again and again as a vision of Sandra McCluskey gradually came to mind, standing on the porch at the old Wade's Creek house, two steps behind Kyle Caldwell. Sandra's mouth was opening in a scream destined to embed itself so deeply in Emma's brain the aural memory could be triggered years later by any high-pitched noise. The screech of tires, the cry of a hawk, a baby's sudden squeal—all caused the scream to echo. Emma had learned to avoid horror movies and television shows that might include screams, knowing that the women's faces on the screen would morph into Sandra's, staring into the house, transfixed by the horror at Emma's feet.

Every time Emma recalled the scene, her memory followed the girl's eyes down to the floor where Jacob Stewart lay, no longer threatening, no longer a slick enabler of his criminal friend, just a boy, unconscious on her floor. Now she opened her eyes and looked again at the strangest words in Maggie's e-mail: *Jacob was really dangerous.* It was hard to imagine that the crumpled body at her feet that night had been dangerous. Surely Emma was the dangerous one, the woman with the bat clenched in her hand, wild with adrenaline.

Outside the screen door, Sandra McCluskey had been gasping, "Oh God, oh God," and the words had merged with Emma's thoughts: *Oh God, what have I done?* She dropped the bat and knelt beside Jacob, reaching to brush the long brown hair away from the side of his face. Her hand emerged warm and wet from the blood flowing in a thin line down Jacob's neck, and she remembered thinking that it looked like a red iPod cord, as if the scarlet bubble in his ear were merely a bright earbud. Emma rose to her feet and swayed, placing her right hand on the hall table until her vision steadied, leaving behind a reddish-brown streak on the wood.

Inside the kitchen she grabbed the telephone.

"We need an ambulance right away at 1634 Wade's Creek Road. There's been an accident . . . A college student. Hit in the head with a baseball bat. A bat . . . In the head . . . No, he's unconscious . . . I have to stop the blood . . . Hurry . . . Yes, 1634 Wade's Creek . . . I have to stop the blood . . . No." She hung up and reached for the two dish towels hanging on the handle of her oven, then ran back to Jacob, whose blood was forming a cauliflower stain on the beige Oriental runner. Lifting his head gently, she placed it in her lap, pressing one dish towel tightly against each ear. *Please God, don't let him die. Don't let him die.*

Looking up, she saw Kyle on the other side of the screen door, staring as he always stared, but this time in terrified fascination, mesmerized by the sight of Jacob's head cradled in her lap. Wood whispered across carpet, and Emma lifted her eyes to see Maggie's bedroom door upstairs, slowly pulling shut. Years later that closing door would strike her as emblematic—the sign of a girl shutting her mother out, closing her door on a chapter of her childhood, never again to be fully opened.

She had wanted to go to Maggie—to fold her daughter into her body and assure her that everything would be all right. And perhaps if she had, their lives would have been different; perhaps she could have shielded Maggie from all the trouble to come. But she couldn't rush to her daughter at that moment, not with Jacob bleeding in her lap. Kyle and Sandra had already turned to run away, and she was left with a boy who should not die alone.

As she knelt on her hallway floor, holding Jacob's head as tenderly as her trembling hands could manage, doubts and self-recriminations had spun through Emma's mind. Why had she done this? How did it happen? She tried to remember Jacob's words as he pushed into her house: "I just want to talk to you . . . just one word." What had been so frightening about that?

The words weren't the problem; Jacob's language was always smooth and reassuring. It was the force of his shoulder, pressing inside, and the leer on Kyle's face, when her strength finally gave way and she released the door. Jacob had stumbled into her hallway with an ominous grin, his right hand reaching forward and touching her hair, as if he might have been a lover, about to draw her in for a kiss. But no—Emma had sensed that he was going to grasp her hair, yank her head back, and lift her off the floor. At six foot one he was ten inches taller than her, and probably fifty pounds heavier. In his hands, she would have been nothing more than a Raggedy Ann.

Too late Jacob saw the bat, swinging toward his legs, cracking across the top of his right kneecap. He fell onto his knees, which must have doubled the pain, both of his hands groping forward toward her thighs. At the time Emma had thought he was reaching for the bat, trying to disarm her, but afterward she had questioned whether he was attempting to shield himself from the bat's returning swing, or raising his palms in a gesture of supplication. Had Jacob been asking for a mercy that she refused?

Ten minutes after her 911 call the first vehicle pulled into Emma's driveway—not an ambulance or police car, but a dented pickup with oversize tires and a red flashing light on the hood, the sort that could be displayed or hidden at a driver's whim. Two boys in jeans, camouflage jackets, and Tractor Supply ball caps hopped out and advanced as far as her front steps, close enough to see the grotesque pietà within the hall. "The ambulance is coming," one of them said, then they both stepped back, clearly embarrassed. Emma knew about these boys, the eighteen- and nineteen-year-old volunteers for the paramedic squad, with special radios tuned to the county dispatcher, enabling them to gawk at accident scenes when they weren't on duty. She figured it was their only excitement in this rural area: car crashes and hunting accidents and boys with cracked skulls. Another pickup with a flashing light arrived, bringing a third gawker who looked scarcely sixteen, and Emma wondered if the paramedics would be as young and hapless as these kids.

The ambulance approached at the same time as the county deputies, sirens converging in stereo from the north and south. Emma's poplar tree flashed red and blue as the ambulance lurched beyond the pickups, onto the edge of her lawn, and to her relief, the head paramedic who stepped onto her porch had a headful of gray hair.

"What happened?" he asked as he opened her screen door, a duffel bag with a red cross slung over his shoulder.

"He got hit in the head with a baseball bat—here." Emma raised her right hand from the dish towel and patted the back of her own skull, leaving a drop of blood that merged seamlessly with her red hair.

The paramedic knelt and placed his fingers on Jacob's neck, feeling for a pulse. "Get the stretcher!" he yelled back to his female partner, and one of the awkward boys ran to help her. Meanwhile the older paramedic lifted Jacob's head carefully off Emma's lap and placed it on the rug while he took out his stethoscope. A steady hand settled upon Emma's arm, and she looked up to meet the gentle brown eyes of a young deputy, wearing a tan uniform and holding his hat against his chest like a humble suitor. Slowly he pulled her up and away from the body, gripping her elbow firmly as her legs, stiff from fifteen minutes of kneeling, staggered beneath her. "Come this way, ma'am," he murmured as he guided her into the kitchen.

Emma held up the two dish towels, as if offering him the blood.

"You can put those on the counter," he said. "Can I get you a glass of water?"

Emma shook her head as she took the seat that he pulled out for her. "My husband . . . Someone needs to call Rob." The deputy nodded to his partner. "Give Fletcher the number and he'll make the call."

Over the next few minutes Emma began to recite her story—how she had heard voices at the creek and seen the students from Maggie's window. They were drinking, she explained, and she had walked down to the water to tell them to leave. She gave the police the names of the boys, and described the trouble she'd had with Kyle's thievery in the past. And then the nameless girl had asked to use the bathroom.

Another deputy entered the kitchen. "Is there a fire somewhere?"

"No." Emma replied, confused. "Why would you think that?"

"There's a ladder hanging down from one of the upstairs windows. The kind used to escape from a house during a fire."

Emma's mind flew to Maggie and she bolted from her chair, running into the hallway and up the stairs two at a time. Pushing her daughter's door open across the carpet, she saw the empty bed, the open window, and the ladder. "Maggie!" She leaned out the window, peering down into the rhododendrons. "Maggie, where are you?" Emma ran past the deputy, who had followed her to the bedroom door. "My daughter," she murmured as she hurried back down the steps, edging around the paramedics, who had strapped Jacob onto a stretcher with an IV, an oxygen mask, and a cervical collar.

Emma rushed down the front porch stairs, scanning the yard, right and left. "Maggie!" Two more police cars had arrived, bringing the total to four, and she recognized the county sheriff, Albert King, a heavyset man in his late sixties with a silver crew cut, adjusting his hat before hoisting his frame out of the front seat. Her driveway was a carnival of spinning lights, and Emma turned away from the crowd, running toward the small white guesthouse behind the oak trees at the opposite end of the driveway. Maggie sometimes used the guesthouse as a play space, so Emma hurried inside and checked the coat closet, underneath the bed, and behind the living room sofa. She even searched the kitchenette's cabinets, having once discovered Maggie scrunched up there during a game of hide-and-seek, but this time she found nothing. Rushing outside, Emma headed for the creek.

In the moonlight the water appeared peaceful, its silver reflections and soft current a welcome antidote to the garish colors and sharp voices at the house. But Emma knew the creek's dangers, with three-foot pools deep enough to drown your average toddler. When Maggie was small, Emma had waded through the water beside her, lifting rocks to reveal crayfish scuttling backward, never letting her daughter wander beyond arm's length. Now five-year-old Maggie could swim, and by daylight she explored the creek on her own, with Emma watching from the porch. Most days, the water was a reliable friend, but tonight nothing was safe.

Emma stood on the long rock where Maggie liked to crouch with a kitchen strainer, catching minnows. "Come on out, Maggie!"

Behind her, the gentle-eyed deputy was approaching with Sheriff King. "Missing child," she heard him say.

"How old is your daughter?" the sheriff asked as Emma climbed off the rock, onto the grass, and headed upstream.

"She's five."

"You think she's run away?"

"She must have gotten frightened."

"There's a rope ladder," the deputy explained, "hanging out of her bedroom window. Looks like she climbed out."

"Tell Sensabaugh to start a search," the sheriff replied. "And put those boys to use." He gestured toward the three teenagers, still watching from the top of the hill. "Your priorities are the creek and the road. After that the woods."

Within sixty seconds the three boys were scouring the creekside while two deputies walked the road, shining flashlights into the ditch beside the edge of the asphalt. The sheriff had gone inside to speak to the paramedics before the ambulance rushed Jacob away. "Call the dean of students," he said to the deputy at his side. "She'll need to contact the parents. Say there was an accident, and the kid got hit in the head with a bat. No more details than that. Tell her he's being taken to the local hospital, but there's a good chance he'll be airlifted to UVA. And see if she has a number and address for this Kyle Caldwell. Tell Fletcher to track him down."

"Damn, I can't get any coverage out here." The deputy put his cell phone away. "Where's the landline?"

Outside, Emma was searching for Maggie in all the best hide-and-seek locations—the two-foot crawl space underneath the front porch and the twelve-inch nook behind the John Deere tractor in their plywood shed. She ducked beneath the branches of their vast magnolia, into the tree's dark tent, where only a few bits of moonlight penetrated beyond the thick leaves. The sheriff joined her, shining his flashlight up into the canopy. "Is she a climber?"

"Sometimes," Emma replied.

"Any favorite trees besides this one?"

"The oak tree over there." Emma pointed as the two of them emerged from the magnolia. "And the big willow by the creek."

"I'll check those," the sheriff said, "then we'll search the woods."

Emma glanced toward the woods as the sheriff walked away, and thought she saw the tiniest flash of white, like a lingering firefly. The woods were the last place she expected to find Maggie—so black and frightening and far from the house, and yet, there it was again, that brief flicker of white. She crossed the grass slowly, calling, "Maggie, are you in there? . . . Don't be scared, honey . . . Everything's all right now."

At the edge of the trees she lifted a branch and spotted a few more white flecks, several yards ahead. "Maggie?" Still barefoot, Emma tiptoed on the twigs and leaves. Without a flashlight, she was quickly surrounded by darkness; only thin strips of moonbeam sifted through the branches. Still, there was enough light to discern her daughter's white nightgown, growing larger as Emma approached.

When she reached Maggie, the girl did not run to her, or even stand up. She remained seated against a tree, her nightgown pulled over her knees in a frail attempt at shelter. The child did manage to lift her face from her kneecaps long enough to look into her mother's eyes, and Emma knelt before her, saying, "Oh, Maggie, I'm so sorry," foreseeing in that moment that she would be sorry for years to come— sorry for what the child had witnessed, sorry for not hurrying to her room after calling 911, sorry that her five-year-old had spent a trau-matized half hour hiding in the woods. What endless river of pain was bound to flow from this?

Emma lifted the silent child who rested her cheek on her mother's shoulder, and together the two of them emerged from the woods.

CHAPTER 14

EMMA stared at Maggie's e-mail, blind to the words, seeing only the white nightgown pulled around her daughter's bony, five-year-old knees. She had no desire to see Sandra McCluskey again—no wish to face the girl whose lies had made a mess of her life. It had taken years to clear the wreckage, gradually rebuilding and beginning to forget, and the resentment remained rock-solid in her stomach; if she must face Sandra, she didn't want Maggie to witness the confrontation. And yet, Emma knew that she could refuse Maggie nothing; her daughter had asked so little of her in the past nine years.

After her traumatic night it seemed that Maggie had never wanted to trouble her mother, making no demands, always carefully obedient. In the months following Jacob's death, Emma had recognized Maggie's sudden taste for cleanliness and prompt retreats at bedtime as signs of fear. The small fragments of rebellion that remained in the child were all channeled toward her father: No, she wouldn't leave the playground when Rob called. No, she wouldn't get into the bathtub when he asked.

But as for Emma—she had merely to raise an eyebrow and Maggie would obey.

Obedience was not the trait that Emma valued most in human beings. She didn't want to raise a fearful daughter, easily intimidated by teachers and boyfriends and husbands, which was why, a few years later, when her marriage unraveled into a hundred broken threads, she had agreed to give Rob custody. Removed from the maternal shadow, Maggie might learn to assert herself.

Emma had other reasons for avoiding a custody battle—mostly the knowledge that she could never win, for what judge would grant custody to a murderess? And beyond that, what ugly domestic secrets might surface if she battled Rob in court? For ten years Rob had borne her most bitter remarks, silently enduring the verbal assaults that surfaced in her fits of deepest frustration with marriage and parenthood and tenure struggles. Once, when she and Maggie threw matching tantrums, he had rolled his eyes and asked, "Who is the toddler?" Emma had never entirely forgiven him. Nor had she forgotten how closely Rob watched her when she first described her encounter with Jacob Stewart, and the seconds of hesitation before he asserted that she had done the right thing. No—she could never have won a custody fight against a man who knew her so well.

Emma wondered if Maggie understood how hard it had been for her to move away—how all of Emma's instincts had rebelled against it. When she decided to take a job in Washington, Emma had spent weeks in advance of the change, assuring Maggie that this was not an abandonment. Every month during the school year Maggie would spend a weekend in D.C., and Emma would come to Jackson with equal regularity; for six weeks each summer Maggie could live at Emma's Dupont Circle condominium, enjoying the perfect blend of city and country life. In Jackson, she could hike in the mountains, learn to kayak, and benefit from small, safe schools with acres of lush green playgrounds. In Washington, she could visit museums and concerts and festivals and eat every kind of food. Didn't it sound wonderful?

In retrospect, Emma probably hadn't needed to soften the blow of her departure, because Maggie showed no hints of sadness or anxiety as she watched her mother packing clothes and books into boxes. While Maggie played in the yard, Emma had taken one of her daughter's many stuffed bears and stashed it in the bottom of her suitcase, wanting something she could hold at night, something that smelled of her daughter's hair and sweet skin. Later, when she loaded her bags into the car with Maggie watching from the porch, the predominant emotion Emma sensed emanating from her inscrutable child was relief. Or was that merely Emma's guilt, clouding her view?

Rob swore for months afterward that Maggie missed her mother, that she slept in Rob's bed for two weeks after Emma moved out not because she wanted her father's closeness, but for the feeling of Emma that lingered in the sheets. He had seen Maggie remove a picture of Emma from a family album and place it under her pillow, and sometimes Rob saw her lying in bed, staring at it.

Emma also noticed that a necklace she gave Maggie on the child's first visit to D.C. was still around her daughter's neck three weeks later, when Emma visited Jackson.

"She never takes it off," Rob explained. Curious, Emma gave Maggie a bracelet the next day, then a ring one month later, watching each item become a permanent fixture on her child's body. Emma hoped that pieces of her love might touch her daughter's neck, wrist, and finger, even if she couldn't yet touch Maggie's heart.

Now Emma offered her daughter the gift of a few, meager words:

You can set something up for anytime Saturday. I will come down on Friday night.

A knock came at Emma's door, and her assistant, Ruth, stuck her head inside. "You wanted me to tell you when Maria Cortez arrived."

"Yes." Emma switched off her computer and tried to concentrate. The past was a deep well into which she often tumbled headlong, and it took a few moments to regain her mental footing. She examined the office around her—cinder-block walls painted eggshell white, a thin brown carpet like the texture of a child's worn teddy bear, a wooden desk and metal filing cabinets donated from the D.C. public schools. Another Wednesday afternoon in the North Capitol Center, Washington's largest shelter for women and children, and the petite woman edging tentatively through her door was one of Emma's regulars.

Maria Cortez was twenty-five, but looked sixteen in her long black braid and Empire-waist dress hanging loose over striped leggings. Each time Emma encountered Maria she thought of a beautiful doll, barely five foot two with mocha skin and eyes like maple syrup. But Maria was a doll with a careless owner; she arrived at Emma's office with a broken arm one month, cigarette burns another. Today, she entered with a cut lip and a black eye that flashed with tears as Emma wrapped her in a delicate hug, careful not to press against any tender bruises.

"I'm so glad you're here. Come sit down."

Emma gestured toward the blue sofa opposite from her desk, the so-called couch of consolation, where hundreds of battered women had shared their stories, or remained silent, as they wished. Emma believed in the healing power of words, but she also understood the value of sitting quietly and holding a woman's hand.

"He said he'd kill me if I came here again," Maria murmured.

"Do you feel that it's a serious threat?" Emma asked, thinking that tomorrow she would need to transfer Maria to a small, anonymous shelter, with an undisclosed location.

"He's probably serious"—Maria nodded—"but I don't care anymore. I'm too tired. I'd let him do it if it weren't for Christian."

Christian was Maria's ten-year-old son, the child of a child, with an unnamed father and brutal stepfather—a boy who relied for all his well-being upon this small, all-suffering woman who had once dreamed of becoming a nurse but who had dropped out of high school when her baby came, and now worked part-time as a maid.

"I'm here because Carlos has been focusing on Christian."

Emma nodded. *Focus.* A favorite word from her previous life. *Your thesis should be more narrowly focused. This paragraph has strayed from its focus. What is the focus of your argument?*

For Maria Cortez, *focus* was a euphemism for beating, kicking, slapping, and above all, burning. Her husband, Carlos, had a fascination with charred human skin, which he sometimes satisfied by practicing a grotesque pointillism on his own arms and legs with smoldering match tips, although more often he "focused" on Maria. Emma glanced at Maria's leggings, wondering what horrors lay beneath. The first time she had met the girl, then twenty-two, Maria had been lying in a hospital bed, admitted for third-degree burns on her arms, apparently from a skilletful of bacon grease.

"Where is Christian now?" Emma knew from years of experience that if the children weren't safe, the mothers could never be secure. Too many times she'd watched women return to abusers who were holding a child hostage under the guise of fatherhood.

"Christian is with my sister, Christina. She's his godmother."

"She lives in the same building as you, right?"

Maria shook her head. "Christina moved in with her boyfriend."

"Where do they live?"

"Just down the street."

"Does Carlos know the address?"

Maria nodded in silence.

Emma sighed. "Christian should be here, with you, where you can watch him and know that he's okay."

Maria stared at her hands. She and Emma had held this conversation before. The young woman didn't want her son to see his mother in a shelter for homeless and battered women—to carry in his mind the memory of the residents in the cafeteria, holding orange plastic trays, waiting for their slush of green beans or slab of boiled chicken, the younger ones using makeup to cover bruised cheekbones while a few of the older, mentally ill women muttered noisy invectives against syphilis and gonorrhea.

Emma appreciated Maria's impulse to protect the boy, but what did she think Christian witnessed at home every day, in the projects? The gangs, the drugs, the violent stepfathers. By comparison, the North Capitol Center was a luxury resort, with a basketball court, a renovated playground, and a new climbing wall supervised by volunteers. Here, there were hot meals and clean beds and six PCs designated exclusively for children, where Christian could play educational games, or surf websites filtered with parental controls. Maria wanted to maintain the fiction that Christian lived in a normal family with a loving mother and father, in a clean, safe apartment, with a cheerful aunt nearby who sometimes picked him up from school for unannounced sleepovers.

"Does Christina understand what to do this time if Carlos shows up?" Emma asked.

"Carlos is working until nine today. He won't know I'm gone until he gets home."

"Carlos is unpredictable," Emma said gently. "He might skip work or leave early. And he suspected you might come here, right? He threatened you?"

Maria understood. "If he shows up at Christina's, she'll call 911." Emma gave Maria a sharp look, and the young woman dropped her eyes, acknowledging with a silent shrug that the police might never come, especially if violence was only threatened, and not yet committed.

In Maria's neighborhood, domestic disputes were common as rainy days.

"Christina's boyfriend will be home by seven. He's big, and he doesn't like Carlos."

"That's good." Emma nodded. Carlos enjoyed terrorizing small women and children, but he usually fell into muted grumbling in the presence of grown men.

Emma reached across her desk, lifted her phone, and placed it on the side table next to Maria. "I want you to call Christina. Tell her to take Christian to the park, or out for a Coke, and tell her to stay away from home until her boyfriend gets there. She should avoid her usual hangouts, where Carlos might come looking, and stick to public, crowded areas. While you make that call I'm going to check to see that your bed has new sheets and your locker has been scrubbed."

She opened her office door and beckoned Ruth to come inside. "Please help Maria with anything she needs." Emma looked back at Maria. "Would you like a cup of coffee, or a soda?"

"Coke, please," Maria answered, and Ruth headed toward the mini-fridge on the far side of the couch.

Meanwhile Emma lifted a plate of baked goods from the corner of Ruth's desk, then walked back into her office, handing it to Maria. "Have some homemade pumpkin bread."

Twice each week local volunteers taught baking classes for the shelter residents, and during off-hours the women had permission to use the cafeteria's large kitchen, to practice the art of flaky pastries and stiff meringues. Emma promoted baking as medicine for the soul; in a world where so many things were beyond a woman's control, baking offered a sense of stability. She hoped that it might provide an illusion of home for the shelter's children; they might find solace in helping their mothers bake banana bread and lemon squares. Emma often told the nearby churches that the shelter needed flour and sugar as much as blankets and sheets, and she viewed it as a moral deficiency each night when she went home and ate raw cookie dough from a tube.

"I'll be back shortly," she said to Maria.

Outside her office door, Emma nodded for Ruth to join her, murmuring, "Bring your first-aid kit, and try to see if there are other injuries." Ruth, a registered nurse, handled the residents' minor medical care.

As Emma headed toward the hallway, the brass letters on her wooden door caught the corner of her eye: *Principal*. Her official title was "executive director," but she had never removed *Principal* because the word seemed fitting. The North Capitol Center was housed in an old school, Fred J. Waring Elementary, a two-story brick building with round white columns at the front door and a semicircle of boxwood hedges surrounding a thirty-foot pole where children from the shelter raised and lowered the flag each day. The school was supposed to have been razed five years ago to make way for new condominiums, but before the developers could descend, D.C.'s mayor had intervened. Due to the recession, the city's homeless population had spiked 20 percent, and the mayor had been under pressure to take action. A ten-million-dollar gift from an anonymous Waring Elementary alum purchased enough mayoral compassion that he had announced plans to transform the school into a shelter.

The neighbors had protested bitterly. North Capitol was a borderline community, poised between gentrification and urban blight. They had hoped for manicured town houses, not a home for crazy bums and drug addicts who would loiter at the property's fringes and spread like lice into the blocks beyond. The most vociferous neighbors, teamed with the real estate firm that had hoped to develop the site, hired a triumvirate of lawyers who threatened to delay the project indefinitely.

That was when Emma stepped in. Prior to coming to the North

Capitol Center, she had spent five years as assistant director, then director, of Kelly's House, a twenty-bed shelter for battered women located in a large Victorian mansion near the Adams Morgan neighborhood. *Mother Jones* magazine had featured Kelly's House as a model shelter, clean and compassionate, with an excellent record of placing its residents in permanent housing and steady jobs. As a result, the *Washington Post* had hailed Emma as an up-and-coming community leader, prompting an award at the mayor's annual dinner for nonprofit directors, along with a seat on his community services board. Ultimately it was Emma who convinced the mayor that the North Capitol neighbors might find a shelter more palatable if it was devoted entirely to women and children. The small network of women's shelters throughout D.C. had never been sufficient, and the coed Federal City Shelter was drastically overcrowded. If the mayor proposed a shelter for women and children as a compromise, he would gain the moral high ground. What lawyer wanted to appear on CNN and object to a safe haven for battered wives?

To the neighbors, Emma had pitched the idea as a female empowerment project. "We are proposing a house of mercy," she had stated at public hearings, "a safe, clean facility with a day-care center and afterschool activities to keep our city's most vulnerable children away from dangerous influences on the streets." She had filled her speeches with soft, feminine words like *mothers, grandmothers*, and *infants*, promising that this would be another model shelter, where women could have access to medical care and a healthy diet. Most of the maintenance would be performed by shelter residents, who would clean and cook and tend the grounds.

"These women want to work," she had insisted. Forty percent of the women residing in the city's shelters were at least partially employed. The new, proposed shelter would provide safe transportation to their jobs, and offer employment training and job-search assistance for all the other residents. "Shelters are only temporary solutions," Emma had continued. "Mothers with children want permanent homes, and we can help them transition into stable housing situations."

The mayor had tacitly assumed that Emma would direct the new shelter, although she had never agreed. She enjoyed the cozy size of Kelly's House, with women sleeping four to a room and all the residents eating together in one large dining room, around two tables. There, the neighborhood was vibrant, full of elegantly decrepit town houses and detached mansions with warped wooden porches, where families gathered on summer afternoons to lament the humidity. A Cuban tapas café stood two blocks away; Brazilian, Thai, and Ethiopian waited within walking distance.

By comparison, the neighborhood at North Capitol was more elderly, more white, and much more bland. For two months Emma had gone door-to-door, distributing brochures from successful women's shelters in other cities, sensing that her white skin was a password that could grant her ten minutes on the living room couches of most of these brick row houses. Like the mayor, the neighbors assumed that they were talking to the future director of the shelter; Emma's acceptance of the post had eventually become a prerequisite for their consent. Looking into the eyes of those exhausted women and men, Emma had developed a sense of obligation, a need to assure them that a shelter would not threaten their fragile hold on respectability. Many of the neighbors had a siege mentality—retired couples clinging to the middle-class decency they had achieved through hard, manual labor, suspicious of a younger generation that lounged in front of screens, and especially wary of the black families a few blocks east, where the city's drifting color line divided white paranoia from African-American ambition.

"A women's shelter will not harm your neighborhood," Emma had promised the North Capitol community. The shelter's residents would behave better than the noisy fifth and sixth graders who had roamed the streets after school, playing ding-dong ditch.

"Public schools are great locations for shelters," she had added. The gymnasium, in partnership with the local YMCA, could offer after-school sports for the children, while outside, a corner of the grassy playground could be transformed into a vegetable garden for the residents to maintain. They could use the cafeteria's kitchen to prepare the food they grew, and cooking classes could be offered twice a week. Meanwhile, the library would be filled with books and magazines and old computers from District government offices, with volunteers on hand to teach literacy skills, hold story-time hours, and help children with their homework. The library was Emma's favorite selling point; she spoke with the passion of an exiled English professor as she reminded the neighbors to be sure to donate their old paperbacks.

With each week Emma added more trappings of upper-middle-class respectability to her vision of the ideal shelter, including composting at the center's garden, art therapy, and a biweekly book club. Of course the neighbors still grumbled—a women's shelter was not going to raise real estate prices. But Emma quietly pointed out that while legal action might delay the process, the anonymous, ten-million-dollar gift had guaranteed that a shelter would come, and the neighborhood would be better off with a women's center than a traditional shelter dominated by men.

What she didn't confess publicly, though Emma knew it all too well, was that even at a women's shelter, the men would come, mostly at night—unusually bold husbands searching for their wives at one a.m., deceptively contrite, making promises of love and reformation. Their sugary facades often reminded Emma of Jacob Stewart, although she tried to discipline her thoughts, to keep past baggage from clouding her present judgment. It was impossible not to think of Jacob as she watched the men's faces darken when they realized she saw through their lies, and was determined to block them. She had witnessed several transformations from Jekyll to Hyde, enduring threats made more ugly by the distortions of peach streetlights. Usually Emma stood on the front stairs of Kelly's House with arms crossed, flanked by young male volunteers from local colleges. Her tactics depended on the history of the batterers; most nights a verbal rebuke could send a man home, but on a few occasions, if a husband had a criminal record, or was known to carry a gun, she locked the doors and latched the windows when she saw trouble coming, calling the police and instructing her residents to get away from any glass. "Tornado drills," she called these rare events. "Looks like we've got a storm at our door. A hurricane named Rodney."

Emma hadn't realized, when she proposed the new shelter, how the authoritative face of a school building would help to minimize these problems. In the coming years she would discover that men who had no qualms about pounding on the doors of an old Victorian house, or trying to climb into a first-floor bedroom window, were reluctant to enter public institutions. The flagpole, the white columns, the heavy metal door opening onto linoleum tile that led to the principal's office—all carried the residual intimidation of their public school days. The few batterers who dared to step inside sniffed the scent of prison and were grateful to exit.

Since the opening of the center only three men had lingered outside to shout curses, but even then, the building thwarted them. They had no idea where a wife or girlfriend might be housed—what side of the structure to shout at—and no assurance that their voices could penetrate brick walls. The men who bothered to come once usually didn't return.

Now, as Emma walked the halls of her shelter, she imagined herself as a mother superior overseeing a medieval convent. Eight centuries ago she might have relished that role, if she could have stomached the celibacy. Almost two hundred women and seventy children lived within these cinder-block walls, 10 percent more than Emma had expected. "If you build it, they will come," she had told the mayor, but she hadn't anticipated how great the numbers would be, and how many women she would have to send away to the Federal Shelter. Some observers complained that Emma had made the center too comfortable; an op-ed in the *Washington Times* accused her of being a home wrecker, an embittered divorcée who encouraged women to leave their husbands. Of course the claims were ridiculous. How could living in an elementary school ever be too comfortable, sleeping on cots, twelve to a classroom, with a one-by-five foot locker for all of a woman's possessions? She had written a rebuttal, mocking those detractors who claimed that she was making it too easy for women to abandon their husbands: *If a man is breaking his wife's ribs, who wants to make it hard for a woman to leave?*

Mothers with young children had first priority at the center, and now, as Emma passed the open doors of the old kindergarten classrooms, she glimpsed each woman's cot paired with a crib or bassinet. These were the shelter's nurseries, for women with babies less than two years old. When infants woke at night, mothers were required to take them across the hall into the teachers' lounge, newly refurbished with couches and rocking chairs for midnight breast-feedings, and a stove for warming bottles of formula. The lounge contained one of the few TVs in the building. In general Emma opposed them, but she remembered, from Maggie's earliest months, the watchful hours at two a.m., pacing a dark room, trying to rock her daughter to sleep while thanking God for late-night reruns of *Law & Order* that glowed from the corner of the family room, the volume tuned to a whisper.

Emma entered a stairwell and headed upstairs to the third- through fifth-grade classrooms along the far side of the building. This was the shelter's most secure location, three stories off the ground, including the basement. Too high for anyone to see into the windows—too high for Carlos Cortez to press his face to the glass. Emma stepped through a doorway into a space almost unrecognizable as a former classroom, where the chalkboards were covered with fabric wall hangings and posters of impressionist landscapes hid most of the cinder blocks. Three bunk beds for children and six cots for women were arranged on a scattering of blue-and-green area rugs; old lamps on bedside tables from the Salvation Army eliminated any need for the overhead, fluorescent lights. The finishing touch hung at the windows—lace curtains handmade by one of the shelter's most reliable residents, Martha Diaz.

Martha was a sixty-two-year-old Jamaican-born widow, white-haired and strong-boned, who was now stripping sheets off a cot and bundling them into a plastic laundry basket. She had worked as a security guard through her midforties, until recurrent spells of depression, aggravated by alcoholism, sent her spiraling from one job to the next. Homeless and rarely sober for three years before she came to NCCW, within these walls Martha had renewed her sense of purpose by serving as den mother for many of the younger women. She had a passion for cleaning, gardening, and decorating, and eight months ago, when she asked for a sewing machine, Emma had bought three, chiding herself for not thinking of it sooner. With fabric donated from two northern Virginia Walmarts, Martha had shown other residents how to make curtains for most of the classrooms, and she had begun to teach a few mothers how to sew clothes for their children.

Now Emma joined Martha, taking the ends of a clean mattress cover and helping to pull it over the cot.

"Maria is here," Emma said.

Martha nodded. "This will be her bed. Is Christian with her?"

"No. He's with her sister."

"Safe?"

"I hope so."

They fluttered a clean sheet above the mattress, then pulled it tight, Emma trying to fold a hospital corner as neatly as the older woman, and failing.

"How does the girl look?" Martha asked.

Emma sighed. "She's wearing long sleeves and leggings, so it's hard to tell, but she's got a black eye and split lip. Ruth is with her now."

"He's a mean one, that Carlos." Martha settled a clean pillow on the cot. "You think she'll go back to him this time?"

"I don't know."

Martha shook her head. "Her little body can't take much more."

"She's tougher than she looks," Emma replied, though secretly she agreed with Martha. Maria's situation was getting desperate, following a pattern Emma had seen too often, the violence becoming more frequent and more severe as the man lost all shame and the woman all hope. This was Maria's third visit to the shelter, and probably her last chance to escape.

"Will Carlos show up here?" Martha asked.

"Probably." Emma nodded. He'd done it before, one of the few men who had bothered to stand outside the building, howling his remorse, begging for Maria to come back. He would never hurt her again if she would please, please forgive him.

On that night Emma had been learning the ropes at her new shelter, and had stupidly housed Maria in the front of the building. There had only been two beds available when the young woman arrived, both in a front-facing classroom on the second floor, but it was a mistake Emma would never repeat. Maria heard her husband's lamentations through the closed windows, and the sobbing wrenched her heart.

"Don't listen to him," the other women had said. "They're always sorry until the next time they get drunk."

When Maria didn't come outside, Carlos had smashed a first-floor window with a rock before running away, and the next morning Emma had gone to the U.S. Attorney's Office to swear out a complaint against him and get an emergency restraining order. But by the time she returned to the shelter, Maria had taken her small grocery bag full of clothes and gone home.

"Has her locker been disinfected?" Emma asked. Like most shelters, NCCW waged a constant war against lice and bedbugs.

"Yes."

"And the same for Christian, if he comes?"

"Of course."

"You are a star." Emma gave Martha a hug, then stepped back, surprised to see the woman blush.

"What will you do if Carlos shows up?" Martha asked.

"Sergeant Rodriguez has agreed to spend the night here. He knows the drill."

Martha smiled. "Sergeant Rodriguez is your special friend, right?"

Now it was Emma's turn to blush.

"He's a good man, that cop of yours." Martha spoke without lifting her eyes from the towels she was folding.

"Yes," Emma agreed. Junot Rodriguez was a very good man.

CHAPTER 15

WHEN she walked back into her office, Emma found Ruth and Maria on the couch, eating pumpkin bread.

"Maria would like to use the sewing machines," said Ruth, "to make some pajamas for Christian."

"Good idea." Emma nodded. "Martha will help."

She glanced at her watch: 5:30—two hours before Junot finished work and brought her some take-out Thai. Not enough time for her to ride home on the Metro, enjoy a shower, and relax before returning, but enough hours to stretch on the couch, close her eyes, and breathe deeply. "If you'll take Maria upstairs to room 209, I'm going to unplug my phone and lie down. If I'm not answering calls again by seven, come and wake me."

With the lights out, and only the evening sun sifting through the windows, Emma pulled two blankets and a pillow from her closet and draped them across her couch, took off her gray ankle boots and the red reading glasses she had almost forgotten on top of her head, then lay down and stared at the ceiling. Light brown cauliflower florets were spreading across the fiberglass tiles, blooming with each heavy rain like all healthy vegetation, and reminding her of the stain on her hallway runner at Wade's Creek. She rolled onto her side, trying to envision the autumn leaves in Jackson: the maples' descending layers of red, orange, and green like children's striped Popsicles, and the dogwoods' crimson leaves falling like drops of—no, she would not think of blood—just red leaves falling.

Emma closed her eyes and forced herself to imagine greens and blues and browns, the colors of life and health and growth, until her mind settled upon Junot Rodriguez's lovely dark skin, the opposite of her porcelain arms with their rashes of freckles. But there, too, she couldn't escape the past, because Junot's complexion gradually merged with the tan shade of Jacob Stewart's face as he lay dying in her lap, and she remembered thinking, as she knelt in her hallway, that somewhere, unbeknownst to her, a dark-eyed mother was losing a very beautiful son.

It was pointless to resist the past; Maggie's e-mail had admitted the entire cast of characters from nine and a half years ago, and after another five minutes of trying to forget, Emma gave up and decided to examine them head-on.

First she thought of the kind-eyed deputy whom she had nick-named Prince Charming because of his name tag—*Prinze*. He had wrapped Maggie in a blanket as soon as Emma reached the house with her, and had brewed a pot of coffee. An hour later, when Rob was home and prepared to watch Maggie, Prince Charming had driven Emma to the sheriff's office to give her official statement. Emma's lawyer, Jed Christianson, met her at the station and didn't advise silence. From what she had told him, hers was a clear case of justifiable homicide, the legitimate act of a law-abiding mother protecting her child from drunk intruders.

"Under the law, your house is your castle," Jed had explained. "It's the place where you are most private and vulnerable, and where you have the most right to defend yourself. The sheriff knows that you killed someone and he hasn't Mirandized you, so he's not treating this as a crime. If there's any point during your statement when I think their questions indicate that they are viewing you as a suspect, I'll stop the interview."

During Emma's hour at the station, the sheriff and his deputies had been surprisingly chivalric, probably because she was the only woman in a building of men, with English-professor sentences so grammatically precise, she figured her statement was the most eloquent prose they had ever typed up. Afterward she wondered if it was just an act, the way Sheriff King made her believe he was entirely sympathetic. Was that a common technique to keep a woman talking?

When her story ended, Emma heard a familiar voice in the hallway—the high-pitched whirlwind of chatter that always accompanied Jodie Maus, Holford's dean of students. Emma liked Jodie. She appreciated the dean's frenetic energy, the perky competence that matched her brown pixie cut and the five-foot one-inch frame that made Emma seem tall. Some of the older male professors had nicknamed the dean "Mighty Maus," and joked about how blithely she scampered through administrative mazes, but Emma didn't laugh. She wondered what subtle disparagements they murmured behind her back.

Jodie, usually immaculately dressed in a wardrobe purchased far from Jackson, was wearing tennis shoes and sweatpants under her knee-length camel jacket. "Emma?" she said when Deputy Prinze led her into the room. "What are you doing here?"

"It happened at my house," Emma replied.

Jodie's brow furrowed. "What was Jacob Stewart doing playing baseball at your house at night?"

Emma stared into her hands. "It wasn't a game."

Jed rose from his chair. "I'm going to get a cup of decaf. Would you two like some?"

Emma nodded. "Thanks."

"Full strength for me," said Jodie.

"Emma," Jed murmured into her ear before leaving. "It's fine to tell Jodie the basic facts that you've explained to the police, but if anything else comes up—anything new that you remember—speak to me first, okay?"

When the two women were alone, Jodie sat down beside Emma. "I just came from the hospital. Jacob has already been airlifted to UVA. They say his condition is critical and he might not survive the night. His mom is flying down from Philadelphia. She's a widow and Jacob is her only child, so this is going to be especially hard. I'm going to have to explain to her exactly what happened."

Emma sensed that this interrogation would be far more difficult than the police's questions. Jodie was mother hen to three thousand students, one of whom Emma had attacked, which placed her outside Holford's protective circle.

"Jacob showed up in my backyard around ten-thirty with Kyle Caldwell and a female student I had last term, I don't remember her name. They were drinking." Slowly Emma repeated the facts she had told the police, how an amicable conversation devolved into confrontation, and how she threatened to have Kyle expelled for theft. Then came the force of Jacob's shoulder pushing into her house, the touch of his fingers in her hair, the swing of the bat, and the vision of his head in her lap.

Jodie interrupted at only one point, early in the story, when Emma explained that she had asked the students to leave.

"You say they had been drinking?"

"Kyle was holding a beer," Emma confirmed. "And the girl seemed tipsy. I figured they had come from the party at Hillyer's."

"And you told them to drive home?"

Emma paused, sensing where this was headed. A professor who had encountered drunk students at her home had encouraged them to drive away.

"I just told them to leave. It was late and I wanted them off my property."

"But you didn't offer to give them a ride, or call the HOTS van?" HOTS stood for "Holford Transportation Services," which included everything from vans for handicapped students to emergency transportation for stranded kids whose cars had broken down, or, more commonly, who were too drunk to drive. The students called it the Shots Van, the Hottie Van, the Party Bus.

"I wasn't thinking about that. It wasn't like I served them the alcohol, or invited them over to my house."

"All right," Jodie said. "But I wouldn't stress that part of the story. Tell me again what happened with Jacob—how you came to hit him."

"It was a sudden reflex. The whole thing took less than ten seconds. He reached for me, and I swung at him twice, as hard as I could." She didn't mention that Jacob had dropped after the first blow. Emma didn't want the dean to envision a student on his knees, reaching out for help from his teacher before she struck him a second time.

"Well." Jodie sighed. "This is going to be hard to explain to his mother. I'll have to wake up Don. He'll probably want to drive over to UVA with me to show that the whole college is concerned."

Don Kresgey was president of Holford, a school small enough to market itself as a family; naturally he would be involved if a student was critically injured. Still, Emma was surprised at the cold pragmatism in Jodie's tone, completely free of anguish or hesitation. She knew Jodie had faced dozens of student tragedies—suicides and car crashes and alcohol poisoning, pregnant girls and drug-riddled boys, expulsions and suspensions. But this event held its own unique terror, and she could see the calculations racing through Jodie's head. A professor had attacked a student, possibly killed him, and now his mother was on her way. What lawsuits might come of this? What nightmarish publicity? The president and dean of students must address Mrs. Stewart with a united front of sympathy and competence.

"Have you spoken to any reporters?" Jodie asked.

"No, and I don't plan to."

"Right. The less publicity the better." Jodie tilted her head and assessed Emma. "Are you okay?" Only now it seemed to occur to her that there was more than one victim in this scenario.

"Physically, yes."

"Do you want to talk with one of our counselors? Paula Harding is wonderful."

"I don't think that's necessary."

"You've been through a huge trauma; you might want some professional help."

Kyle Caldwell's words, *crazy bitch*, rang through Emma's ears and she bristled. "I don't need professional help."

Jodie hesitated, prepared to say more, but instead changed the subject. "Is Maggie all right?"

Emma dropped her eyes. "She witnessed the whole thing."

"Wow." Jodie shook her head. "I'm so sorry, Emma." She began to bite the inside of her left cheek, a nervous habit she sometimes betrayed at committee meetings when pondering a difficult question. "All of this is so hard to believe. I mean, Jacob Stewart is such a good student. He's on the student council, and the soccer team. I just can't believe he'd do this."

In the coming months Emma would hear those words over and over—*It's so hard to believe! I can't believe it! Completely unbelievable!*—and every time the words carried a hint of indictment, the implication that she was not credible.

Jodie lifted her purse. "I've got to make some more phone calls and get on the road to UVA."

"Damage control," Emma murmured.

"Yes." Jodie nodded. "Damage control."

Jed drove Emma home at 2:30 a.m., telling her not to worry, he didn't think the sheriff would press charges. Albert King attended the same church as Jed, and as the lawyer put it: "Al and most of his deputies have wives who are alone at home right now, some of them with small children. If some drunk guy was to come to their house and try to push his way inside, I bet they'd want their wives to do exactly what you did."

They were pulling into Emma's driveway, where a squad car was still parked, and she saw a deputy peer out from the kitchen window. Rob emerged from the guesthouse and met Emma in the driveway, wrapping his arm around her right shoulder while Emma stared at the yellow police tape stretched across the main house's porch stairs.

"Don't worry about that," said Jed. "It's standard procedure. You should be back in your own bed by tomorrow night."

"I convinced the sheriff to let us stay in the guesthouse for now," said Rob.

Jed smiled. "Small-town rules."

"What's that?" Rob asked.

"It's a term that some of the local lawyers use. In a big city the police would never let you stay anywhere on the property after a homicide. But Al King is playing by small-town rules." Jed turned to Emma. "The fact he's letting you use the guesthouse shows that he trusts you."

Rob thanked him, then led Emma inside. "Let me fix you a cup of chamomile." The guesthouse had a kitchenette, where he boiled water on a two-burner stove while Emma looked at the living room bookshelves, thinking that the framed family photos seemed oddly arranged.

"They searched this place before letting me in," Rob explained. "Stuff got shifted around."

Emma lifted a picture, trying to remember where it used to go. *Everything is wrong now.*

"How is Maggie?" she asked, glancing toward the closed bedroom door.

"She fell asleep an hour ago. Hasn't said a word about what's happened." Rob brought over a cup of tea and pulled up a chair beside Emma at a small round table. "I don't really understand it myself."

For the fifth time that night Emma recited her complete story, including the details of her search for Maggie, finding their daughter in the woods, her little nightgown pulled tight over her knees. The recitation seemed to have become Emma's purgatory; she imagined herself as Coleridge's Ancient Mariner, the killer of a living creature doomed to repeat her tale forever. Her only consolation was that Rob never said, "I can't believe it." He believed it all too readily, coming from a working-class background that prejudiced him against the Holford students. In his eyes, they were too rich and presumptuous, all too likely to challenge any teacher who threatened their privileged lifestyles.

"Little bastards," he muttered as Emma recalled Kyle and the girl walking down from upstairs. He paused only when she described the rush of anger that had driven her to swing the bat into Jacob's body, first his knee and then his head. Emma saw Rob squinting at her and she lowered her eyes, wondering what ugly memories were running through his head. "You did the right thing," he asserted after a few seconds. "The son of a bitch deserved it."

Emma didn't know what Jacob Stewart deserved. She doubted whether he deserved to have his life hanging by a thread at age twenty-two, but events had moved so far beyond her control, words like *deserve* had lost all meaning. Life was a series of random occurrences, not a world where people got their just deserts. Was this what she deserved, to be caught in a vortex of guilt and humiliation?

"You're exhausted," Rob said. "Try to sleep."

She did try, slipping into the guest room and lying down beside Maggie with her clothes on. She stared at the ceiling until six a.m., when the sun spread a peach-and-lavender glow over the Blue Ridge. Emma could see the pools of their creek forming a meandering pastel thread outside her window as her eyes finally closed.

Three hours later there was a knock at the door. "She's sleeping." Emma heard the edge in Rob's voice, out in the living room. "Can't it wait?"

"Who is it?" she called from her pillows.

"The sheriff," said Rob, looking into the bedroom, where mother and daughter were both awake, looking exhausted.

"We need to clarify a few things," Albert King called from outside. His voice sounded less compassionate than before, more noncommittal. "Mind if I come in?"

"Sure. I'll be out in a minute," Emma called back. "What's the problem?"

"Just part of the investigation."

He hadn't uttered the word *investigation* last night. Then his manner had been consoling, almost paternal, but now, in the light of day, the sheriff's tone was strictly professional.

Emma put her hair up into a bun while Maggie sat up in bed, watching in silence. The child's eyes seemed to focus on the knee of her mother's blue jeans, and Emma looked down, noticing a spot of blood. She walked into the bathroom and scrubbed at the spot with warm water and hand soap, wondering if the sheriff would want the pants as evidence.

When she came back out, Maggie was still staring at the wet patch on Emma's knee. "Try to go back to sleep," said Emma, and closed the bedroom door.

She sat with the sheriff at the kitchenette table, Rob brewing coffee while Albert King explained that Sandra McCluskey's story did not match hers.

"I don't understand," said Emma. "Who is Sandra McCluskey?"

"The girl who was here last night."

Ah yes. Sandy. The invisible girl who had blended into the classroom walls. Emma should have remembered her name, because she recalled thinking, midway through the semester, that "Sandy" matched the shade of the young woman's hair—not the soft white sand of the Caribbean, or the black volcanic sand in parts of Hawaii, but the grayish-tan sand at Maggie's preschool, hauled in a dump truck from the local quarry.

Sheriff King had bluish circles under his eyes as he scribbled notes on a small black pad. "You said the students came into your house, right?"

"Yes." Emma nodded.

"And you say that they were drinking at your creek?"

"Kyle had a beer in his hand." It occurred to Emma that she hadn't seen Sandra drinking, and Jacob had appeared very lucid. "I can't be sure about the others."

The sheriff looked into her eyes, noting, Emma supposed, these first cracks in her story.

"You're sure they came into your house? What rooms did they visit?"

"Kyle and Sandra entered the house to use the downstairs bathroom. But when I came inside with Jacob, they were walking down from upstairs."

"So they could have gone anywhere up there?"

"Yes, what's the problem?"

"Just a discrepancy in the stories." The sheriff wrote another note. "Sandra McCluskey claims that she and Kyle never entered your house, or went down to the creek. According to her, the three of them stopped here for directions, and Jacob went inside. She and Kyle never saw the reason for your altercation."

Emma sat in stunned silence. She had never imagined that the students might lie about last night; the truth was damning enough. What more did they need to say except that Professor Greene had swung a bat and smashed their friend's skull? But of course Kyle wouldn't want to discuss the bracelet or the Polly Pockets, or her threat to have him expelled, and he wouldn't want to admit that his kleptomania had sparked this whole tragedy. If not for the bracelet, the students could have walked away.

Kyle had every reason to lie, but why Sandy? Why did she have to strip Emma's crime of any excuse? Emma had wanted to imagine Sandy as a silent, unperjured groupie whose only guilt lay in her choice of companions. But maybe Rob was right about the students' selfishness—they viewed her as a stepping-stone in the rush to save their asses.

"She's lying," Emma murmured. "Sandy is lying."

"Kyle's story is the same," said Sheriff King, "but we have reason to doubt him. Anyway, this should be easy enough to clear up. Our forensics man is coming back to dust for some more fingerprints, if you don't mind?" Another car was pulling into the driveway as he spoke.

"Of course," said Emma. "Kyle was holding the banister when he came downstairs, and Sandy's fingerprints must be all over the bathroom . . . Can you force the students to be fingerprinted?"

"When we ask nicely, most people cooperate. It looks bad when someone is not willing to be fingerprinted. But we can get a court order if the students refuse; we'll need one to get prints from Jacob Stewart, since he can't give consent."

Emma nodded, relieved that the students' story could be so easily disproved. How stupid for Sandy to have told such an insupportable lie. It must have been Kyle's doing; he must have pressured the girl. But although she knew the fingerprints would exonerate her, Emma could feel the lie wrapping itself around her arms, as if the false story was a straitjacket that the young people were trying to strap onto the crazy professor's body. *Take her away, the hysterical female; lock her in a lonely room where she can't hurt anyone else.*

Rob brought Maggie out of the bedroom, the child's arms held tightly around his neck while her face leaned sideways against his shoulder, watching the scene at the kitchen table.

"Well, hello there." Sheriff King smiled when they entered the room, but Maggie did not smile back.

"We'll need to speak to Maggie again today." The sheriff spoke quietly to Emma.

"Why?" Rob interjected.

"Just to verify a few things."

"Not without our lawyer present." Rob made no attempt to mask his belligerence, and although Emma valued her husband's logic, she felt ashamed of his manners. Hard times brought out Rob's aggressive side, while she, the daughter of a history professor and a lawyer, both of whom had died years ago, had inherited a legacy of words to handle most crises. Why had those words abandoned her last night?

"Jed would probably prefer that Maggie and I both consult with him," she said to the sheriff.

"Of course. Give him a call." Sheriff King rose from the table. He hadn't slept all night and had no desire to get into a pissing match with a protective father.

Emma stood as well, reaching out to lift Maggie from Rob's chest, but the child turned her face away and buried it in her father's flannel shirt. Emma blushed, knowing that the sheriff was watching, and she forced herself to speak to Maggie in a bright, casual voice. "Would you like to make some chocolate chip pancakes?" Maggie nodded without turning to look at her mother.

"Can I get some ingredients and pans from my kitchen?" Emma asked the sheriff.

He nodded. "I'll go with you."

Ten minutes later they were back in the guesthouse, the sheriff writing notes at the kitchen table while Maggie helped Emma measure Bisquick and milk into a glass bowl. In silence Maggie cracked the egg and stirred the batter; in silence she poured it into the greased skillet with Emma's hands directing her own. Into the pale viscous circle Maggie placed ten chocolate chips, arranging them into a face with a forced smile, while she remained ever-conscious of the tall stranger visible outside the kitchenette window, swishing a layer of dust across their house's front porch, with a brush that resembled the one her mother used for rouge. Small white clouds rose at each step while the stranger's twitching wrist slowly advanced up the porch railing.

Deputy Prinze, who had been absent thus far that morning, knocked on the guesthouse door.

"I'm looking for Sheriff King," he said when Rob answered, and seeing King still writing at the table, he held up a Bud Light can in a gloved hand. "I found this by the creek."

Albert King followed Prinze outside while the guesthouse phone rang.

"It's Jodie," said Rob. "Do you want to talk to her?"

"Sure." Emma took the phone into the bedroom.

"I'm at the hospital." Jodie's voice sounded strained. "Jacob died a few minutes ago."

Emma sat down on the bed and closed her eyes, surprised by the chill that swept her body. She had been expecting bad news, sensing that Jacob's life was slipping away as he lay in her lap, but some part of her brain—the emotional, spiritual, desperately hopeful part—had clung to the illusion that somehow everything could be made right. The doctors would fix her mess, Jacob would recover and grow into a healthy adult, all memory of violence would fade, and her world would return to the measured, predictable routines of academia, last night surviving only as a painful aberration in a life otherwise marked by normalcy. But now that Jacob was gone, nothing could be fixed. The finality of death had left a wall between past and present.

"There's another problem," Jodie continued. "Jacob's mom has been talking to Kyle Caldwell, and apparently he's told her that you attacked Jacob without provocation. According to him, Jacob wasn't pushing his way into your house, and he hasn't mentioned any confrontation over theft. As far as Mrs. Stewart is concerned, the students were just stopping at your house for directions and you and Jacob got into some sort of fight."

Emma sighed. "It's a lie, Jodie. Kyle and Sandra are both lying. The sheriff is here and he's told me all about it. He has a man dusting for fingerprints right now, which will verify that Kyle and Sandra were all over our house. This story won't hold up for long."

"That's good. The sooner this is settled, the better. I've got to warn you, Jacob's mother is not the silent suffering sort. Stewart must be her married name because she's got some kind of Greek or Armenian thing going on. You can't imagine how enraged and vengeful she is. There's a reporter here from Charlottesville's *Daily Progress*, and Mrs. Stewart has been repeating Kyle's story as if it's gospel. She's basically calling for your head on a stake."

"How did the press find out about this so soon?" Emma asked.

"This isn't soon. More than ten hours have passed since I got the first call from the sheriff's department, which is enough time for the students to have e-mailed all their friends and family. By now it's probably on every campus gossip site in the country. The AP issued a two-paragraph report a half hour ago."

Outside, Emma could hear Rob's voice, shouting, "Get the hell off our lawn!" Glancing out the window, she saw a television news van with a satellite dish, backing off their grass as Rob waved his arms wildly.

"The press are here too. Looks like TV from Roanoke."

"The *Washington Post* will be next," said Jodie. "Don will have to issue an official statement."

"Tell them what happened." Emma's tone was almost pleading. "The police just found a beer can in my yard—I know it's from last night. Tell them that the students were trespassing on a professor's property and Jacob forced his way into my house."

The silence on the other end of the line was long and deep. "In these cases, we can't get into any specifics. Don will probably just verify that a student died after an incident at your home."

"I'll tell the press the full story," said Emma.

"I don't know if that's wise." Jodie hesitated. "Ask Jed what he thinks. Reporters have a way of warping whatever you say, getting the facts all wrong. If there's any possibility of legal action, it's usually better to stick with 'no comment.' Right now I've got to make some more calls—this is going to be a nightmare right in the middle of graduation—but I'll be back in Jackson in two hours. Come see me, okay?"

Emma hung up and walked to the window, watching a female reporter try to question Sheriff King while he inspected the area around the creek. A television cameraman, scanning the front of the house, turned his lens upon Emma's window, and she backed away from the glass, hoping she hadn't been caught on film—the guilty woman slinking off.

Returning to the kitchenette, she found Maggie eating in slow motion, one chocolate chip at a time, gradually dismantling her pancake's smile. "Would you like another glass of milk?" Emma asked, and Maggie shook her head without speaking.

Rob entered from outside, the tops of his ears bright red. "I think we should get Maggie away from all this. Have her spend the day at a friend's house."

"Would you like to play with Kate?" Emma asked Maggie, and the child nodded.

"She'll have to stay here until Jed arrives, to talk with the sheriff." Emma turned back to Rob. "But I'll call Sarah and see if Maggie can go to her house after that."

Sarah McConnell was Emma's closest friend, an English department colleague in her midforties. The two women shared lunches, coffee, and campus news, along with all the trials of motherhood.

"My God, Emma, how awful," Sarah said when Emma called. "Of course Maggie can stay with us. I'll be there as soon as I can to pick her up . . . No, you don't need to come to town . . . Is there anything I can bring you?"

Thirty minutes later a silver Volvo wagon pulled into the driveway. The woman who emerged had several gray streaks in her dark, shoulder-length hair, and a flicker of crow's-feet framed her eyes as she squinted at the yellow tape around the house, but her clothes had a youthful style—skinny blue jeans, a long silk blouse with a wide belt slung around her waist, and a scarf hanging over her shoulders with beaded fringe. Reporters swarmed as soon as she stepped forward. Did she know Emma Greene or Jacob Stewart? Did she have any comment on the killing? With a graceful sweep of her crimson fingernails, Sarah lowered her sunglasses and walked toward the guesthouse as if no one was present. When Rob opened the door, she smiled grimly, kissing him on the cheek and murmuring, "Damn buzzards."

Emma appeared in the bedroom doorway and Sarah opened her arms. "Oh, honey, I'm so sorry." Exhausted from shock and sleeplessness, Emma allowed her first tears of the day to fall on her friend's shoulder, and the two of them settled on the sofa while Rob took Maggie outside to play in the sandbox. The women remained silent on the couch for several minutes, Sarah with an arm around Emma's shoulder, Emma dabbing at her eyes with a Kleenex. Sarah seemed wholly unruffled, marked by a perpetual air of quiet reserve that never ceased to impress her younger friend.

"You always seem so calm," Emma had remarked two years earlier, when Sarah was in the throes of her tenure year.

"You should have seen me when my husband died," Sarah had replied. "I was a complete mess . . . Going up for tenure is a piece of cake."

Now Sarah asked no questions, allowing Emma to tell her story in her own time, her own way. *Recitation number six*, Emma thought as she shared the most important details, the woods becoming darker and Jacob's blood more red with each telling. It seemed that all her life had been whittled down to one tragic night, and she wondered how many people had experienced the same narrowing phenomenon— one incident becoming their world's focal point, erasing everything prior and warping everything to come. By the end, Emma had fallen into a mire of apologies. She was sorry for Jacob's death, sorry she couldn't have handled things better, sorry for the trouble this was heaping upon everyone.

"Oh no." Sarah cut her off. "You have *got* to be kidding. There is no way you are going to apologize for this . . . Look at me, Emma." Taking her friend's hands firmly into her own, Sarah stared directly into Emma's eyes. "This was *not* your fault. You must get that into your head—none of this was your fault. I know Holford likes to pretend that the students are a bunch of kids and we are all supposed to be acting in loco parentis, but these young people are *not* children, and we are not responsible for taking care of them. Jacob Stewart was a twenty-two-year-old man who showed up at your house in the county late at night and tried to push his way inside, after you clearly told him to leave. You were absolutely justified in what you did. I would have done the same thing."

She paused, looking out the window. "Remember how I told you that I knew one of the professors who was killed at Virginia Tech? Well, he died trying to hold a door shut against Seung-Hui Cho long enough so that his students could climb out the windows. And just now, when you described trying to press the door shut against Jacob, that's what I thought of—how my friend kept the killer out for as long as he could while Cho shot him through the door."

The two women leaned their heads together as Sarah continued. "Just two weeks ago there was that student at a community college in Nebraska who showed up with a gun because he didn't like his math grade, and in the past year there have been at least three cases of college students killing their classmates. It's like we've got this culture of young people who are either depressed, or overly ambitious and stressed out, and they are saturated with scenes of violence from TV and the Internet. Most of them turn out fine, but you never know what the worst are capable of. So don't you dare apologize to *anyone* for what you did—least of all to the police, or to Jodie Maus. That could be used against you as an admission of guilt, and you are *not* guilty."

Emma exhaled a long, shaking breath as Sarah put her arm around her shoulder. "We are going to get through this."

"I'm worried about Maggie," Emma murmured. "She's not talking."

"That's understandable," said Sarah. "Maybe she'll open up once she has some playtime with Kate."

"Where is Kate now?"

"She's with my friend Margaret . . . You know Maggie can stay all day with us, and sleep over if you'd like. Why don't you pack a bag for her, just in case?"

"That would be great."

"What about you?" Sarah asked. "Are you planning to hunker down here and ride out the storm?"

"I'm supposed to go to town to see Jodie a little later, and I want to get out of this guesthouse. It's too claustrophobic. The only problem is that gauntlet of reporters."

Sarah thought for a moment. "I have an idea." Ten minutes later she stepped outside, hesitating at the door's threshold while the press rushed forward. She lifted her long blue scarf over her hair and tied it around the back of her neck *hijab*-style, with the fringe falling behind her blouse. The reporters aimed a barrage of questions: Would Professor Greene be coming out to make a statement? Had she heard that Jacob Stewart was dead? Sarah put on her sunglasses, then silently walked to her car and removed a book, which she held in front of her face as she returned to the guesthouse, reporters still trailing her.

One woman from Channel 10 News yelled in a nasal voice: "Did you know that Professor Greene has a history of mental instability?"

At that, Sarah stopped abruptly, lowered the book and head scarf, and took off her sunglasses. "I am Professor Sarah McConnell"—she spoke directly into the nearest camera—"and I can state absolutely that Emma Greene is the kindest, most reasonable professor at Holford College, and all actions she has taken were justified in the name of self-defense." She put her sunglasses back on with a flourish and continued to the house, but before stepping inside, Sarah looked back. "Emma will not be coming out today, so you might as well go away."

After another fifteen minutes the press saw the door open again, but it was only Sarah, holding the same book in front of her face, her scarf still wrapped around her hair and her sunglasses covering her eyes. She hurried to her car unmolested, and drove away. No one noticed that she had shrunk two inches, or that the hair peeking from beneath her scarf glinted with a tinge of copper.

In town, Emma drove with the scarf and sunglasses on, hoping to

remain anonymous for as long as possible. Stopping at a park beside
the Shannon River, she watched a pair of fishermen in plastic lawn
chairs, reeling and casting between sips of beer wrapped in small brown
paper bags. A jogger trotted by to her right, but otherwise the park
was empty, granting Emma a few minutes to clear her head. She rose
from Sarah's car and walked toward the old red railway bridge that
extended over the water, part of an historic trail that wandered south
twenty-three miles, following the Shannon out of Jackson, through
pasture and woods skirting the edges of two more small towns. Halfway across the bridge, she stopped to lean against the railings and stare
into the current, where a trout flickered just beneath the water's surface, darting into the shadows under a large rock, far from the fishermen's lures. It was reassuring, thought Emma, how nature remained
oblivious to human tragedy, making all events trivial, even the unnatural death of a twenty-two-year-old student. Jacob Stewart was nothing to this river, nothing to the rocks and trees and fish, and she was
equally insignificant, another shadow passing across the water's surface.

She could feel the eyes of one of the fishermen and wondered if he
knew about the killing. The radio at his side was playing country
music, not local news. He was probably worried that she would scare
the fish, or perplexed by her head scarf. With a wave of her hand Emma
lowered the scarf and freed her hair, letting it flash in the sun like a
red flag of defiance. *I have nothing to hide,* she told herself, and she gave
both of the fishermen an unsmiling nod as she returned to Sarah's car.
She drove the rest of the way to the college, where Jodie's brick colo-
nial house stood in a wooded enclave at the edge of the campus, on
a winding drive that led uphill to the president's mansion. Jodie's
husband, Will, greeted her at the door, saying, "Ah, Emma—such
terrible news." He pointed down the hall. "She's in the study."

Emma knew the way. She had often come to this house for faculty
cocktail parties and Christmas open houses, and whenever the rooms

overflowed, she had gravitated toward the study, preferring the stillness of books over the noise of crowds. Kierkegaard, Nietzsche, and Hannah Arendt always waited on the top shelves, testifying to Will's early career as a philosophy professor. In recent years Jodie's salary had freed her husband to teach part-time and devote more hours to his true passion: gardening. Apparently the image of a tulip sprouting into life answered all of his questions about the nature of reality. Jodie had contributed few books to the shelves other than a dozen volumes on adolescent self-esteem, learning disorders, and drug abuse. By her own too-frequent admission, Jodie was "a people person, not a book person," as if the two were mutually exclusive, implying that faculty bookworms, like the one she had married, suffered from stunted social skills. Her job was to serve as a conduit between awkward professors and their more socially gifted students.

As Emma crossed the study's threshold, Jodie rose from her desk and glanced briefly at Emma's enormous blouse, hanging almost to her knees, before ushering her toward one half of a leather couch. "What a nightmare." Jodie collapsed onto the other half. "I've gotten over two hundred e-mails in the past three hours."

"From who?"

"Parents, students, and a few persistent reporters. I'm directing them all to Brent in public relations. He issued a statement this morning saying that a student had died after being struck in the head during an incident at a private residence. We haven't said anything more, but the rumors on the Internet are getting pretty nasty. There's a lot of speculation about what happened between you and Jacob when you were alone in the house."

"We were never alone," Emma objected. "Kyle and Sandy were inside the house when Jacob first entered, and later, when he pushed his way back in, they were standing on the porch behind him."

"Well, the Internet is not known for factual accuracy. According to the student gossip, you and Jacob were alone when the incident occurred."

"My story will be confirmed by the police. They dusted for fingerprints this morning."

"That's good. How soon will they have those results?"

"It should take about eight days."

"Eight days!" Jodie gasped. "Don't they have computers that can do that right away?"

"Not in this town. They have to send it to the state crime lab in Richmond, and there's a backlog. Priority goes to cases where there's a criminal on the loose. There's no danger to anyone in this case."

"There's a *big* danger to your reputation. Eight days is an eternity in cyberspace. By then this thing could get completely out of control."

Emma shrugged. "The folks in Richmond aren't going to care about my reputation. And I can't control what the students broadcast on the web. I think there are enough students who know me well—they should be able to set the record straight."

Jodie shook her head, looking at Emma as if she were a naive child. "You should understand"—the dean lowered her voice—"some of the boys from Kyle and Jacob's fraternity are spreading nasty rumors. They're saying that you are a radical feminist who doesn't like men."

"I *am* a feminist. So what? I tell that to my students, just to show them how normal feminists are. That doesn't mean I'm a man hater. They know I'm married, and I have plenty of male friends."

"I realize that," said Jodie. "But a few students are claiming that your grading is prejudiced in favor of women."

Emma stared. "Did Kyle Caldwell start this? He was damn lucky to get a B in my class; he deserved a C. I'm probably one of the more generous graders in our department."

"They're saying that Jacob was unhappy with his grade," Jodie continued. "They think you two were arguing about that when you were alone inside the house."

"I was never alone with Jacob in my house!" Emma's mind was racing. "And I don't even remember his grade. I think he got a B-plus. You're saying he wanted an A? Everybody thinks they deserve an A."

"And you don't think the women are being favored?"

"Christ, Jodie. You know how the grades work at our school. If you look at my grading sheets, yeah, the women are probably doing better on average, but I think that's true in most of the humanities classes at Holford, and at plenty of other colleges too. The women are making higher grades because of the amount of effort they are willing to put in, and because of the distractions that the fraternities pose for the men. It has nothing to do with gender bias."

"The students also claim that your class content is anti-male."

Emma rolled her eyes. "If Virginia Woolf's *A Room of One's Own* is anti-male, and Zora Neale Hurston's *Their Eyes Were Watching God*, then sure, you can call my readings anti-male. You know what I teach, Jodie. There's nothing radical in it—these are canonical texts. My classes are practically right-wing compared to the women's studies offerings at other colleges."

"They're also complaining about how you handled the Bible course."

Emma threw up her arms. "That was four years ago! Will they never give it a rest?" During her second year in the department an elderly male colleague had suffered a heart attack over Christmas break, and the newest assistant professors had been assigned to teach his spring classes at the last minute. Emma had gotten stuck with the Bible Then and Now, a subject in which she had no expertise, and she had approached the book with the same lens of gender and power that she applied to all texts. She hadn't realized that most of the students who signed up for the course were coming straight from Bible study groups and Young Life camps, and that the professor she was replacing had traditionally balanced his lectures between scholarship and evangelism. He had been comfortable with students who used their papers to proclaim their enthusiasm for Christ, but Emma had no patience for it. On the first paper assignment she had felt magnanimous, even saintly, when she gave half the papers back ungraded, telling the students to start over or risk failure. She had expected them to be grateful, but instead their resentment had scarred the class discussion for the rest of the term. Supposedly the problem was her, not them. She was the heathen in their midst, preaching her feminist agnosticism. Parents had sent e-mails to the dean of the faculty, claiming that she was biased against Christian students, and unduly irreverent toward the Good Book. The students' course evaluations at the end of the term had been scathing.

Emma sighed as she thought back on the squabbles. "I still don't know how you can talk about Adam and Eve without discussing gender bias."

"Some male students are saying you were enthusiastic when a woman in the Old Testament killed a man?"

"That's the story of Judith," Emma said. "And the students liked her too . . . If they are comparing me to Judith, I'll take that as a compliment."

"And you've taught other books where women kill men?"

This is ludicrous, thought Emma, noticing how her shoulders had stiffened; her anger always manifested itself as a case of rigor mortis. *Let it go*, she thought. *Let it all go.* "They must be referring to the murder in *Tess of the d'Urbervilles*, but I think most readers feel that Alec had it coming."

"I don't want you to think that I agree with any of these claims." Jodie was watching Emma closely, noting the edge in her voice. "I've supported the women's studies program one hundred percent. I just thought you should get a heads-up so you'll know what kind of wild accusations are flying out there. You say you've told your students that you are a feminist. Well, for half the kids on this campus 'feminism' is a scary word. Our young women all want equal access to education and jobs, and equal pay for equal work, but most of them would never think to call themselves feminists. All it takes is a few rumormongerers, calling you an angry Feminazi, to make a vicious lie spread all over the web. It's hard to compete with that."

"So you're saying that I'm a victim of cyber-bullying?"

"I'm saying that this is already getting ugly."

"How is Don handling it?" Emma imagined Don Kresgey under siege in his castle fifty yards up the hill, beyond the putting-green lawn, the flat-topped boxwoods and cut-glass windows, pinned down by a flurry of phone calls with her name repeated ad nauseam: Feminist Emma, the femme fatale.

"He's not making any public comments," said Jodie. "And he's not taking sides. Don says we'll let the investigation run its course before the college issues a more detailed response. He's only expressing regret that a student has died."

So, thought Emma. She was on her own to face a tsunami of student-generated slander. "I assume I shouldn't come to any of the graduation-week events?"

Jodie ignored Emma's sarcastic tone. "Your presence might be inflammatory. This has already cast a pall over the week. Jacob had a lot of friends."

Emma clenched her jaw. "Sorry to have inconvenienced everyone."

Jodie sighed. "You are in a lousy situation, and the next few weeks are going to be rough. But once the students disperse for the summer, I think this should ease up. They will all be busy with their separate lives, and an incident on one campus is not going to interest the press for long. In the meantime you are lucky to have Sarah as your PR person."

Emma's eyebrows lifted, and Jodie pointed toward a flat-screen TV in the corner, where a muted CNN was running headlines beneath the face of a twentysomething anchorwoman in heavy mascara. "Sarah's comment is all over the news, saying how kind and reasonable you are, and how justified you were in your actions. That sort of statement will go a long way. If the fingerprint evidence clears you, you should be okay."

Emma noticed the qualifier in Jodie's sentence. Not "when" but "if." She rose to her feet. "I better get going."

Jodie escorted her to the front door. "I'll keep you posted on all developments. For now you can lay low out in the county."

As Emma descended Jodie's front stairs, a dark green Mercedes pulled into the driveway and an older man in a well-tailored dark jacket and tie emerged from the driver's seat. He opened the back door for two women, the first one pale and blond in pearls and gold earrings, wearing a navy-blue suit that seemed to match the driver. Probably his wife, Emma guessed, from the way he held the woman's elbow with a courtesy just shy of love. The second woman to rise from the car was very different—black hair pulled in a tight bun, eyes circled with heavy liner, lipstick like blood. She moved stiffly, as if each step was painful, and although the mid-May heat had reached eighty-nine degrees, the woman was shivering. The blonde had one arm around her, helping her negotiate the walkway while the husband followed two paces behind, occasionally examining the woods around him with a distracted gaze. Emma stepped to the side, making room for the trio, and as the dark woman passed, her eyes, red and swollen, briefly settled on Emma.

Goose bumps rose along Emma's arms. This was Jacob's mother; they had met at Parents' Weekend in October, when Mrs. Stewart had attended Emma's class on Tennyson. The woman had shaken her hand afterward, and Emma remembered the mother's eyebrows, penciled in with too much arch, her face locked in perpetual inquiry.

The question those eyes seemed to ask at this moment was "Why?" and Emma froze, unsure if she should try to express some awkward sympathy. The mother's face first registered perplexity, followed by a slow hardening of her mouth. Emma turned without speaking, heading toward Sarah's car, while behind her she detected a long, growling "herrrr" suddenly changing to a clipped shout—"That's her!"—followed by quick footsteps. Emma scarcely had time to glance back before Mrs. Stewart's left hand had grabbed her hair, yanking her head around, while her right hand dug sharp fingernails into Emma's right biceps, twisting her backward and throwing her to the grass. Emma shielded her face while Mrs. Stewart pounced, purple fingernails raking across Emma's forearms. The blond woman stood frozen and appalled, but her husband reacted instantly, reaching down and pulling the enraged harpy off Emma, saying, "No, no! Come away." He held Mrs. Stewart's arms back, so that her final act was to spit upon Emma. *Cobra mother*, Emma thought, and she realized, as she looked at the gray-haired man restraining Mrs. Stewart, that this must be Mason Caldwell, Kyle's super-rich dad.

Behind them, Emma saw Jodie running down from the house. Emma imagined that her friend might rush to her aid, but when Jodie reached the gathering, she did not kneel to help. Instead she stood beside the Caldwells while Emma lifted herself from the grass with what small shred of dignity she could muster, pushing her hair from her face, then rising to the most erect five foot three she could manage in the presence of these tall parents, noting the brief flash of surprise in Mason Caldwell's eyes, as if he was taken aback at how small and unthreatening the murderess was. She turned her back and continued walking, her legs shaking while she opened the car door. Behind her she heard another low noise gradually crescendo as Mrs. Stewart released a long, keening cry of despair, falling into Mr. Caldwell's arms while she howled with grief and rage.

Ashamed, Emma closed the car door and pulled out of the driveway, glancing in the rearview mirror at the anguished tableau on Jodie's lawn. She drove a mile past the college campus before stopping at the curb of a quiet residential street, where she pressed her forehead against the steering wheel and sobbed. Why was she the guilty one? She, who had been robbed and threatened and nearly attacked, was now branded an outcast, exempt from sympathy.

Emma allowed herself five minutes of self-pity, and when she could breathe calmly, she drove to Sarah's small house on the outskirts of town, where Emma's white Toyota waited in the driveway.

"My gosh, what happened?" Sarah met Emma at the door.

Emma glanced at the grass stains on Sarah's blouse, and the bleeding scratches on her arms. "I ran into Jacob's mother at Jodie's house."

Sarah held open her door and Emma entered tentatively, primed for another ambush.

"Is Maggie here?" She glanced around the house for children.

"Not yet." Sarah guided her toward the living room sofa. "The sheriff was still talking to her when I left, though from what I could tell, she wasn't saying a word. Rob will bring her over when they're done, and my friend Margaret will bring Kate home then."

"I wish the sheriff would leave Maggie alone." Emma sighed.

"She's a witness. If she would speak, she could corroborate your story about the students being inside your house."

Emma nodded, although she wondered what Maggie would say if she did speak. Would she tell the police that her mother was a murderer? That she had slammed a baseball bat into the head of a boy who was on his knees? She didn't know how much Maggie had heard or seen, but the child couldn't have understood about the bracelet, or the school's honor code, or what the threat of Kyle's expulsion might have meant to him and Jacob. All Maggie would know was that her mother had committed an unspeakable act of violence.

"Did you get out of the guesthouse without a hitch?"

Sarah laughed. "Oh yes. The reporters gave quite a double take when they saw me exit the place a half hour after I'd already driven off."

"Do you think anyone followed you?"

"I took the long way home and stopped by the grocery store for good measure, but I didn't see anyone tracking me. I bet they're looking for you at your office."

Emma returned the scarf, sunglasses, and keys. "Jodie says that some of the students have targeted me for a smear campaign."

Sarah dropped her eyes. "I know. I've been online."

"Is it bad?"

Sarah sighed. "Everyone who knows you will understand that it's all a bunch of vicious crap, but yeah, a lot of nasty e-mails are flying around. Are you going to give a statement?"

"I called Jed on the way over, and he thinks I should lie low. The media might distort anything I say. But Jodie says your vote of confidence has appeared on CNN."

Sarah smiled grimly. "I was thinking of sending an e-mail to our department and to all our closest friends in town—to let them know the full story about what happened. If I get the word out to about thirty people in Jackson, and to some of the colleagues we know at other campuses in Virginia, the truth should establish a foothold. Whatever I do can't compare to the students' Internet blitz, but it should make it a little easier to hold your head up in Jackson. Is that okay with you?"

"Sure, thanks."

"Is there anything else I should know about last night? Any other facts?"

"You mean, am I hiding something?"

"No," Sarah replied. "I don't mean that."

A car pulled into the driveway, and Sarah pushed back her living room curtain to see Rob approaching the house with Maggie.

"Hello again." Sarah smiled as she opened the door. "I've made homemade banana muffins, Maggie. Would you like one?"

The child nodded without speaking, and Rob gave Sarah a grateful look as she took Maggie's hand and walked her back to the kitchen. He stepped into the living room and sank onto the couch beside Emma.

"What a nightmare."

"Did Maggie say anything to the sheriff?"

"Not a word." Rob shook his head. "Jed says she is silent as a church mouse, and he approves."

"I can't imagine what's she's thinking," Emma murmured.

From the back of the house they heard Maggie's voice, speaking tentatively to Sarah. "Yes, please" and "thank you" and "I like bananas."

"Sarah is so terrific," said Rob. "It will be good for Maggie to stay here with Kate, away from the house." He placed an awkward hand on Emma's knee. "I'm sorry I wasn't there last night. I shouldn't have left you and Maggie alone."

"That's ridiculous." Emma looked away from him, out the window. "There was no way to know that something like this would happen."

"But if I had been home, I could have handled it."

Rob didn't add the final word, but Emma completed his sentence in her mind: "I could have handled it *better*." For Rob, the bat was a prop, not a weapon; he would have scattered the students without violence.

"You think I went too far."

"Not at all." Rob shook his head. "You did the right thing. I'm just disgusted with myself. I could have been home by eight o'clock yesterday. There was no need to spend the night."

That fact had crossed Emma's mind as well. In the midst of her self-rebukes she had also condemned Rob for all the nights he had left her and Maggie alone—late evenings at work, nonessential business trips, too many visits with his mother.

"It's pointless to blame ourselves," she said. "We shouldn't even talk about it."

Rob stopped speaking, knowing that in their marriage Emma set the rules of conversation, deciding which topics were worth discussion and which were fruitless. A mountain of unspoken thoughts loomed between them, with Jacob Stewart's death the crowning weight on a crumbling precipice. Gently, Rob lifted his hand from Emma's knee and they sat together in silence, each of them alone in their separate guilt.

Chapter 16

A knock at her door roused Emma from the depths of sleep, and she opened her eyes to see Ruth leaning her head inside the office.

"You told me to check on you by seven."

"Thanks." Emma sat upright and tried to get her bearings.

Junot was due to arrive anytime, so she fumbled through her purse for a hairbrush and lipstick, then staggered into the small bathroom that extended from her office. The fluorescent lights gave her face a jaundiced glow; sighing, she pinched her cheeks, fluffed her hair, and regretted the wrinkles carved deeply around her eyes and above the bridge of her nose. In two more weeks she would be forty-five, and although her occasional gray hairs could still be plucked one by one, their Brillo-pad texture warned that age would not come gracefully. It would emerge in brittle strands, tinged with melancholy.

She had never seen a fleck of gray in Junot Rodriguez's black hair; he was her younger man, her trophy lover—as if she had ever done anything in her life to deserve a prize—and she often marveled that he had stayed with her for so long.

"You are his MILF," Maggie had stated last year in one of her belligerent moods.

Emma had chosen to ignore the remark, lamenting the vulgar world her daughter was growing up in. "Junot likes me," she had replied, "because he feels guilty about something that happened to another woman over a year ago."

Emma had gone on to tell Maggie the story of how she met Junot one night after finishing dinner at a friend's house in Cleveland Park.

"Cleveland Park is a very ritzy neighborhood, which is why it surprised me when we heard a husband and wife having a loud fight next door. Rich people fight just as much as poor people, but they're usually quieter, trying to keep up appearances. My friend, Michelle, told me that things had been going downhill for this couple ever since the guy lost his job at Merrill Lynch."

"So you had to get involved?" Maggie rolled her eyes.

Emma's jaw tightened. Her daughter rolled her eyes way too much. "You should never ignore domestic violence. We heard a sound like glass shattering, so I told Michelle to call 911, and I went over to pay a helpful neighborly visit."

"And the man let you in?"

"I didn't exactly wait for an invitation."

Emma still remembered the scene: the blond husband deceptively handsome, looking like he'd stepped out of a Ralph Lauren catalog, and the living room so coldly clean—white walls, white sofas and cushions, a white fireplace where a woman stood with her back turned.

"Are you all right, dear?" Emma had ducked under the husband's arm and hurried to the wife's side before the man could stop her.

The woman's hands seemed to be holding her nose in place, cupping the blood that had already left a few dark drops on the snowy carpet. Turning toward Emma, she had lowered her fingers enough to reveal a nose folded sideways, as if turning its face away from a blow, a thick red mustache growing beneath her nostrils. Slowly the woman held her hands forward, palms out, offering handfuls of blood to this strange visitor in her home, and Emma saw in those dripping palms her own bloody hands, presenting her ruined dish towels to the kind-eyed deputy.

"The police are on the way." Michelle was standing inside the doorway, staring at her neighbor's mangled nose.

"Come and help this woman clean up." Emma beckoned Michelle over.

"This is a *private* matter," the husband stormed. "You both need to leave." At which point Emma saw the boy, sitting at the top of the staircase, watching in silence. Maybe eleven years old, she thought. Maybe twelve.

"*You* need to be quiet." She spoke over her shoulder to the man as she directed Michelle and her neighbor toward an open bathroom door in the hallway. "You're keeping your son awake."

She had expected the husband to fall silent. Most fathers could control themselves in the presence of neighbors and young children, but although this man's eyes glanced briefly at the stairs, his tone didn't soften.

"My son is none of your business."

What was this guy on? Cocaine? Amphetamines? Emma could smell liquor, but there had to be something stronger giving him the sharp edge.

"Get the hell out of my house," he said, before adding: "you bitch."

There it was, thought Emma. The single, harsh syllable that had provided a staccato accompaniment to the most bitter scenes of her life: stupid bitch, crazy bitch, angry bitch. The word had become an alarm bell, clattering through her brain, its ugly sound inescapable, omnipresent on TV, in movies, and on the Internet, repeated constantly in the lyrics of popular songs, as if *bitch* were synonymous with *woman*, and it wasn't. Whenever she heard shelter residents toying with the insult, lightly calling each other bitches as if their lives were one big, crude joke, she rebuked them. Appropriation by women didn't take the sting from the word or erase its history of violence.

Turning toward the husband slowly, Emma had flicked open the blade of her sharpest smile, murmuring in a seductively low voice: "Ooooohh . . . So now you're flirting with me?" She gave a bright laugh as she stepped closer to his face, barely whispering, "What an impressive man you are. Such a good husband and father. So considerate, and so eloquent. Your son"—she nodded toward the stairs—"must be so proud."

She had been ready for his fist, or perhaps his open hand, thinking it might be time to test her five years of karate lessons, and learn whether a black belt on a five-foot-three, middle-aged woman amounted to anything. Emma had become a regular at the dojo up the street from her home ever since the occasion when, one block from Kelly's House, a large man had pushed her down onto the sidewalk. He hadn't taken her purse or assaulted her further. Instead he had kept walking as if nothing had happened; he had simply knocked a short, stupid woman out of his way. Emma would have preferred a traditional mugging, something with material motivations that might have made the act less reminiscent of playground bullying. Twice in her life she had been knocked to the ground, and it wasn't the physical injury (a few bruises to her arms and knees), but the mental outrage that had sent Emma to the sensei two days later. Since then she had frequented the karate center as methodically as some women attended church.

Just try, Emma had thought as she glared at the hyped-up husband, *just try to knock me down.*

"You are always putting yourself in those positions!" Maggie had interrupted the story. "I'm the only kid at school whose mom has bruises all the time."

"I don't put myself in danger," Emma replied. "Stuff just happens . . . Anyway, Junot saved the day."

She could vividly remember the dark-haired sergeant with the name tag *Rodriguez* stepping through the door of that cold white house, saying, "Whoa now, folks, hold on there."

Emma had been surprised to see the police arrive so quickly, being accustomed to no-shows or thirty-minute waits. But then again, this was Cleveland Park, home to millionaire lawyers and future senators, where taxpayers demanded prompt attention to their pettiest grievances.

"Is there a problem, ma'am?" The sergeant was looking at Emma's face and arms, clearly searching for injuries, assuming she was the battered spouse.

"Go into the bathroom and take a look at his wife's face," said Emma. "Then you tell me if there's a problem." Sergeant Rodriguez gestured for his partner, who was entering the door, to check out the bathroom.

"And who are you?" He continued to focus on Emma.

"Emma Greene. I was eating dinner next door with a friend when we heard the fight over here and called 911."

"Officer." The husband's voice was suddenly calm—the polite tone of a financial professional who might have been discussing the yield on a small-cap fund. "This woman and her friend are trespassing in my house."

"We're going." Emma gave the husband one final, contemptuous glare. Then she turned her full attention upon Sergeant Rodriguez's eyes and was surprised to see, in those dark brown pools, the same gentle expression she remembered from the deputy in Jackson, as if the two men were cousins. Despite being a city cop, this sergeant didn't speak to Emma with jaded impatience; nor did he wear that slight smile of amusement she had noticed too often on the lips of tall men when confronting short, angry women, as if the height of a woman gave her rage legitimacy, and Emma was merely an irate toy.

She suspected that her instinctive confidence in this sergeant was simply her preference for brunettes. Forty-three years as a freckled redhead had left Emma envious of Starbucks skin—shades of cappuccino or mocha or warm chocolate—rich colors than didn't turn pink in an hour of sunlight. As for eye color, she was suspicious of pale blues, sensing that the deeper the iris, the deeper the heart.

What nation was it, she wondered as she looked at this anonymous policeman, that produced such lovely brown eyes? Staring into his serious gaze, Emma tried to silently infuse a sense of crisis, to communicate the urgency of the situation without actually pleading. "I leave this in your hands."

Together, she and Michelle had returned next door and watched from the porch, joined by two other neighbors attracted by the ambulance that had arrived just after the police. When Emma saw the dark-eyed sergeant and his partner emerge from the house without the husband in custody, she ran over to him.

"You're leaving?"

"The wife claims she ran into a door."

"You know that's bullshit. We all heard the fight."

"But did you see anything? Did anyone see anything?"

"You saw her face. What more do you need to see?"

"If nobody saw him hit her, and she insists that she ran into a door, there's nothing we can do."

"You must persuade her." Emma knew that her "must" sounded too demanding and professorial, and she tried to ease her tone. "You can convince her that she will be safe. Tell her to think of her child."

The sergeant shook his head. "This woman refuses to even go to the hospital. The paramedics have set her nose and given her some painkillers, and she says she'll see her regular physician in the morning, but she won't go anywhere tonight."

"Look." Emma tried one last strategy. "I run a women's shelter, so I see this every day, and it's very clear that this woman is in serious danger. Normally a husband from a neighborhood this upscale wouldn't hit his wife in the face; he wouldn't want anyone to see the bruises. But this guy doesn't care anymore—you can tell he's crossed a mental line. He doesn't give a damn about what the neighbors think, or what his son sees, and that's a huge red flag. Most men in his income bracket would be horrified if they broke their wives' noses. They would be all contrite and begging for forgiveness, but this guy shows no remorse— like he's not even trying anymore."

"If the wife won't cooperate, there's nothing we can do."

"What about a drug charge? He's clearly wound up on something."

"There's no obvious drug use, and we haven't got a warrant to search the place."

"That woman"—Emma pointed to the house—"is in imminent danger." But she could tell from the sergeant's face that he saw no danger in Cleveland Park. Danger resided in Anacostia, or on South Capitol Street, in neighborhoods without gazebos and fertilized lawns.

"I'll come back in the morning to check on them," the sergeant tried to reassure Emma. "For now, everyone needs to settle down and get some sleep."

When the police car pulled away, Emma glanced at the house and saw the living room curtain fall into place.

Back in her bedroom in Dupont Circle, she couldn't sleep for more than two hours at a time, her mind filled with the woman's bloody palms outstretched like the hands of Christ. At five-thirty the call came that she had been expecting: a panicked Michelle, woken to gunshots from next door. Michelle had phoned 911, but apparently she wasn't the first. Sirens were already approaching, and neighbors were emerging in bathrobes up and down the street.

"Was the woman dead?" Maggie asked when Emma paused in the middle of her story.

"I expected everyone to be dead—the whole family," said Emma. But according to Michelle's neighbors, and confirmed later by the *Washington Post,* the twelve-year-old son, who hadn't been able to sleep, had seen his father enter the family's study around five a.m. Through the cracked door, the boy had watched his dad remove a wooden box from his lowest desk drawer, and unlock it with a small key. The box contained a pair of handguns that the boy had seen before—on his tenth birthday his father had taught him how to load and unload them, clean them, and check that the safety was on. After watching his father take one and insert a few bullets, then leave the room without locking the box, the boy entered the study and copied all of his father's movements, before going in search of his dad. He had found his father in the master bedroom, standing over his sleeping wife, and when the man began to lift his weapon, the boy had shot him—once in the back shoulder, then twice more in the chest and stomach when his dad turned to face him. The boy had been the first person to call 911. Later he told the police that he didn't know whether his dad intended to shoot his wife or himself, a question Emma imagined would plague the boy for the rest of his life.

Emma's interest in the story would have ended there, except that two days later, when she was sitting at her desk at Kelly's House, absorbed in yet another grant application, she had heard a knock at her office door and looked up to see Sergeant Rodriguez, wearing blue jeans and a button-down shirt. "May I come in?" he asked.

Emma rose from her chair and gestured toward her brand-new blue sofa. "Please."

He had come to apologize—to say he was sorry for not taking her advice more seriously. He should have gotten the mother and son out of the house.

Emma shook her head. "They would have been back there soon enough, if the mother wasn't ready to make the break."

"But it would have defused the tension for that night," the sergeant said.

"And left it for another night," Emma replied.

The man was quiet for a while, looking at Emma's walls, and she did not rush him; after traumatic events, witnesses often needed extra time to gather their words. "When I went into the house in the morning," Sergeant Rodriguez began, "and saw that boy sitting on the couch with his mother, I thought that I should have done what he did—not killed the man, but stopped him. I left that boy to do my work, and now he has to live with the knowledge that he killed his father."

"He'll also know that he protected his mother," said Emma.

Sergeant Rodriguez didn't respond. He merely shook his head and said, "I didn't think the man was dangerous. He seemed to have calmed down by the time I left."

Suddenly Emma was impatient with this cop for taking up her time. She had heard all this before—the remorse of family members who never saw it coming, friends who had noticed bruises and heard arguments but who could never imagine the worst. Something pliable and hopeful in human nature made them blind to imminent tragedy, seeing only the possibility of improvement. It was Emma who always anticipated the worst, who saw death lurking in every corner, digging its trench of pessimism into her soul, so that right now she wanted to shake this man out of his naïveté, or at least shrug her shoulders and say, "Good riddance to bad rubbish."

Still, she didn't ask him to leave, because it was unusual to hear a policeman expressing regrets. Emma expected a city cop to remain hardened to the ugliness of his job, but something in that house in

Cleveland Park must have disturbed him, and she wondered what details the newspapers hadn't reported—whether the dying man had spoken a few, haunting words, or whether something in the boy's violence and the mother's helpless acquiescence had hinted at family traditions destined to be repeated. Looking into Sergeant Rodriguez's troubled eyes, Emma saw a capacity for suffering that seemed at odds with the apparent strength of his late-thirties body, and she thought to herself: *Well then. Welcome to my world.* But aloud, she simply asked, "What is your first name?"

"Junot," he replied.

"As in the goddess?"

"No—as in the writer, Junot Díaz. The one who won the Pulitzer." Emma smiled at her own prejudices. She hadn't expected a cop to know any Pulitzer winners.

"Well, Junot Rodriguez, would you like to walk up the street with me and have a cup of coffee?"

From that day forward, she had gained not only a lover, but a private bodyguard. After observing her work at Kelly's House, Junot had insisted that the shelter needed a strong male figure of public authority, and he had begun to volunteer on difficult nights, bringing a bedroll and sleeping bag and camping on her office floor like a faithful Boy Scout. Emma understood his motives; she had seen the same behavior in her ex-husband. Having failed to make the woman in Cleveland Park safe, Junot had decided to ensure the safety of Emma Greene. It was a touching gesture, though she doubted whether guilt could be the bedrock for a lasting relationship.

RUTH knocked at Emma's door again.

"Sergeant Rodriguez is here."

Emma pulled her blouse over her hips, trying to smooth the wrinkles from her clothes, if not her face. "Send him in."

A scent of coconut and cumin announced Junot's entry, and he lowered two white paper bags onto her coffee table.

"I brought your favorite, yellow curry."

When she kissed him on the cheek, Emma inhaled deeply, knowing Junot to be an olfactory buffet, full of hints of wet leather and spicy food, ever-changing shampoos and semisweet colognes. Today she smelled pine and cardamom and chili peppers.

"You're expecting a bad night?" he asked as he opened the boxes.

"Carlos Cortez," Emma replied, retrieving paper plates and plastic forks from her closet. "I've told you about him."

"I thought you got a restraining order."

"That won't stop him. He's never been to jail, and the one time he got arrested, Maria wouldn't cooperate with the prosecutor and Carlos was out within half a day. He thinks the criminal justice system is a joke."

"I've come prepared." Junot held open his jacket, and Emma thought he meant to display the gun that he carried at all hours. But instead he reached inside his breast pocket, pulling out a pair of handcuffs. "These are my idea of a restraining order."

Emma's eyes were drawn to the nine-millimeter at Junot's hip. The first time she had put her arm around him, outside a movie theater, she had been surprised to feel the hard metal.

"Do you always carry that?" she had asked.

"Force of habit." He nodded. "I feel too light without it. I need the weight."

He called the gun his *camarado*, and Emma had been embarrassed by the thrill she felt at the sight of it, considering herself above such base reactions; guns were the ugly, crude accessories of criminals and rednecks and men who couldn't feel masculine without a weapon. And was she now dating one of those men? Was she falling for the machismo she had always held in contempt?

"Have you ever shot anyone?" she had asked Junot on one of their earliest dates.

"Once, in the arm."

"So I'm the only killer in this relationship?"

Junot had not smiled. "I see no killers here."

That was more than a year ago. Now the gun, the cuffs, the badge, were as commonplace as the BlackBerries, iPhones, and laptops that Emma's former lovers had brandished. Every man carried the tools of his trade, and Emma supposed she was abandoning her liberal inclinations, to find so much comfort in the nearness of a weapon.

She and Junot ate their curry in silence, while outside her window the moon rose over block after block of old brick town houses.

"I'm going to have to cancel our date this weekend." Emma spoke at last, then took a bite into a spring roll.

Junot paused over his *satay*. "You said you were dying to see this show. We've had the tickets for weeks."

"I know—you should definitely go, and take a friend."

"My friends don't go to musicals."

"I'm sorry, but I got an e-mail this afternoon from Maggie and she has a crisis going on at home."

"Teenage problems?"

Emma shook her head. "Mommy problems . . . Do you remember the name Sandra McCluskey?"

"Sure. She was the girl involved that night at your house."

Emma admired how Junot never forgot a name, especially those tied to a crime. "Apparently Sandy has returned to Jackson and now she's Maggie's math teacher."

Junot's eyebrows raised half an inch. "Doesn't the school see the problem in that?"

"I don't think they know who she is. Her married name is Murdock, and Rob didn't even recognize her on back-to-school night. Maggie's been in a classroom with the woman for weeks and only now figured out who she is. Apparently she had a talk with Maggie recently and told her some new information about Jacob Stewart. Maggie wants me to come down this weekend and hear Sandy's story. I think the woman plans to apologize."

Junot watched Emma's eyes. "Do you think an apology is worth anything?"

"No, not anymore. But it seems important to Maggie, so I need to show up."

"Do you want me to go with you?"

Emma shook her head. She had been promising for months to take Junot to Jackson, to meet Sarah and Kate and go hiking in the mountains. But not this weekend, not under these circumstances.

"Did I tell you about the shelter fashion show?" Emma smiled, grasping for a new subject. "You know how we get all these donations of clothes and toys and books, and I've told you how some people give us horrible, worthless stuff—used underwear and broken toys, like they think women in a shelter should be grateful for rags? So whenever some piece of clothing arrives that is especially tacky, we save it, and next Thursday evening we've got about twenty residents and volunteers who are going to be our models, and we'll put on a show. Each year we set up a runway in the gym, and some colored lights, and we have an announcer—it's funny, in a kind of grotesque way—and the children love it. There are five little girls who are going to be modeling. For them it's like playing dress-up."

"Or dress-down," Junot replied.

"I'm going to model too." Emma rose from the couch. "Here's my favorite outfit that I've been saving since June." She opened her closet door and reached into a large cardboard box, pulling out a wedding dress with a vast hoop skirt.

"What do you think?" She pressed the dress against her torso, revealing a froth of shiny white satin, puffy round princess sleeves, and a scalloped top with tiny fake pearls arranged in dozens of hearts. Across the front, an enormous yellow-brown stain extended from the bust to the waist—one large smear followed by dribbled splotches.

Junot smiled. "Looks like Cinderella got sick at the ball."

Emma glanced down at her torso. "Or else some drunk groom threw up on his bride. Either way it doesn't bode well for the marriage." She carried the dress back to its box and stuffed it inside. "I can understand a woman wanting to get rid of the evidence, but why give a ruined wedding dress to a shelter for battered women, unless it's meant to be sarcastic?" She returned to the couch and lifted a spring roll. "Martha is going to raise the hem about five inches so that I can wear it without falling on my face, and after the show she's going to make pillowcases out of all the satin that's clean . . . Will you come to the show?"

"Sure." Junot nodded. "It will be the highlight of my year."

For the next two hours they remained secluded in Emma's office, eating and talking and dealing hands of gin rummy. She told him about the latest round of budget cuts to community services, and the hopes she had pinned on one federal grant, while Junot explained the slow progress in the case of a Georgetown doctor found in a dumpster outside the clinic where he performed abortions.

"In bad economic times the violence gets worse," he said.

"I see it every day," Emma replied.

By ten o'clock they had blown up an air mattress for Junot and were pulling a fitted sheet over the corners when they heard a voice outside the building shout: "Maria!"

Twice more the caller barked the name before stretching the syl-lables out, as if a father was calling a child acres away. "Mariiiiaaaa . . . Mariiiiaaaa!"

"Sounds like *West Side Story*." Junot smiled weakly.

Emma shook her head. "More like Marlon Brando in *Streetcar*, howling for Stella after he hit her."

"That's the English professor in you." Junot lifted his jacket from the hook on the door. "Showtime."

When the two of them entered the hallway, Emma found a hand-ful of women gathered near the front entrance, mostly the leaders of the kindergarten and first-grade rooms.

"I know this guy." She waved to them. "Go back to your rooms and tell everyone to try and sleep. Sergeant Rodriguez and I will handle it."

Outside, the moonlight on the shelter's concrete walk formed a bright circle around the flagpole. Carlos was not visible, though Emma could hear him to her left, shouting toward the upper windows on the west side of the building: "Maria, are you there? I love you, Maria. *Te amo*. Can you hear me? *Te amo*."

"Maria is in the back of the school, third floor," Emma murmured to Junot. "I'm hoping she's asleep." Carlos returned to the front of the shelter, still shouting at the windows, "Maria! *¿Me puede oir?*" Getting no reply, he turned to Emma: "I want my wife."

The last time Carlos had come to the shelter he had been on his best behavior, addressing Emma with a saccharine mask until he real-ized that she wasn't buying it. Now his belligerence was unchecked. "The center has a restraining order against you," Emma replied. "If you don't leave immediately, you'll be arrested."

Carlos ignored her, shouting again toward the second story, "Maria! *¿Estás allí?*"

"This is your last warning, Mr. Cortez." Emma spoke mechanically, as if she uttered the words a hundred times each day.

From his spot near the classroom window, ten feet away, Carlos turned his head and leveled his contemptuous eyes upon Emma. "Fuck you, bitch."

Junot took a step forward, but Emma placed her hand across his path. "This is my job," she said. "You just back me up."

She cocked her head and eyed Carlos, staring into his pupils without blinking, then approached him with a smile poised somewhere between seduction and madness. When she had come close enough to smell the cigarette stench in his hair and clothes, Emma spoke in a hissing whisper that only Carlos could hear.

"You like insulting women, don't you, Carlos? You like hitting us and burning us, and putting us in our place? We're all bitches, aren't we? Uppity, smart-ass bitches. We deserve to be brought down. I bet you want to hit me now, don't you? It makes you feel like a big man, right? But I know what you really are, Carlos. You're nothing but a tiny little prick." At that, she lowered her gaze to his crotch and laughed out loud. Emma did not duck when Carlos raised his hand. She didn't close her eyes or flinch, or turn her face away from the blow. She planted her feet and allowed his fist to land squarely on her left cheek, surprised only by the force of the impact, stronger than she had anticipated, knocking her to the ground.

Damn! she thought as she lay there. *Son of a bitch.* Nothing was more insulting than getting knocked down. She could still feel Mrs. Stewart's fingers, yanking her to the ground, and the sudden push of that strange man who had not even paused to look back.

Junot had bolted forward the moment Carlos lifted his arm, but was too far behind Emma to stop the impact. Now he leaped over her and tackled the man face-first onto the ground, wedging his knee between Carlos's shoulder blades while he grabbed him by the hair and dug his left ear into the concrete. "You are under arrest," he said. "You have the right to remain silent."

"Get off me!" Carlos sputtered as Junot Mirandized him, then yanked him to his feet and handcuffed him to the flagpole. Pressing the speed dial on his cell, Junot called for a squad car then hurried over to Emma, who was sitting up, rocking back and forth to ease the pain.

"Jesus, Emma," he said as he knelt, stroking her face tenderly with a bemused expression. "What did you say to him?"

She answered only with a smile, revealing a bloody gap where her left incisor should have been.

"You look like a hockey player," Junot said. "Let's go inside and get an ice pack for your cheek."

"No," she refused. "I want it to be as swollen as possible when I face the judge at Carlos's arraignment."

Junot gently inspected the side of her face. "You did this on purpose."

Emma shrugged. "Maria might never press charges against Carlos, but I sure as hell will. Between his prior attack on her, the violation of the restraining order, and now this assault, I figure he should get locked away for at least six months. That might buy Maria enough time to get on her feet."

Junot sighed. "You are one determined little woman." He held her arm as she rose to her feet. "You know, there are better ways of doing this."

"No," Emma replied as she swallowed a mouthful of blood. "There aren't."

CHAPTER 17

EARLY the next morning Emma woke to a throbbing cheek, and her left arm groped toward the bedside table, feeling for the Advil and bottled water that had sustained her all night. Beside her, Junot lay in a deep sleep, and as she swallowed the pills Emma felt an almost aching gratitude for this man in her bed. She had enjoyed the progress of their relationship, from coffee, to lunch, to dinner, then long walks through Rock Creek Park, visits to new exhibits at the Corcoran, and Sunday mornings lounging in each other's arms. Like Emma, Junot Rodriguez was divorced and skeptical about love; for now, neither of them wanted to move in together, valuing their separate spaces, his neat and hers messy, and inviting each other to spend the night only as the mood struck.

Emma had never thought she would date a man without a college degree. In the past she had maintained the usual prejudice of professors, not based on race, but intelligence. Intellectual snobbery was the nerd's best defense, a remnant from public school days when she had fostered contempt for the popular boys who dismissed brainy girls, berating them in response as jocks or rednecks. How would she have labeled Junot if she had known him as a teenager? She probably would have grouped him under the catchall term *migrant,* no matter how long his family had lived in America, and recognizing no difference between Mexican, Guatemalan, or in Junot's case, Chilean, descent.

The labeling had continued throughout her academic life. Were you a Ph.D. or an A.B.D.? Associate, assistant, or adjunct professor? Or were you a college dropout like Junot, preferring a police academy over a university lecture hall? It was only on her first visit to his apartment, when she felt relief at the stack of books on his bedside table, that Emma realized how deep her prejudices ran.

She supposed that if the stars aligned, she could marry him, although these days most marriages struck her as ill-advised compromises. The last two years of her marriage had been painful, riddled with repercussions from Jacob's death. As she closed her eyes and tried to get another hour of sleep, scenes from the past flashed through Emma's mind, and she saw herself walking through her old kitchen, into the troubled hallway where Rob stood waiting, ever pragmatic and capable.

Rob had asserted from day one that the media interest in their house would be short-lived. Once they had their footage of the porch, the door, and the creek, and understood that Emma wasn't talking, the reporters would settle for archived video footage of her, available at the English department's website. And Rob was right. Emma had been relieved, after three days, when the phones stopped ringing and the e-mailed interview requests slowed to a trickle. It was a blessing on those May mornings to wake in a quiet house, with no watchers outside except the half-dozen deer that lingered at dawn under her crab-apple tree. When she stepped onto the porch, they lifted their heads in silence, assessing her with frozen calm before lowering their noses to the wet grass. In those early morning hours the trees were filled with cardinals and mockingbirds, and theirs were the only sounds Emma wanted to hear, other than the rise and fall of Maggie's quiet conversations with Rob, upstairs, in the child's room.

Maggie no longer wanted her mother in her bed. Two nights earlier Emma had felt Maggie's body stiffen when she snuggled beside her five-year-old to share a bedtime story—the tale of the one-legged, faithful tin soldier. Emma had hoped that a lesson of loyal affection might plant roots in her daughter's mind, but in the meantime she had delegated to Rob the precious evening and morning hours, when their child was tender with the weight of sleep. Rob would be the parent who kissed Maggie at the beginning and end of each day. He would hold earnest conversations with her at dawn, while Emma stood outside the house, beyond the family's shelter, wading into the cold grass to pluck a few sprigs from the dwarf lilacs beside her porch.

One morning, four days after Jacob's death, as Emma bent above those lilacs, admiring how each millimeter blossom combined with a hundred others to make a handful of lavender, she had thought of Walt Whitman's "When Lilacs Last in the Dooryard Bloom'd," *ever returning spring, trinity sure to me you bring.* She envisioned Lincoln's coffin, traveling by train from Washington to Illinois, and as she inhaled the lilacs' perfume she thought how Jacob Stewart's coffin had been advancing on its own slow procession from Virginia to Philadelphia, accompanied by his mother. That morning was Jacob's burial day, and she imagined Mrs. Stewart rising from a sleepless bed in a silent house, putting on the same black-and-white dress she had worn when she attacked Emma, the only dress Emma could envision her wearing, with long white sleeves that widened like open petals at the wrist.

At that moment, lost in thought, Emma had raised her eyes from the lilac bushes and seen a dark blue Ford Explorer stopped in the road. Inside, a balding man in wire-rimmed glasses was watching her—

a reporter, Emma thought, except that he didn't approach to ask questions. Instead he assessed the house, the creek, her lilacs, and her face, with an unapologetic gaze, as if taking inventory. Emma instinctively pulled her robe tight over her chest, and the man smiled, made a slight bow of his head, then drove on.

I have a stalker, Emma thought, for she remembered seeing the man yesterday, rolling silently past the house. Probably a crime addict, some mystery lover curious to see the murder scene. Would he come every day? Would he step from his car when she was away, to peer inside the windows, or linger on the porch and fondle the railing? She could never let Maggie out to play, with a man like that lurking. Emma went inside and locked the door.

The next day Jodie called to set up another meeting.

"Not at your house," said Emma.

"No," Jodie agreed. "We shouldn't meet on campus at all. Tomorrow morning is the baccalaureate, so all the families are arriving in town."

"Come to my place," Emma said. "It's quiet out here."

She could detect the brief hesitation in Jodie's voice, the reluctance to visit the blighted home.

"Okay. I'll be there in half an hour."

Emma spent that time washing dishes and making a pitcher of iced tea with sprigs of mint from beside her creek. She resolved to meet Jodie at her car—to lead her to the screened porch at the back of the house so that the dean wouldn't have to cross the threshold Jacob had entered, see the floor without its rug, and sense the invisible traces of blood between the polished pine boards that Rob had scrubbed for two hours. All the details from that night had been circulating through town via grocery-store encounters and book-club conversations, both Emma's version and Kyle's given equal credence, and Emma knew it would be awkward for Jodie to stand twenty feet from the house and see the offending door, the porch where the students had lingered, and to the left, the second-story window where Maggie had climbed out.

When Jodie arrived, she did pause as she stepped out of her car, staring at the house, and Emma hurried to lead her away. But what Emma couldn't guess was Jodie's surprise at seeing how innocuous the place looked, and how pretty, with its peonies lining the walkway to the stairs, its hanging baskets of petunias, and white porch railings. With every petal the house proclaimed its innocence, as if nothing bad could happen in a structure so inviting.

Emma led Jodie around the side, toward the back porch, where they sat in white wicker rockers and watched cloud shadows rippling across the mountains. The foothills flashed a vivid, sparkling emerald wherever the sun broke through, while the dark, murky shadows moved like folds of thin fabric pulled along the treetops.

"It's peaceful out here," said Jodie, and Emma nodded.

"There is no peace when you live on campus," Jodie continued. "People think your home is another office, and they show up on weekends to discuss the most trivial things, as if Will and I had no life beyond the college." She paused before adding, "I had absolutely no idea that the Caldwells were coming over with Mrs. Stewart on the day you visited me. Apparently Don told them I was home."

"It's not your fault," said Emma.

Jodie sighed. "The whole thing is such a mess. Did you know that a private investigator is looking into the case? He came to my house this morning—couldn't find me at the office, so he just stopped by, without calling first. Have you met him?" At Emma's blank stare, Jodie added, "A bald man, around fifty, with wire glasses?"

The stalker flashed across Emma's mind. "I've seen him drive past the house, but I didn't know who he was."

"His name is John Rivers. He was hired by Mason Caldwell."

Emma didn't try to hide her confusion. "I don't understand."

"Apparently Kyle is still claiming that you attacked Jacob without provocation, and Mr. Caldwell wants to get to the bottom of this. I don't think he trusts the county sheriff to handle things properly."

Emma stared at the mountains in silence as Jodie continued.

"Mr. Caldwell probably has his own doubts about whether Kyle is telling the truth. My sense over the past four years is that Mason Caldwell has never been very impressed with his son. He knows that you accused Kyle of stealing, and he probably wants to dig up some dirty laundry about you—to challenge your credibility if you were to take Kyle before the honor court. This all began with your stolen bracelet, right?"

Emma looked into Jodie's eyes. "With everything going on, I'd forgotten about that."

"At this point it's probably best if you don't initiate an honor-court case. Since graduation is only two days away, and with all this trauma in the background, it would be hard to carry out a fair investigation before Kyle leaves."

"Could they suspend his diploma?"

"We tried that once, about eight years ago, when a student attacked a classmate a few days before graduation. But the parents filed a legal injunction, saying we couldn't withhold his diploma. All we could do was prevent him from walking the stage and shaking Don's hand.

"Anyway, I don't think this private investigator is entirely Mason Caldwell's idea. I get the impression that Mrs. Stewart is pressuring the Caldwells to manufacture some kind of justice for her son. She could never afford an investigator—Jacob was getting by on work-study funds. So she must have asked the Caldwells to pay the bill."

"The fingerprints will clear me," said Emma.

"Let's hope so. But did you know that Mrs. Stewart is threatening to bring a wrongful-death lawsuit against you?"

Emma stared back at the mountains. "Can she do that?"

"I've spoken to our lawyers, and they say that if the police don't find enough evidence to charge you, there's little chance she could win a suit. She would need a preponderance of evidence that it wasn't self-defense, and that's probably why the PI is snooping around. To see if there's anything the police are missing."

"I have nothing to hide," Emma murmured.

"No principled attorney would take the case," Jodie added. "The problem is that with an ultrarich client like Mason Caldwell, his lawyers will do whatever he says, regardless of whether or not the facts support the allegations. Caldwell has plenty of money to waste, and he's probably willing to make some gesture to appease Mrs. Stewart, but I don't think he'll want to take it very far."

"Why not?"

Jodie lowered her voice. "I'll tell you something confidential, that you can't share with anyone." She took another sip of iced tea.

"Two years ago Kyle was caught shoplifting in town, at Sophie Miller's shop. She saw him take a necklace and called the police. They arrived just after he left the store, and found him one block away, with the necklace in his pocket. I know all about it because the police tend to contact me whenever they arrest a student. They thought I should call the Caldwells to tell them that their son was in jail, because Kyle hadn't called them. At first I said no, that was Kyle's business, but then I asked Don, and he spoke to the Caldwells himself, since he knows them personally. Kyle's mom flew down on their private jet, and the next morning Sophie dropped the charges, saying it was all a misunderstanding. I heard later that Mrs. Caldwell had given Sophie a mother-to-mother talk about the struggles she'd had raising Kyle, and how he's really a good kid deep down, and she offered to compensate for his theft by doing her own shopping spree in Sophie's store. The rumor in town is that Mrs. Caldwell ordered twelve thousand dollars' worth of jewelry and clothes, which helped to keep Sophie in business during the recession. She might not have taken the bribe if the economy hadn't been so bad.

"Anyway, it backs up what you said about Kyle and the bracelet. His parents know he's got a problem, and Sheriff King must know about it too, since Kyle spent a day in the county jail. Kyle might have other shoplifting charges on his record, and that's the kind of information that would come up in a wrongful-death suit."

Emma shook her head. "That won't keep Mrs. Stewart from taking me to court. It might stop Mason Caldwell from paying the bills, if he thinks his son's reputation will be damaged, but Jacob's mom wants revenge. You should have seen the way she looked at me at your house. She wants to hurt me as badly as I've hurt her, and I don't blame her."

Jodie watched the shadows rolling over the mountains. "Mrs. Stewart has been in my office every day since the incident, demanding that the college take some kind of action. That's one reason I'm avoiding the campus—she's like this raging Fury, badgering me and Don. I got a break yesterday because she and the Caldwells went up to Philadelphia for Jacob's burial, but I expect she'll be back this afternoon . . . And you should know that she's also threatening to sue the college. She claims we were negligent in hiring you—that you were unfit to work as a professor."

"Why?"

"According to this private investigator you were in some sort of drug trouble when you were younger?"

Emma flushed. "That was in high school. They raided student lockers and found one joint in mine. Just one joint. Fourteen of us were arrested, and since I had turned eighteen three weeks earlier, and they wanted to make an example of the older kids, it's on my permanent record as a misdemeanor . . . But c'mon, Jodie, we've got faculty members who are smoking every day, and the students use drugs that are a lot stronger than pot. I haven't touched anything illegal since high school."

"It's not the marijuana that's the real problem. This investigator also says you were charged with assault when you were at Berkeley."

"I didn't touch anyone," Emma protested.

"What happened?"

"I threw blood."

"Blood?"

Emma sighed. "I was a member of PETA, and we were protesting at a lab outside of San Francisco. They were doing some horrific experiments on monkeys, so when the board of directors came for a visit, we threw blood. I didn't actually throw mine onto anyone. I poured it onto the ground in front of their feet, in a symbolic way, to have them wading through blood. It was a few other members of the group who threw it right onto the people's suits and hair, and into this one man's face. I would never attack a person directly like that."

"Where did you get the blood?"

"Christ, I don't know. Our PETA chairman always had access to blood. I guess he bought it online."

"And you spent time in jail?"

"Two weeks," said Emma. "If we'd thrown blood on the scientists, we probably would have gotten our hands slapped. But the board was full of rich lawyers, and they charged us with conspiracy to commit assault. The leader of our group served two months."

"I'm told that this PETA group bombed a laboratory in Los Angeles?"

Emma hesitated. "I wasn't a member anymore by the time that happened. But yeah—they blew up the electrical station behind a Dow Pharmaceuticals lab. No one was hurt. The idea was to disrupt the power."

Jodie took a long sip from her drink. "Mrs. Stewart claims that we should be doing criminal background checks on all of our employees, as part of the job search. She says that's where the college was negligent."

"What kind of background checks do you perform?"

"Almost none. We look at CVs and letters of recommendation, not at police files. A job search committee will usually check a candidate's references, and I'm pretty sure the English department did a Google search on you, but I never heard about any of this coming up."

"It all happened before I was married," said Emma. "The department would have needed to search under my maiden name."

"This investigator also claims that you have a history of mental instability? You were taking Zoloft?"

"How does he know about that?"

Jodie threw up her hands. "How do these investigators know about anything? I imagine it's all on computer files somewhere—your medical records, your prescriptions, your insurance claims. Or maybe he's been talking to people in town who know something about your past? I have no idea."

Emma stared at the mountains. How could she tell Jodie, the childless, career-driven dean, about her months of postpartum depression—how she had been paralyzed by the terror of holding newborn Maggie in her arms, knowing that none of her books or brainpower would get her through this. She couldn't be perfect at this task; she couldn't make straight A's. She could fail for the first time in her life, fail horribly, painfully, floundering in the basic role expected of all women.

She shrugged, trying to seem casual. "It was never a big secret. I went through some postpartum depression after Maggie was born, so I got a prescription for Zoloft and did about six months of therapy with a counselor at UVA. I didn't find the sessions helpful, so I struggled through it on my own."

They remained silent for several seconds while a blue heron tiptoed across the grass beside the creek. Then Emma looked again at Jodie. "Do you think Mrs. Stewart will really file a lawsuit against Holford?"

"Considering how angry she is right now, anything is possible. And honestly, if she were to press it, the college would probably settle with her. Even if she doesn't have a case, they'd want to give her a few million dollars just to put this to rest—mostly because of her ties to Mason Caldwell. He's the ace in her pocket. We count on him for about a million dollars every year; he gave twenty million to help build Caldwell Hall. Now the development office is worried that this whole affair will leave a bad taste in his mouth, so the priority is to keep him satisfied that the college is handling everything in a professional, discreet manner. If they settle with Mrs. Stewart, in the end her payment will come out of Mason Caldwell's checkbook."

The priority is to keep him satisfied. Emma smiled bitterly. Naturally the priority was not justice, or the safety of faculty members. Not the disciplining of students who stole from teachers' offices, trespassed on private property, and threatened women's lives. The college's priority was to keep the money flowing, fatten the endowment, build more halls.

She looked into Jodie's eyes and saw the administrator and the woman at odds, the impulse toward compassion restrained by the obligations of authority. Jodie lowered her gaze, and with that gesture a sudden conviction spread through Emma's body, certain as death: *She would not get tenure.* Not now. There was no chance. Her tenure committee was scheduled to meet the following winter, and even if they recommended her, the administration would never approve it. Not if there was a lawsuit pending, and not if she had been publicly lampooned as a pot-smoking, blood-tossing, radical nutjob.

She wondered if Mrs. Stewart understood the precarious position of an assistant professor—how every career move was gauged toward pleasing the college. After a lifetime of testing, from grade school through college through graduate school, tenure was the final examination, and Mrs. Stewart would guarantee that Emma failed.

Her chances for tenure had always been shaky. She had alienated the English department's old guard in the spring of her first year, when she announced that she was pregnant. It was terrible timing, after only one year of teaching, to request maternity leave for the coming semester. Registration for the fall had been completed weeks earlier, and she could see the calculations running through her department chair's mind when she told him the news—he would have to hire someone to teach her three classes, and it was so awkward to hire for only one semester, especially late in the spring.

The pregnancy had surprised Emma as much as her department; her ob-gyn had been so contrite when she explained that Emma's IUD had somehow shifted out of place. Emma and Rob had wanted children, but not so soon, not like that, not before she could get her career established.

"English departments deal with pregnancies all the time," Sarah had assured her. "It's not a big deal." But Emma had sensed the eyes of her older colleagues focusing on her belly as Maggie grew, and she had felt both defiant and apologetic—paradoxical impulses inspiring an emphatic need to prove herself. She'd spent the months before Maggie's birth shaping two dissertation chapters into articles published over the course of the following year. Since then, one more article had appeared, but Emma knew now that it wouldn't be enough. If she had been the English department's rising star, the young professor with the critically acclaimed book, the article in *PMLA*, or the NEH grant, her light might have outshone the pall of a lawsuit. But she had no book contract to wear as her armor, no article impressive enough to wield as a sword. Her achievements were middle-of-the-road: conference papers that sparked no fiery debates, publications in respected journals read by a handful of specialists. Combined with her teaching, it might have been sufficient for tenure under normal circumstances, but not with this firestorm raging around her.

Emma glanced down at her hands and noticed how tightly she'd been wringing them; multiple indentations starred her right palm where her wedding diamond had pressed into flesh. She must master this habit of displaying her agitation so blatantly. All of her emotions were revealed in her hands, and right now Emma's hands expressed despair. Eleven years of effort, between graduate school and Holford, were slipping through these anxious fingers, and she foresaw that in the coming months she would never be able to piece together the ruins.

"I should go," said Jodie, rising to her feet.

Emma stood and walked the dean to her car.

After settling into the front seat, Jodie rolled down her window and turned to Emma, apparently grasping for some final, consolatory statement. She managed only "This too shall pass."

Emma smiled sadly, thinking that silence was better than clichés. Of course this would pass. All things passed. Years passed, people passed. Youth and happiness and hope passed. The question wasn't whether this would pass, but what would remain?

Justice

CHAPTER 18

AT six a.m., while Emma Greene was swallowing Advil and trying to fall back asleep, Grace Murdock lay wide-awake, watching the dawn trickle through the window of her parents' house. She had no lover on the pillow beside her, no man to console her for the troubles of the week. Instead, when she turned onto her side, she lay face-to-face with four-year-old Lily, whose breath was causing a soft flutter in a strand of dark hair tossed across her cheek. *Nothing more beautiful than a sleeping child,* thought Grace, which was why she let Lily climb into this bed whenever she pleased. It had comforted Grace, after her divorce, to feel her daughter warming the other half of the sheets, even though Lily rotated like the hands of a clock in her sleep, her head at one o'clock and legs at nine. Sometimes Grace built a boundary of pillows to protect herself from the small, kicking heels, but usually she let Lily curl beside her, knowing this shared bed to be a temporary pleasure.

Maggie Greene probably hadn't slept beside her mother for years— so Grace told herself as she watched her daughter, wondering when her conscience would stop pairing the girls. She had begun her official penance two days earlier, after leaving the yellow note on Maggie's desk. Within an hour Maggie had sent a text message agreeing to meet at the public library at five. The location and time had struck Grace as fitting; Maggie had chosen a setting where they would not be alone; nor were they likely to be overheard in the low-traffic hour before closing time. The library was a safe, impersonal repository of stories where Grace could share her own painful narrative.

When the designated hour came, she had found Maggie sitting in an alcove in the back, occupying one of two leather wing-back chairs between the Mystery and Biography shelves. There, in the company of thousands of fictions, Grace had tried to tell Maggie the truth. She had murmured her confessions as if the girl were a priest, capable of granting absolution, but Grace's words did not describe her own sins so much as the sins of Jacob Stewart. In a low monotone Grace had explained how she had come to know Jacob as Kyle's best friend, and how she had initially been charmed by his handsome face and habits of flattery. She had told Maggie about Jacob's false friendships with men, and his sly compliments to girls that devolved into crude sexual comments in their absence. She had described how he plagiarized papers, stole library books, and drove through the county tossing beer bottles from his car window, delighted by the shatter of glass against trees, and encouraging Kyle to follow his lead.

Maggie grew impatient. "You said my mom was right to kill him, but none of these things are so terrible." Yes, but Grace knew worse things, much worse. A rumor had spread during senior year that Jacob had beaten up a girl, and Grace believed it. She had thought he was going to hit her once when she, Kyle, and Jacob were walking home from a frat party. They were all a little drunk, and when Jacob tripped on the roots of a tree and fell to his knees, she had laughed, calling him the epitome of grace. Rising slowly, Jacob had approached her and lifted his hand, and she knew he would have slapped her if Kyle hadn't been present.

"But he didn't hit you," Maggie said. "He never hit you?"

"That's right." Grace nodded. "But he did something else." Something unforgivable.

In the crawl spaces beneath the old fraternity houses there were several stray cats, sustained by table scraps from well-meaning students. During Grace's college days a litter appeared under the SAE house almost every year; the brothers coaxed girls over by offering to show them the kittens. One evening after dinner, around eight o'clock, Grace was hanging out at the house with Kyle when Jacob said he wanted to take a look at a litter of four newborns. The mother was an orange tabby, and she had given birth on a shredded tarp under the house, so Kyle found a flashlight and they all went outside to the back porch.

The porch was high off the ground, with storage space below for bikes and lawn equipment, enclosed by latticework and a wooden, crosshatched door that was almost never locked. When Grace, Jacob, and Kyle first stepped underneath the porch, they could stand erect, but the ground sloped up toward the house, and the mother cat was sheltering her kittens at the narrowest part, against the outer wall, where the earth was only about two feet from the wooden planks above. Kyle was crouching low, shining his flashlight on the kittens, and they were blinking and moving with the stiff, jerking motions of infancy, the mother lying on her side, nipples exposed to kneading paws, looking too hot and exhausted to bother with any students.

Jacob wanted to hold a kitten, although Grace begged him not to—they were too young, only four inches long, and it would upset the mother. But he crawled over as close as he could, then went down on his belly and reached forward. The mother spat and hissed, rising up to arch her back, while Jacob grabbed one of the kittens and carried it over to where Kyle and Grace were standing. It was the smallest kitten Grace had ever seen, gray and puffy and making a high-pitched mewing that set off its brothers and sisters, while the mother growled. Jacob put the kitten's hind legs on the ground and held its front paws up, moving it around as if it was break-dancing, which Kyle found hilarious. Then Jacob lifted it by the scruff of its neck, holding it up to his lips, where he could blow into its nose and watch its eyes scrunch, its paws brushing at its face.

"You're going to drop it!" said Grace, and Jacob grinned at her.

"What?" he asked, and let the kitten go.

She screamed as it fell from Jacob's right hand, but he stuck out his left and caught the creature before it hit the ground. While Kyle laughed, Grace insisted they put the poor thing back. Bored, Jacob went to return the kitten, getting down on his knees and then his stomach, but when he reached forward to settle the kitten in its litter, the hissing mother slashed out. Jerking his head up, Jacob hit the bottom of the porch, then scrambled out backward, muttering a chorus of obscenities.

"Shine that light on my arm," he told Kyle. Three bleeding claw marks extended from his elbow halfway to his wrist.

"Damn cat probably has rabies." Jacob took the flashlight from Kyle's hand and shined it back in the litter, right into the eyes of the spitting tabby.

"You want a piece of me? Hey, *you* want a piece of *me?*"

At first it seemed funny, Jacob's Italian mobster voice, but then he started moving back toward the cat very slowly, with the flashlight in his left hand, still shining it into her eyes. Reaching forward with his right, Jacob murmured in a low, sweet voice, "Here, kitty kitty. Did I scare you? I'm not going to hurt you. Oh no, no. I'm not going to hurt you." The cat's tail twitched as the flashlight advanced: "I just want to pet you. Just let me pet you once."

Suddenly Jacob lurched forward and grabbed the cat by the tail. She hissed and tried to bite him, but he yanked her away from the litter with her claws scraping across the ground, then he ran past Grace and Kyle, through the door and into the empty backyard. The cat was dangling in the air by her tail, trying to bend her body upward to attack Jacob's hand, but he was laughing: "Not so tough now, are we?

"Watch this." Jacob started swinging the cat in circles over his head like the blades of a helicopter. With each loop he counted aloud—"One . . . two . . . three!"—and suddenly he extended his arm to the left and bashed the cat's head against an oak tree.

It happened so quickly Grace didn't have time to shut her eyes. She heard the crack of the animal's skull and saw its body fall limp out of Jacob's hand—not dead yet, but nearly there, with one eye popped out of its socket and blood running from its mouth and nose. Jacob lifted a stick and started to poke at the protruding eye while Grace started to sob so hard she could barely breathe.

"For shit's sake," said Kyle. "Jacob! Leave it alone."

Jacob shrugged, reached down, and lifted the cat by its tail one last time. By then the animal was completely limp, and Jacob swung it around his head, let go, and the body went flying behind the bushes to the right of the fraternity house. Meanwhile they could hear the kittens crying under the porch, desperate for a mother who was never coming back.

"Can't you get her to shut up?" Jacob scowled at Grace, and Kyle walked her home to the student apartments.

Kyle came over the next morning to sit with her, but Grace told him she felt sick and didn't want visitors. That afternoon she heard stories about how the mother cat at SAE had abandoned her litter; some of the brothers had crawled under the house and found two kittens dead. Now they were trying to save the other two, feeding them warm milk from a medicine dropper. In the coming days, whenever

Grace walked past the house, she thought of the cat's body rotting behind the shrubs. Even after nine years, when she first returned to Jackson, Grace had envisioned the skeleton lying undiscovered behind the bushes, its broken skull buried beneath almost a decade of earth, waiting.

Grace had shared all of this with Maggie, watching the girl flinch as she described the cat's head hitting the tree. But she didn't confess one detail—that when Emma Greene's bat cracked against Jacob's head, Grace's first thought was that the cat had been avenged. Terrifying as the scene had been, it had struck her as a form of Karma.

She should have broken up with Kyle after the cat's death. The Spring Fling was long over, the year was ending, and Kyle and Jacob were soon leaving for the beach. Graduation, however, was such a convenient ending point, they wouldn't even need to break up, so much as say good-bye and drive in opposite directions.

It was easy now, after so many years, to recognize her mistakes and regret her cowardice. At the time Grace's only resolution had been to avoid Jacob for the few weeks that remained in the school year. Which was why, when Kyle asked if she wanted to go to the party at Hillyer's farm, she had made sure that Jacob wouldn't be riding with them. Of course Jacob would be at the party, but in a crowd of hundreds she might avoid him.

Kyle was driving to the party in the dark green Range Rover his dad had brought him to carry home his college things, and Grace met him at the SAE house with a sleeping bag and pillow, planning to sleep under the stars. Her heart had sunk when she found Kyle and Jacob sitting together on a couch. Apparently Jacob's ride had fallen through; he was coming with them after all, and he and Kyle had already started their own party, swilling cheap cans of Bud Light. They had a twelve-pack in the back of the Range Rover, along with more sleeping bags, and although Grace thought to make an excuse and walk home, the party sounded too good to miss. She offered to drive, since she hadn't been drinking, but Jacob said no, he was sober enough, and he escorted them into the countryside with windows open and stereo blaring, singing the whole way. Grace had never seen him so happy. Between the job in New York and the summer vacation at Kyle's beach house, everything was working out perfectly for Jacob. She remembered him yelling "score!" when he tossed a half-full beer can out the window and dented a mailbox.

The only problem was that Jacob didn't know how to get to Hillyer's. He knew the general area, and there weren't many roads in that part of the county, but at night, with no streetlights, all the pastures and woods looked the same, and they wasted twenty minutes before Jacob recognized Professor Greene's house. Apparently he had dated an English major named Lauren who had been there once for a department picnic, and she had pointed it out to him. He knew that Hillyer's was a mile farther up the road, but Jacob needed to pee, and he said he might as well piss on the professor's lawn, since she hadn't given him the grade he wanted, so they all headed down to the creek.

With all of Jacob and Kyle's talking and laughing, Grace knew they would wake up anyone in the house, and it wasn't surprising when Emma appeared. She was very nice, considering the circumstances, and everything would have been fine if the students had left right away, but Grace made the mistake of asking to use the bathroom, which gave Kyle a chance to go inside and hunt for a souvenir.

Emma Greene was the first person Grace had ever known to catch Kyle stealing, and the professor was so angry—Grace had never seen a woman get so angry. Professor Greene was very calm in class, maintaining a sense of humor when students hadn't done the reading, or had failed a midterm, but when she saw the dolls Kyle was trying to steal, and all the little clothes he had stuffed in his pocket, she was beyond furious.

Grace hadn't needed to tell Maggie the next part of the story, the child had witnessed it all—the shouting, the obscenities, the acceleration to violence.

"Why didn't you tell the police about any of this?" Maggie asked.

"I was scared, and ashamed."

"But you told them other things. Things that weren't true."

"Yes." Grace looked down at her hands. "I have no excuse."

She and Kyle had fled the scene while Jacob lay bleeding in Emma's lap, running back to the Range Rover, where the keys were waiting in the front seat. Kyle raced down the country roads, turning any which way whenever a road ended. With five beers in his system, he was veering around the winding curves while Grace cried and begged him to slow down, until eventually he stopped at the side of the road in a quiet area with only one distant house at the top of a hill. Kyle got out and started pacing, muttering about how crazy Professor Greene was and saying they should come up with a plan.

The police would come looking for them, once they reached Professor Greene's house. They'd want to hear the students' story, and Kyle would have to sober up fast. He went to the back of his SUV, took out the case of Bud Light, and hid it in the woods behind a tree. Someday he might go back to get it, but for now he couldn't have beer in the car.

Kyle explained that they would have to wait there in the county until all the alcohol was out of his system; he'd apparently had several problems with Breathalyzer tests and DWIs in the past. The two of them found a big rock on the side of the road and sat for a long time while Grace crafted the most extravagant lies of her life, piecing together a story for the police. They hadn't done anything that gave Professor Greene the right to attack Jacob, but it would look bad if the police knew that they were drinking and trespassing, and that Kyle had tried to steal some things.

Grace and Kyle agreed to tell everyone that their threesome had been looking for the party at Hillyer's when they got lost on the rural roads. They would confess that each of them had drunk one beer before leaving the SAE house—other students had seen as much—but they would insist that there hadn't been any drinking on the way. That was one of the reasons they were going to Hillyer's—to get the free beer. They would say that they recognized Professor Greene's house, and Jacob decided to stop to ask for directions. Kyle and Grace had waited in the SUV while Jacob knocked at the door. They saw Professor Greene let him inside, but they didn't see what happened between them. Jacob must have been in the house for ten minutes before they heard yelling. When they got out of the car and walked up to the porch, they could see inside the screen door, and Professor Greene was standing with a baseball bat in her hand while Jacob lay on the hall floor with his head twisted to the side in an unnatural position, blood coming out of his left ear. They had panicked and run away, and were lost in the dark on the country roads, completely traumatized, which is why it took them a few hours to get back to the college.

That was Grace's story, a shaky product of panic and fear full of obvious holes, but her gift for lying seemed to abandon her under pressure. She insisted that Kyle rehearse it with her several times so that they would be consistent when the police asked questions. Once they had the story memorized, they climbed back into the Range Rover and drove until Kyle got his bearings. At the 7-Eleven south of town they bought two black coffees, and by the time they arrived at Kyle's house it was almost two a.m. Kyle's other roommate, Nolan, was watching TV in the living room, and he said that the sheriff's department had been there twice, looking for Kyle—at which point Kyle broke down. Grace had never seen him cry before, and she put her arm around his shoulder, telling Nolan to get them both another cup of coffee. Sitting on the couch, Kyle gave their story to his housemate just as he and Grace had rehearsed, except he embellished, saying he thought Professor Greene was a psychotic feminist who hated men— a statement that made Grace cringe. It was true that Professor Greene was a feminist; she included feminist literary theory in her classes and made no apologies about it. But Grace could tell that Kyle and Nolan assumed all feminists were a bunch of angry lesbians, and over the next twenty-four hours the SAE brothers would latch onto that idea and spread the tale around campus of how Professor Greene was a hotheaded man hater who had murdered one of their brothers.

In the meantime Grace walked back to her apartment, where a pair of county deputies came knocking within a half hour. She gave them the same story Kyle had repeated, minus the feminist part, but she could tell they didn't believe her. They kept asking questions, like where was she standing when she saw Jacob's body? And why hadn't she called 911? That was their biggest issue—Jacob was bleeding on the floor of his attacker, and she and Kyle had abandoned him without calling the police?

Jacob was dead, Grace had answered, and Professor Greene was holding a bat, so she and Kyle had run for their lives. That was when Grace learned that Jacob hadn't died yet—he was in a coma, and the local hospital had helicoptered him to UVA. The deputies claimed they understood why Grace and Kyle might drive off, but why hadn't they called 911 once they left the house? It wasn't like Emma Greene was chasing them down the road with her bat. Why couldn't they get on a cell phone and try to help their friend? "You can't get cell-phone coverage that far out in the county," Grace explained, which was true, and it would have been a terrific excuse if she had thought of it sooner. But by then she'd mumbled lots of other explanations, and the damage was done.

"I think you know the rest," she had said to Maggie in the library, and the girl had nodded. Maggie knew all the dismal consequences that could face a professor who was accused of killing her student.

"I was especially sorry," Grace added, "because your mother was nice to me." Once, when Grace had gone to Emma's office for help on a paper, she had admitted to the professor that she didn't like poetry, and Emma had merely smiled, taking a book down from her shelves and turning to a dog-eared page. "Read this."

Even now, sitting up in bed, Grace could remember the words. She had memorized them at the end of the term for Professor Greene's recitation requirement:

Poetry . . . I too dislike it. There are things that are important beyond all this fiddle. Reading it, however, with a perfect contempt for it, one discovers in it, after all, a place for the genuine.

Professor Greene had told Grace all about Marianne Moore—how the poet liked to count the syllables in each of her lines, and arrange her stanzas into syllabic patterns. Knowing that Grace was a math major, interested in anything that could be tallied, balanced, and verified, Emma had shown Grace how traditional poetry had rhythmic structures similar to the mathematical foundations of music, and she talked about numerology and the patterns that some Renaissance poets embedded in their work.

"Your mom was a really good teacher, and I never thanked her."

Tears pooled in Maggie's eyes, and Grace thought she knew why—the shame Emma had endured, the parents' divorce, the years of separation between mother and daughter. But Maggie wasn't thinking about any of that. No one had ever told her before that her mother was a good teacher. Why had it never occurred to her as a possibility? Why had she never considered that some students might actually have liked her mom—that her mother might have been someone's favorite professor?

"I should never have gotten involved with boys like that." Mrs. Murdock was still talking. "I hope my daughter never does."

For a moment Maggie thought of Mike Hodges, and wondered what vices she would be willing to overlook to be with someone like him. What would she do if she found the bones of a dissected cat among his science experiments?

"I wish I could make it up to you." Grace's final words sounded contrived, and Maggie wondered how this woman could make anything up to her.

"There is one thing you could do."

"What?"

Turning to look her teacher in the eye for the first time that afternoon, Maggie chose her words carefully. "I want you to tell your story to my mom. I want her to hear about it in person. She lives in Washington, three hours away, but she comes to town every month to visit me, and she stays at the McConnells' house. Do you know Kate McConnell? She's a ninth grader."

Grace shook her head.

"Kate's a friend of mine, and her mother used to be one of my mom's colleagues."

"Professor McConnell from the English department?"

"Yeah." Maggie nodded. "Ever since my parents got divorced, my mom has stayed with Mrs. McConnell whenever she comes to town. She's planning to visit for Thanksgiving, but that's almost a month away. If I send her a note about you, I bet she'd come down here this weekend."

"Your mother won't want to see me."

"She will when she understands what you have to say . . . Look." Maggie hesitated. "All these years I think my mom has never known whether she did the right thing. Teachers are supposed to be supportive of their students, not aggressive, and she once told me that she liked Jacob, up until the moment when he turned mean. There's still a lot of confusion about that night, in her mind and in the minds of most people in this town, and your story might give her some peace."

Grace shook her head. Maggie didn't know what she was asking. Professor Greene would not care about Grace's explanations; an apology nine years after the fact was useless. Besides, Grace had been prepared to bare her soul to a fragile fifteen-year-old, a girl she could address as a mother might speak to a child. There was nothing intimidating about Maggie Greene. In any meeting with Emma, Grace would be the student facing the teacher she had wronged, a woman smarter and more poised than herself. What could Grace say except "Hello, Professor, sorry for screwing up your life?"

Now, as she watched the full sunlight falling across her wedding-ring quilt, Grace realized there was one thing she could say to Professor Greene. Something she hadn't told Maggie at the library—one last fragment of unrevealed truth.

Leaning over to open the drawer of her bedside table, Grace reached inside to the very back and pulled out a small velvet pouch. She had kept this item for nine years, always hidden behind stockings or scarves or sweaters, never opened but never forgotten. And now, for the first time, she held it upside down over her bed and allowed the contents to fall onto her covers. Professor Greene's charm bracelet.

She touched the tiny ballet slippers, the silver horseshoe and pewter book that opened to reveal three engraved letters: *EMP*. As her fingers traced the initials, Grace thought of Tolkien—the power of the cursed jewelry that warped the wearer's soul. She supposed it was time to carry this stolen bracelet back to its owner, although the task seemed like a monumental exercise in humiliation.

So be it. Penance was never meant to be easy. It wasn't something she could accomplish in one afternoon. Of course there would be multiple trials, each one more difficult than the last, as it was for Peter and Paul and all the early Christian saints with their mountains of sin to atone for.

"I will do what you ask," Grace had told Maggie before leaving the library. "Just tell me when."

CHAPTER 19

"FOR nine years I wondered if my mom was a murderer."

Maggie was sitting on Dr. Riley's couch, leaning forward with her elbows on her knees, wringing her hands. She pulled her fingers apart and leaned back, fixing her eyes on the swirl of dark hair on the doctor's left forearm. He had rolled up his sleeves within five minutes of her arrival, which Maggie viewed as a personal triumph. She liked to see him agitated.

She had called the doctor at his house the previous evening, after her library meeting with Mrs. Murdock, welcoming him back from San Francisco, and asking if she could see him, sooner rather than later. Of course the good doctor had made time, because Maggie had never before requested an appointment; they had always taken place at her father's insistence. For the past twenty minutes Maggie had been sharing everything—her recognition of Sandra McCluskey, the yellow note, the meeting at the library, and all the crimes of Jacob Stewart.

"So has this changed your feelings about your mom?" Dr. Riley asked.

"I don't know. It's confusing."

Dr. Riley watched her eyes, waiting.

"I can't even be sure that Mrs. Murdock is telling the truth," said Maggie. "She's been such a liar up until now. I mean, everything she told me sounded true, but I don't know if that's just because I want to believe that Jacob Stewart was really bad, and that my mom was justified in killing him."

"Why have you doubted that she was justified?"

Maggie hesitated, thinking back to that night years ago. At the time she knew only what her eyes had absorbed—that when a tall college boy with dark hair pushed his way into their house, her mother had swung a baseball bat into his right leg so that the student fell to his knees, uttering the ugliest curse Maggie had ever heard. Then with one fatal motion, smooth as the returning arc of a pendulum, her mother had swung the bat in the opposite direction, into the base of the student's skull, which made a cracking sound like a wooden log popping in a fire.

The whole thing had probably taken five seconds, although Maggie's memory played it over and over in slow motion—her mom with the bat in her left hand, reaching over with her right to guide it low into the side of the boy's right knee, using a backhand swing perfected through twenty-three years of tennis. And then the boy was kneeling in front of her, his skull a waist-high target, which, warped as it might sound, always reminded Maggie of T-ball: the round object poised at the top of the stick, the batter taking a full swing, trying to knock the ball for a home run.

Next came the scream, repeated often in Maggie's dreams, a sound she had initially attributed to herself—a preschooler's horrified cry at the quantity of blood that could run from a person's ear. Or was it her mother's scream, realizing what she had done? Until yesterday Maggie had never been certain, but sitting in the library, with Mrs. Murdock murmuring secrets in a rural southern accent, she realized that the scream had come from her teacher, standing on the porch, witnessing Jacob's death from a few feet away.

Maggie knew because yesterday, as she sat in that library chair, she could remember a woman's gasps of horror, her exclamations of "Oh Gawwd," in an accent neither hers nor her mother's. She also remembered looking down through the banister that night and seeing that her mom was not making a sound. Emma Greene's lips had been frozen in a tight, unflinching line as she gazed upon her handiwork.

Maggie looked up at Dr. Riley. "Do you want to know why I didn't speak to you about Jacob's death during our first few months of therapy? And why I didn't speak to the police?"

"If you want to tell me," the doctor replied.

"I didn't speak because I knew too much. I was worried I'd get my mom in trouble."

Having seen her mother's hard, silent assessment of Jacob's body, Maggie had resolved to be equally silent, quietly closing her bedroom door and removing the rope ladder from beneath her bed without a whisper. Silence was imperative; it was the only gift she could offer her mother when Emma found her in the woods half an hour later, because, after all, what could she have said? *Why did you kill that person? Will you go to jail?* And the biggest question of all: *Would you ever do that to me?*

Maggie had said nothing when her mother lifted her into her arms, weeping. She had said nothing to the police, whose cars' blue lights glared as she and her mother emerged from the woods; nothing to the sheriff who sat beside Maggie on the playroom couch, asking questions while a deputy kept her mother in another room. The sheriff had wanted to know about Polly Pockets and baseball bats and bracelets, and did her mommy have a bad temper? Did she get angry very often? Had her mommy gotten angry that night?

Five-year-old Maggie never said "mommy," and she thought it sounded foolish on a grown man's lips. In response, she had uttered the only words she remembered from TV crime shows, then had lavished all her concentration upon Sophie, who was clearly distressed. Maggie could hear her mother's voice growing frantic in the next room—"I want to see my daughter. You can't keep her from me!"—and eventually her dad had burst in, sweeping Maggie up from the couch and shouting at the sheriff: "What the hell do you think you're doing?"

In the coming days, whenever the sheriff or his deputies returned to speak to Maggie, Jed Christianson, her mom's lawyer, had always joined her on the couch, patting her knee. He approved of Maggie's silence toward the police, especially since she wasn't talking to him either. "Don't say anything," he had advised, "unless you want to tell me first." But her silence also extended to her father and mother. She would answer their questions about toys and books and favorite breakfast cereals, but when they tiptoed around the subject of what she had seen in the hallway, Maggie fell mute, which had prompted her dad to call Dr. Riley.

Emma had objected strongly. "Maggie will talk when she's ready."

"And when will that be?" Rob had replied. "When she's sixteen, and suicidal? You know she's not sleeping, and her appetite has shrunk. She needs help."

Her mother's reluctance only confirmed Maggie's vow of silence, and for months Dr. Riley had enjoyed no better luck than the police. As Maggie saw it, she should let her mom do all the talking, because Emma used words like *self-defense* and *protecting my child*, which sounded more reasonable than anything Maggie could offer. For years after the incident Maggie had tried to assure herself of her mother's reasonableness, eager to block out the adjectives she overheard in the conversations of preschool parents: *volatile, temperamental, erratic, unstable.* She didn't understand those terms when she was five, fathoming only a single word, *crazy*, spoken by a grocery-store clerk who had blushed and looked away when Maggie stared into her eyes.

So her mother was a crazy lady—that seemed to be the town consensus—and a part of Maggie feared that the rumors were right, for hadn't her mother often said that her work was making her crazy, or that Maggie was driving her insane? Maggie knew that her mother was hot-tempered and prone to raging outbursts, and she worried that if she spoke to the police, she might reveal the truth—that her mom had killed before.

First had come the small deaths, like the plastic brontosaurus her mom had sliced with the lawn tractor. Four-year-old Maggie had heard the crunch and seen the machine spit the purple creature six feet across the lawn. When she ran over to pick it up, it was headless.

Her mother had offered no apology or excuse. "You had plenty of warning to get your toys out of the grass before I mowed. You know I can't see them when the grass is long."

Then came the night when Maggie woke from a nightmare, crying out to her parents across the hall. She heard their bedroom door creak open, followed by slow footsteps and the snap of her mother's voice: "Ow, shit! Goddammit!" Maggie had never before heard a parent curse, and she was struck by how harsh and frightening the words sounded. Her mom must have stepped on the landscape of dolls and plastic furniture Maggie had left on the hallway floor, because Emma entered the room limping, touching only the toes of her right foot to the carpet. "I told you to pick up your toys before bedtime."

The next morning, when Maggie inspected her hallway menagerie, one of the Polly Pockets was missing.

"Where is turquoise Polly?"

"I threw her in the bathroom trash after I stepped on her last night." There was no remorse in her mother's voice.

Maggie had run to the bathroom to find the can newly emptied.

"Your dad must have taken the garbage to the dumpster this morning on his way to work," her mom explained. "I'm sorry."

The apology had been mechanical, not sincere. *I'm sorry you didn't pick up your toys. I'm sorry your doll's plastic fingers are so sharp. I'm sorry I gave birth to a child who leaves land mines in the carpet at three a.m.*

Then came the death of a living creature, two weeks before the college students' appearance. Maggie and her mom had been driving to town in the morning, ten minutes behind schedule for the preschool drop-off and speeding around the curves, when Maggie saw a squirrel crossing the road.

"A squirrel! Up ahead!"

Her mom didn't slow down. The squirrel was scurrying toward the grass on the right, with plenty of time to cross, but in typical squirrel fashion he froze, then darted in the opposite direction, back toward the middle of the road. Although her mother jerked the wheel left, Maggie could still feel the small, sickening thud.

"You hit him!"

"It was an accident. He ran right in front of the car."

"Go back! He might still be alive!"

"He's not alive, and even if he was, we couldn't help him."

"We could call Animal Control." Maggie had seen their show on Animal Planet, a team of men saving a deer that was mired in a swamp.

"They don't rescue squirrels that are almost dead."

"If he's dead, we should bury him, or at least get him out of the road." By now Maggie was sobbing.

"Honey, I'm sorry. I didn't mean to hit him. But squirrels run in front of cars all the time, and we can't go back. I've got to get you to preschool and go prepare my class before the students arrive."

"I hate you." Maggie had choked back tears. "I hate you so much."

Nine years later she understood her reactions to these deaths for what they were—childish protests against the cruelty of the world and the insensitivity of adults, who didn't understand that toys and squirrels had complex emotions. Since then she'd seen dozens of dead animals in the road—squirrels, groundhogs, rabbits, and possums. Her father had once hit a deer that rebounded off his right bumper and fled into the woods, probably headed for a slow and painful death. Once he had killed a skunk whose spray had left the car stinking for weeks, but Maggie hadn't blamed him.

Perhaps it would have helped, all those years ago, to have explained to the sheriff that her mother had killed a squirrel and a few plastic toys. It might have shown how innocent Emma Greene was, this woman whose greatest crime was hitting a rodent with her car. The sheriff and most of his deputies were probably hunters—men who shot squirrels for fun, along with birds and rabbits—the sort who could take a blade and carve the antlers out of a buck's forehead without flinching, throwing mutilated corpses next to the county dumpsters, where they would be discovered by children like Maggie.

Still, Maggie didn't speak to the sheriff, for fear of whatever else she might confess. From her preschool perspective her mom was guilty, not because she had hit a squirrel or a boy, but because she hadn't slowed down. That was the damning factor behind both deaths. In the squirrel's case, her mother should have braked at the first glimpse of an animal. It was the approach of her speeding car that had confused the poor thing; he had been crossing the road peacefully, enjoying a pleasant morning, until the sound of the engine frightened him. Where was safety? Where was comfort? The squirrel had heard death coming, and had scurried back and forth in frantic terror until it smashed open his skull.

So too for the dark-haired student in their hallway, another victim of Emma's haste. Once he pushed his way into the house she hadn't brandished her weapon and warned him to get out. She had reacted the second he stepped through the door, and when he fell to his knees, she still hadn't paused. Her second blow had followed immediately, like the implacable metronome on Maggie's piano, ticking right and left.

Couldn't her mother have dropped the bat once the student was kneeling? Couldn't she have locked the door against the others, and called 911? The sheriff might have asked those questions, if Maggie had opened up to him when she was little. He might have asked the most incriminating question of all: Does your mother ever hit people when she's angry?

And then what would Maggie have said?

Yes, yes, yes.

THREE months earlier, when Emma was cleaning the house for a dinner party, she had left Maggie playing upstairs while she prepared the lower level, vacuuming and sweeping, Windexing glass doors and tables, picking up books and socks and shoes and candy wrappers, emptying the dishwasher, loading the dishwasher, scrubbing the kitchen and the downstairs bathroom. For two hours her mother had worked steadily, with Maggie interrupting every fifteen minutes to say: "I'm drawing a picture. Come and see."

"I will when I'm finished, honey. You just stay busy with your art, and don't mess up your room."

And so Maggie had kept on drawing—animals and rivers and trees with leaves like clusters of grapes, her most beautiful drawing ever, with all the colors available in her set of Magic Markers—until she heard the vacuum rattling as it rolled away to a closet, and she called to her mom one last time: "Come see my picture!"

Her mother's tired footsteps had approached slowly, heavily, up the stairs; she had half an hour to get dressed before her guests arrived.

When she reached the topmost stair, Emma had turned to face the hall, where Maggie was standing with a smile, anticipating her mom's approval. To this day she remembered how her mother's eyes had widened and her mouth opened, before a high-pitched shriek ripped from Emma's throat. "What is *this*! What are you *thinking*!"

Maggie had created a hallway mural, just like the one in the children's section of the public library, with an entire rain forest, featuring monkeys and parrots and snakes.

"You know better than to draw on walls!" Emma looked at the floor, where thick permanent markers were lying capless, bleeding into the white Berber carpet. She ran over and picked them up, staring at the green-and-purple Rorschach test on her carpet.

"I'm sorry," Maggie mumbled.

Her mother grabbed Maggie's arm with such force, the child thought it was being yanked from its socket. Emma lifted her daughter off the floor and dragged her into her room, shouting, "Here I'm trying to clean the house, and you are busy ruining it!"

With one quick stroke she had given Maggie the first spanking of her life, a smack aimed at her bottom, landing instead on her bare thigh with a force that wasn't as painful as it was humiliating. Maggie responded with screams and howling tears, while Emma retreated to the bathroom in search of the Resolve carpet cleaner. On her knees, wiping the carpet with a yellow sponge, her mother had wept as the colors merged into an oil slick.

Rob had arrived ten minutes later to find his wife and daughter in their separate bedrooms, still crying.

"I can paint the wall tomorrow," he had assured Emma. "It needed a new coat anyway."

"You can't repaint the carpet," she said. "That stain is permanent. And our guests are coming in fifteen minutes."

"Your friends have kids—they know all about it. It will make a good story."

His nonchalance had infuriated Emma. Rob had a way of always implying that the problem was within her; she was making a big deal out of nothing. "You said you'd come home early to help today. You were supposed to be here almost two hours ago. If you had been here, you could have been watching Maggie."

"I got stuck at work with last-minute problems—everyone seems to have a crisis at five o'clock."

"You didn't call to say you'd be late, and I tried your cell three times. You know this happens every week—I'm stuck here doing overtime with Maggie when you are nowhere to be found . . . Change your clothes . . . the guests are coming soon. And don't wear that green shirt—it's hideous."

When the first guests pulled into the driveway, Maggie was still sobbing in her room. Her mother came in and muttered, "For God's sake be quiet." Behind her Maggie saw her dad, putting a finger to his lips and giving a wink, so she choked down her tears.

"Once you've cleaned your face, you can come downstairs," Emma had added. "The Petersons are bringing their girls."

Her mom had been right about the carpet. After the dinner party Rob scrubbed at it with bleach cleansers for twenty minutes, but the damage was permanent. From that day forward, whenever Maggie walked through the hall, the gray ghost of that afternoon gazed up at her from the fibers, a reminder of her mother's anger and her own guilt.

"All those little events," Maggie explained to Dr. Riley, "the dinosaur and the squirrel and the spanking, they all made me think that my mom was a mean person—that she hurt things, and hurt people."

"Do you feel different about your mom now?"

"You want to know if I love my mom?"

"No, I didn't say that."

Maggie looked down at her left wrist, where a bracelet of blue indigo beads served as a small, secular rosary. Her mother had given her the bracelet two years ago, and Maggie had worn it ever since, making wishes as she ran her right-hand fingertips over the beads.

"It's hard to love a person when you're afraid of them," she murmured.

In elementary school, the primary emotion Maggie had felt toward her mother was shame. Shame at her mother's anger and lack of control. Shame at the disgrace it had brought to their family. Shame at being known as the daughter of the nutty professor, the loony bat-wielding redhead. All the other mothers appeared pleasant and calm, baking brownies for school fund-raisers and chairing PTA committees, but after Jacob's death those women had held Emma at arm's length, eyeing her with a mixture of pity and fear, and Maggie had shared their apprehension, wondering if she would eventually become a target of her mother's fury. The TV news told stories of mothers who killed their children—smothering them, drowning them, beating them to death. What might her mother do if Maggie was really, really bad?

When Emma moved to Washington, Maggie had begun to pretend that her mother was dead—her mom was the person killed on that dark evening, not Jacob Stewart. Sometimes that's how it felt to Maggie, as if she had lost her mom forever on that night. Nothing had been the same afterward. Once her mom was gone, Maggie had kept a picture of her under her pillow for years; she had seen a girl in a movie do that, after her mom died of cancer. It was a way of grieving, and grief was an easier emotion than shame or fear. It was almost comforting, to look at her mother's face and mourn the parent she had lost. Her mother's monthly visits never fully brought her back to life.

Only in the past two years had Maggie's feelings started to change. As an adolescent, she had begun to sympathize with her mother's rage. She had read Truman Capote, and knew that life could be dangerous. But beyond the rare threats from violent strangers, there were plenty of mundane reasons for a person to be furious, and anger was not a male prerogative. The world needed more indignation, more outrage against political and moral corruption, more intelligent protests against the general stupidity. She had been ridiculous to fear her mother—this woman who had never raised a hand against her child except for that one, single slap on Maggie's thigh. If anything, her mom's behavior had become muted after Jacob's death. From that night forward, her instincts toward Maggie had been entirely protective, while all her frustrations had been channeled toward Rob.

"Did you tell your dad about Mrs. Murdock's identity?" Dr. Riley asked.

"My mom beat me to it. She called him yesterday right after I e-mailed her."

"So your mom knows about all of this?"

"Not all of it. I just said that my math teacher was Sandra McCluskey, and she'd told me a lot about the past. I asked my mom to come down this weekend so I could explain everything . . . Mrs. Murdock says that my mom was right to kill Jacob. Jacob was evil."

"Is 'evil' the right word?" the doctor asked.

Maggie shrugged without answering. She wanted to pin a label on Jacob Stewart, to pretend that life was black and white. "I think I've been kind of hard on my mom, and I'd like to make it up to her. That's why I've invited her here for the weekend; I've asked Mrs. Murdock to meet with us."

Dr. Riley's eyebrows arched ever so slightly. "What do you hope to accomplish by bringing Mrs. Murdock and your mom together?"

"I don't know . . . maybe air things out—set the record straight. Do you think it's a bad idea?"

"Is your mom comfortable with it?"

Maggie paused. "I don't know about *comfortable*, but she said she'd come." She looked out the window at the nodding trees, thinking it was time to change the subject. "I haven't had any bad dreams for the past three days. Is that a good sign?"

"Having all of this out in the open should help."

A maple leaf blew against the window, and Maggie watched it pulse briefly like an orange jellyfish.

"It would be nice . . . " she murmured.

"What?" the doctor asked.

Maggie turned her face toward his. "It would be nice for the dreams to end."

CHAPTER 20

ON Friday afternoon Maggie paused in the hallway outside Mrs. Murdock's classroom, jostled by the current of students flowing by. After the library meeting she had thought she would feel comfortable enough to sit through geometry, watching the back of Mrs. Murdock's head and imagining yet another game of KerPlunk. She couldn't afford to fall further behind, so she had tried attending class on Wednesday and Thursday, noticing how Mrs. Murdock occasionally managed to look her in the eye, although not for long—the teacher always dropped her gaze after a few seconds. Still, it was enough time for Maggie to understand that this felt wrong. She no longer dreaded her teacher, but neither did she respect her. She recognized in the woman's fingers, flicking across the chalkboard, the gestures of an impostor, and she couldn't sit for fifty minutes absorbing descriptions of parallelograms as if everything was okay. If Mrs. Murdock offered to speak about the past, giving faces and colors and definition to the college students who had existed for so long as hazy shadows, then Maggie would listen. But she couldn't pretend that Mrs. Murdock's presence in Jackson was normal.

When the seventh-period bell rang, Maggie lingered in the hall, far enough from Mrs. Murdock's door so that she wouldn't be seen. She was about to turn away when a voice at her back interrupted her thoughts:

"Miss Greene, I'd like a word with you."

Officer Petty loomed in his blue uniform, gesturing for Maggie to follow. She obeyed in silence as they walked by open classroom doors, down the stairs, and through another hallway, past the cafeteria, before stepping into "Carver's classroom." Today the space smelled of fried chicken. Or was it fried fish, or home fries, or chicken-fried steak? Maggie couldn't distinguish the subtleties of grease.

Carver sat down in a student desk beside Maggie. He had been thinking about this girl ever since he found her in the woods, although he hadn't told the principal about Mrs. Murdock's identity—he was waiting a few days to see what developed, and he'd been keeping a close eye on Maggie in the meantime. But now, as the child sat next to him in her usual defensive posture, arms crossed and slouching, he wondered what Mrs. Murdock, aka Sandra McCluskey, could have written on that yellow slip of paper that would make this tough kid cry.

"I noticed you standing outside Mrs. Murdock's classroom. You didn't look eager to go inside."

Maggie didn't reply.

"You might not be aware that I was a police officer in Jackson back when all that stuff with your mother happened, and I thought it was terrible, all the cheap shots she took."

Maggie slouched a little lower. So Officer Petty knew about the crazy professor, the pot-smoking Feminazi who loved monkeys but hated men. Maggie had been too young, at age five, to absorb the blizzard of gossip during that first, harrowing summer, but the remnants had lingered for years in the town's folklore, repeated on Internet sites, at dinner-table conversations, in newspaper articles revisiting the events long after. In a town of eight thousand people Emma Greene was notorious, the Lizzie Borden of the new millennium, wielding a bat instead of an ax. Her life provided better entertainment than the local drive-in—with real violence, real cops, and a female protagonist with hair too red and eyes too green to be entirely innocent. Maggie understood why her mother needed to move away, to leave this glorified fishbowl and find a place where she could be anonymous. If she hadn't been tethered to Maggie, she probably would have fled farther— to the West Coast, or Europe, someplace where Jackson was too insignificant to register in anyone's mind.

"You should realize," Carver continued, "that the sheriff believed your mother's story from day one. Policemen can usually tell when someone is lying, and your mom came across as an honest woman with a good heart. I know because I was friends with several deputies, and our police chief in Jackson, Chris Miller, had a little talk with Sheriff King the day after the killing, to give him background information in case King had any doubts about those students. He told him that Kyle Caldwell had been accused of shoplifting by a local merchant a year earlier, although the charges were dropped because his parents bought off the store owner."

Maggie knew this much already, having overheard a conversation between her mom and Jodie Maus shortly after Jacob Stewart's death. Although she hadn't been talking in those days, Maggie had been listening, tuned to every scrap of information floating through the house—every argument, every clash between her parents, every fit of her mother's tears.

"There was something else the chief shared, that I bet your mom never knew."

Carver hesitated, trying to decide how much he should tell this child. "You know those two-story rental houses at the end of Preston Avenue, the ones painted tropical colors?"

Maggie nodded without speaking.

"You know the bright pink one?"

Maggie nodded again. "You mean the brothel."

"Yeah." Carver smiled. "I didn't know you kids were familiar with that name." For the past fifteen years the house had been rented to groups of college girls, so the police called it the brothel, the cathouse, the red-light district.

"Ten years ago I responded to a 911 call out there." Carver paused again, trying to measure his words. The incident he had in mind was confidential but not tied to any active investigation. It was almost a decade old, and a few small revelations couldn't do any harm, but the scenes now running through his mind were R-rated, and Carver often had trouble gauging how much information a ninth grader could handle. He was so accustomed to the toughest, most jaded teenagers, he questioned what level of innocence might still exist in a girl like Maggie Greene.

"It might be best if I showed you something."

Carver stood and walked to his filing cabinet.

"When you were in this room before, Mrs. Murdock handed you a sheet of paper, and I've been thinking that I have my own sheet of paper that you should read."

After flipping through several folders, he extracted an eight-by-eleven sheet of white paper curling at the corners.

"I've kept this for years. Just for the record."

He placed it on Maggie's desk, and she looked down at the xeroxed image of a five-by-seven handwritten letter—three short paragraphs and a signature she didn't recognize.

"Who is Lauren Cross?" she asked.

"Jacob Stewart's girlfriend."

Maggie paused to read the letter, blushing as she absorbed the contents. More revelations, more secrets, more shadows from the adult world.

"I think you should show this to your mom," said Carver. "But nobody else, okay?"

"Yes," Maggie agreed. Nobody else.

"Will you promise to bring it back to me?"

"Yes." She placed the letter, smooth and unwrinkled, into the side pocket of her three-ring binder. She would see her mother that evening.

Carver exhaled. "I suppose you don't want to go back to your geometry class . . . "

No, thought Maggie. *Please no.*

"I don't mind if you stay here and get started on your homework. Why don't I drive up to the Dairy Queen and bring you back a Blizzard."

"Thanks." Maggie smiled. "Make it Oreo."

Chapter 21

EMMA was finishing her last paperwork for the week when she paused to send an e-mail to Maggie.

I should arrive in Jackson by six o'clock. Sarah is fixing dinner for us all, so make sure you and Kate are at her house by six-thirty.

She glanced at the time: 1:25. If she reached Highway 66 by two, she might beat the Friday-afternoon rush hour. Years of experience driving from D.C. to Jackson had taught her that if she wasn't out of town by two-thirty, she might as well wait until after dinner. Even this early in the day, traffic would be crawling from Fairfax to Manassas.

Emma rose and walked into the bathroom beside her office. Staring into the mirror, she turned her face to the right so that the bruise on her left cheek showed purple and green in the fluorescent light. Emma lifted the makeup brush from her counter, and for the third time that day she dipped it into a vial of mineral powder and dusted her cheek with skin-colored foundation, just as she had seen shelter residents do for years. *Now I really fit in here*, she thought. Wasn't it always that way in the nonprofit world? The directors and volunteers needed as much care as their clients; they came to the job because of their scars, in search of mutual healing.

Emma examined her powdered face, hoping she didn't look too scary. Maggie had seen her mother's bruises before—on Emma's knees and right palm when the stranger knocked her down, on her forearms when karate classes got intense. But Emma had never been punched in the face before. She bared her teeth in the mirror, reached in with her thumb and index finger, and popped out her new, fake incisor, attached to a pink plastic mold shaped to the roof of her mouth. "The best we can do on short notice," her dentist had said that morning, showing her the type of three-part screw-in tooth she'd eventually have. The plastic and metal in Emma's hand resembled Maggie's retainer from a year ago, and she thought briefly that she might show this to her daughter, as a curiosity. But when she looked into the mirror and examined the gap in her smile, she looked like a gargoyle. Better not to mention this, she thought, and pressed the plastic back into the roof of her mouth.

Emma returned to her desk, shut down her computer, and lifted a stack of grant application papers she'd been struggling with for weeks. Hurrying to her door, she grabbed the coat and overnight bag that were lying on the couch.

"Ruth," she said as she passed through her assistant's area, "make sure this gets FedEx'd today. I've already submitted the online forms."

"No problem." Ruth smiled. "Have a nice time with Maggie."

Emma hadn't revealed the purpose of her trip—only Junot and Rob knew about Sandra's reappearance. For the rest of the world, this was merely another mother-daughter visit, too infrequent in these busy fall months.

Stepping outside, Emma had a brief vision of Carlos Cortez pinned on the walkway with Junot's knee in his back. Carlos was now in jail, with no chance of raising the substantial bail assigned by an unsympathetic judge who had seen too much domestic violence. Over the next few weeks Maria would have to learn to support herself and Christian without Carlos's income, but she seemed determined, shocked into resolve by the sight of Emma's swollen cheek. She had imagined herself as Carlos's only victim, his anger triggered by her personal flaws, but now, between his threats against Christian and violence toward Emma, she had sworn she would file for divorce, double her housecleaning jobs, and accept her sister's help in finding a new apartment. Emma hoped it was true; she hoped Maria would stay resolute after Carlos was released. "Look at my face," she had said in her last moments with Maria before Christina arrived to take her sister home. "If you let Carlos come back, he will do this to your son. You must never let that happen."

Now, as Emma drove down Constitution Avenue, past the National Gallery on her left and the Archives on her right, she felt that her life in Washington was moving in the right direction. Maria had turned a corner, the grant was finished and likely to be approved, and Junot had promised to be waiting at her condo on Sunday night at seven, with dinner on the table.

Stopped at a light beside the Washington Monument, she saw that the sky was full of enormous dragons, long-tailed fish, and boxy, geometric marvels, rippling and dodging, gathered for the annual kite festival. The wind had dispersed all traces of the humid murk that often settled over the city on warm days, and as she crossed the Potomac, with the Kennedy Center growing distant behind her, Emma thought how lucky she was to be living in this city with a handsome policeman-friend who bought tickets to *Billy Elliot* solely for her pleasure, even though he didn't like ballet.

As she passed the exits for Falls Church, Fairfax, then Vienna, her mind began to slip into the old memories. The drive back to Jackson was a time machine perpetually tuned to one spring and summer, so that by the time she reached the open highway east of Manassas, where the suburbs disappeared into rolling, forested hills, she was back at the house at Wade's Creek, contemplating the husband she had left behind.

She often wondered if she and Rob would have stayed together had it not been for Jacob Stewart's death. There had been problems in their marriage for many years, though the two of them might have soldiered forward, for Maggie's sake. But the pressures in the wake of Jacob's killing had stretched the marriage thin until it finally snapped.

First had come the arguments about Maggie's therapy, which Rob had insisted upon, just as he had insisted on sessions for Emma after Maggie was born. Rob bore the conviction, garnered from years of watching his mother and sisters, that women constantly needed to share their feelings. He didn't believe in women's silence, or in solitary women. Solitude and reticence were traits for brooding men. Women should chat.

"People who are quiet aren't always depressed," Emma had said after Maggie's birth, when Rob pushed her toward postpartum therapy.

"The breast-feeding isn't going well," he had replied.

Emma hated when men talked about breast-feeding as if reading a few chapters in a pregnancy guide made them experts. Yes, her nipples had been cracked and bleeding, so that Maggie looked like a little vampire with drops of blood running down her chin as she nursed. At night, when Emma resorted to bottles, knowing that Maggie slept longer when filled with Similac, Rob had warned of "nipple confusion," flaunting words learned from books while Emma carried the painful knowledge of her body.

Those first cracks in Emma's marriage had formed long before she ever met Jacob Stewart. Every time she heated a bottle of formula, she had known that Rob was watching with critical eyes, and she had wanted him to disappear, although she never said it aloud. She had learned to covet the hours when he was at work, and to cringe when she heard his car in the driveway, anticipating his judgment of the bathrobe she had worn all day, the laundry spilling from the hamper, the telltale baby bottles in the kitchen sink.

In the end Emma had consented to a few months of postpartum therapy, just to stop Rob's cajoling, but she had dismissed the sessions as nothing more than expensive chitchat. Which was why, when Rob insisted on counseling for Maggie, Emma had felt the same gut-level resistance, the same anger that he was pressuring their child to open herself to a stranger, when she wanted silence.

Leave the girl alone, Emma had wanted to say. *Leave us both alone.*

Nevertheless, she had let Maggie go, sensing that her authority as a parent had been lost the moment she struck Jacob. Rob was the responsible adult in the household—the reasonable, calm, guiltless one, while she was the irrational female who might fly off the handle at any moment.

Rob had also insisted that they sell their house—another fight that Emma would ultimately lose. She loved the house at Wade's Creek, even with the violent memories, but Rob said that the location was too isolated and vulnerable; he could never go on a trip or work late at the office without fearing for Emma and Maggie. He wanted them tucked safely into a friendly neighborhood with children biking on slow streets, husbands grilling on back decks (*and mothers inside sticking their heads into ovens*, thought Emma). But she didn't say it aloud. Never aloud. In her mind Rob's concerns were tainted with a wish to make himself feel less guilty. She told him that more crimes occurred in busy neighborhoods than in remote country areas. In town there were more thefts, more drunk students, more opportunities for strangers to show up at night at one's doorstep. Above all, Emma dreaded the close quarters with neighbors who would whisper behind her back, observe her movements for hints of violence, and fear her contact with their children. She needed separation from gossiping townspeople, not immersion in their world.

But she worried about Maggie, every time the child walked through the lower hallway of their house, or stared out her window at the dark trees. Could Maggie ever be happy playing in those woods again? Could she kneel beside their creek in unself-conscious innocence, scooping minnows with a kitchen strainer, knowing that the students had stood drinking at that spot? Had every acre of their property been contaminated?

For all Emma knew, every day at Wade's Creek was reinforcing Maggie's timidity, and so she agreed to buy the house that Rob wanted: a small, yellow Cape Cod in a cozy, in-town neighborhood with mature trees—walnut and pine and pink dogwoods—where a sidewalk marched in a straight line, four blocks, to Maggie's elementary school. What could be more comforting than a cottage in pastels, with freshly painted white trim and ivory Berber carpet with no stains?

The clean carpet had impressed Emma. For three days after Jacob's death she had tried to scrub the blood from her Oriental runner before finally throwing it out, but inside the citric bungalow the rooms were spotless, almost to the point of erasure, as if the dark, rich colors of human life had been bleached down to their palest ghosts.

Standing in the living room of that sunny Cape Cod, while their realtor praised the tidiness of gas fireplaces, Emma had stared out the open window, beyond the twenty feet of grass and azaleas, into the living room of their neighbor, where a child was playing piano. She could hear a fractured "Für Elise," accompanied by the yaps of a lapdog and the shouts of a teenage boy demanding his mother's attention. A garbage truck passed outside, heaving and clanking, and she knew that she would need to keep her windows closed and shades drawn to enjoy any peace in this house. For the next two years Emma would reside in thickly insulated, air-conditioned, spotless sterility.

Her sole consolation had been the nearness of Sarah, less than a mile away. Sarah applauded Rob's wish for a new house, and his insistence on therapy for Maggie. She and Rob usually saw eye to eye.

"Believe me, I understand the impulse to be alone," she had assured Emma. "When I lost my husband, I tried to stay secluded for months, but in the end I had to break free before it drove me crazy. I sold my house, which was a beautiful old Victorian, but much too big for me and Kate, and too heavy with memories."

In the midst of her traumatic summer, the burden of moving had been loaded on top of Emma's shoulders, day after day spent packing her former life into cardboard boxes. Of course they hadn't been able to sell the Wade's Creek home—they hadn't even tried for the first three months, for who would buy the murder house? In September, when their realtor announced his first open house, the visitors had been more curious about the crime than the kitchen. They wanted to see the floor where Jacob had fallen, not the newly updated appliances. They wanted to push open the door, and imagine the bat leaning against the coatrack.

Emma had been pleased when the house didn't sell right away. Several times during that first autumn she had returned to Wade's Creek to walk the five acres, citing the need to trim the dwarf lilacs and mow the lawn, and on each occasion Maggie had asked to come along. When their apples ripened in October, they returned to pick two bushels, and in early November they had raked the front-yard leaves into enormous piles deep enough for Maggie to jump in and disappear. Mid-December had brought the winter's first snow, and when Maggie said that Jackson had no sledding hills as good as their backyard at Wade's creek, Emma had brought her back with their toboggan and together they had raced from the ridge outside their back door down to the base of the creek.

Pulling the toboggan back uphill, Maggie had assessed their house's empty porches and dark windows. "Our house looks lonely."

"Yes," Emma agreed, "but soon another family will move in and they'll bring it back to life."

That family did eventually materialize, but not soon enough to save Emma and Rob's marriage. Over the next year they crumbled under the stress of two mortgages, a situation exacerbated by the anxiety of Emma's increasingly uncertain employment.

As she drove through the Blue Ridge Mountains, turning south into the Shenandoah Valley, Emma recalled the strange course of her last year at Holford. She hadn't lost her job in the way she expected—not rejected by a committee that used her meager publication record as an excuse to deny tenure. In the immediate wake of Jacob's killing, her department chair, Joe Williams, had recognized that Emma's tenure review should be delayed, and Emma had appreciated the reprieve, since each month was bringing new upheavals.

First had come an article in the *Chronicle of Higher Education*, written by an old friend of Sarah's named Janice Lee. Two weeks after Jacob's death Sarah had persuaded Janice to write a feature telling Emma's side of what was then being called "the Holford Murder." Janice was the only reporter whom Emma agreed to speak with, and the article became a springboard for a larger discussion about professors' safety on college campuses, with a litany of violent tales from professors she never knew—a chemist in Chicago, badly burned in a lab explosion orchestrated by a disgruntled graduate student; a math professor in Nevada, shot in the head by a sophomore who failed calculus; an English-composition instructor in New York plagued by a month of e-mailed death threats from an irate mother who claimed that his unfair C had cost her daughter's scholarship.

In the midst of the story stood Emma, the professor who had fought back. It helped that she was female and her attacker male, enabling Janice to give the article a feminist refrain, to the tune of "Take Back the Night." Janice rebutted all previous claims that Emma was a liberal wacko. Sure, Professor Greene had supported PETA; her desire to protect abused animals foreshadowed her impulse to protect her daughter.

Sarah had loved the article, reading it aloud to Emma at her kitchen table. But Emma had cringed, especially at Janice's attacks against Holford's administration, which implied that the school had a chauvinist bias against female professors and was throwing Emma to the wolves. *This won't help my tenure chances,* Emma had thought as she sipped her coffee, listening to the enthusiasm in Sarah's voice. If she were an administrator, she would have handled the situation the same way Jodie and Don Kresgey had. They didn't witness the incident, and weren't in a position to take sides.

Janice portrayed Emma as a feminist avenger, but Emma saw nothing heroic in her actions. When Jacob Stewart entered her house, he had stepped into a maelstrom of anger that had nothing to do with him. The truth was, it had felt good to hit someone, good to see Jacob fall. Emma had been raging against the world when that bat struck his head, and she had continued to rage for the past nine and a half years—against her husband, against Carlos Cortez, against all of life's daily vexations. She knew the precise extent of her guilt, and to be beatified was little better than demonization.

Still, the article seemed to strike a chord far beyond Jackson. Within three days the *Chronicle* had received over two hundred e-mails and letters from professors sharing stories of smashed car windows, vicious graffiti on office doors, and computers hacked by vengeful techies. A few professors had quit their jobs to escape a culture of harassment—and these weren't jobs at the inner-city campuses of lower-tier colleges, where the students might be expected to have rough edges. Often the most elite, privileged universities contained the most antagonistic students and parents—young people insistent on their right to high grades, or parents enraged by professors who did not recognize their children's brilliance. Janice's article became a rallying cry for professors who wanted severe penalties for students who sent threatening e-mails, or who deliberately damaged professors' property. Campus codes for cyber-conduct should include tough sanctions against students who responded to low grades by slandering professors, and all legal action in a professor's defense should be funded by the university's dime.

Just when the media interest in Jacob's death had been cooling down, Janice's article set Emma's phone ringing every five minutes. Sarah encouraged Emma to accept an interview with NPR, as a chance to broadcast her story to a wider, educated audience, but Emma decided instead to offer an op-ed to the *New York Times*. It seemed the best way to control her story, and the *Times* editor agreed that if she would limit herself to eight hundred words, he would not cut her piece. If he needed to adjust any sentences, he'd promised Emma, she'd be able to approve the final version. Under those circumstances she had written her first paragraph:

> *My life changed irrevocably one night last May when three college students showed up uninvited at my home. In our rural area of Virginia, eight miles from the nearest town, houses are divided by acres of pasture and woods, with no neighbors within sight. On that night in May my husband was out of town, leaving me alone with my five-year-old daughter to handle any problems the students might pose. And the problems came quickly.*

From there, Emma had followed the trail of Kyle's fingerprints: from the beer can tossed in her yard, to the banister as he invaded the private spaces of her house, to her bedroom dresser, her jewelry box, her pillow and bedspread. Most damning were the prints on Maggie's dresser, raising the specter of a drunk male college student secretly entering a little girl's bedroom.

Every sentence cried out with violation, culminating in the image of Emma's bracelet on the wrist of Kyle's girlfriend. Emma explained how she had called Holford's honor-court president weeks earlier to complain about Kyle's stealing, and how, when she saw her bracelet, she threatened to have him expelled. In retrospect, the op-ed's publication was probably the moment when her fate at Holford had been sealed: the day she announced in the *New York Times* that Mason Caldwell's son was a thief and a liar.

The response to the piece was swift. Where the *Chronicle* piece inspired letters from professors, now came confessions from high school instructors and middle school teachers, lamenting classroom cultures where they routinely felt threatened. The combination of high-stakes testing and cutthroat college admissions had produced students and parents who responded to low grades not by working harder, but by attacking teachers, calling for them to be demoted, or fired, or in extreme cases, killed. And the problem wasn't only a lack of respect for teachers—there was antagonism toward doctors who would not prescribe on demand, threats against financial advisers when the stock market fell, violence against policemen and politicians, as if Americans believed they were entitled to perfect lives and someone else must be held responsible for every setback.

Emma got interview requests from the *Today* show, *Good Morning America*, and Fox News, but she turned them down. The first invitation she accepted came from the National Association of Women Professors, who asked her to give the keynote address at their huge spring conference. Sarah thought it might help her tenure chances.

Now, driving south through a corridor of pastures and shriveled corn, Emma smiled sadly at Sarah's mistake. Perhaps a more flamboyant school like Berkeley or Bennington would have welcomed a new feminist icon on campus, but dignified Holford didn't appreciate the fuss. They wanted their English professors famous for books on Shakespeare, not for rabble-rousing.

She remembered the morning when Joe Williams invited her into his office, shortly after her April speech at the NAWP conference. High on the applause of two thousand women, Emma had assumed that her department chair would congratulate her. She had already scheduled three more events, partly because of the money—a single keynote address doubled her monthly salary from Holford. But she also appreciated all of the e-mails from women around the country, supporting the action she had taken to protect her daughter.

Joe hadn't been impressed. "I was curious about how your work on Charlotte Brontë is coming along?"

He had never asked about her research before, and Emma managed only a few baffled sentences about new critical approaches to *Villette* before it dawned on her that this wasn't a question so much as a warning.

"You are scheduled to go up for tenure next year," Joe continued, "and there's a sense that you have gotten off track. You might want to focus more on your research, and your teaching." Emma had blushed, then felt ashamed for doing so, which made her flush all the deeper. Joe obviously had in mind the dismal enrollment in her courses. In previous years her classes had always been full, but when the fall registration window opened after Jacob's death, the students who were preregistered for her classes dropped them in droves. The few who remained were loyal junior and senior women, who knew her well enough to accept her explanation of the events. The department had canceled her British survey, which had only six enrollees left of the initial twenty-seven, and although they had kept her seminar on Virginia Woolf, only five students remained out of fifteen. Emma also appeared among the list of freshman-composition instructors, prompting dozens of phone calls from parents who didn't want their children assigned to her section.

Initially Emma had enjoyed her minimal enrollment. Small classes meant fewer papers to grade and fewer questions to endure. But it also meant more work for her colleagues, who picked up the slack by accepting extra students into their classes. Among the few upperclassmen who took Emma's fall seminar, she realized that some were merely gawkers, less interested in the syllabus than in spending a few hours each week in the presence of the local legend. Emma suspected that she was becoming a case study for psychology majors.

Her course counts improved slightly in the spring semester, and she expected that enrollment would slowly climb term by term as all the students who knew Jacob graduated and moved away. In the meantime Joe gave her extra committee work in the spring, to counter the impression that she wasn't pulling her weight. Still, she felt bored and resentful at every meeting.

All of these thoughts had flown through her mind as she sat in his office that April, babbling about *Villette* and pondering her lackluster tenure chances. She had walked out feeling chastened, briefly determined to squeeze another article out of her dissertation, but she found over the coming months that she couldn't concentrate on Brontë; all the writing she produced was on cyber-bullying and campus safety. By midsummer she had abandoned any hope of tenure, and told Joe that she planned to resign after the coming year. She wanted to get a job at a new college in a new town, secretly hoping for a more liberal climate where *feminist* wasn't a dirty word and PETA might appear mainstream. Rob, who enjoyed his job at Holford, hadn't been pleased; he had maintained a stony silence at the breakfast table in October as she studied the MLA's Job Information List. The market was bleak; nationwide, fewer than ten jobs came close to Emma's field, and she sent letters to them all, even the tiny midwestern schools she had never heard of. Only one listing seemed ideal; Barnard's Center for Research on Women was searching for a new director, a professor with a background in women's studies who could handle the center's administration while teaching part-time for one of the humanities departments. The current director, Laurie Copeland, was a friend of Emma's; they had gone out to dinner during the NAWP conference and maintained a sporadic correspondence. After mailing her cover letter and CV to Barnard, Emma had sent Laurie a chatty e-mail, letting her know that she had thrown her hat into the ring.

She was surprised when two weeks went by without a reply, either from Laurie or from the Barnard search committee. Eventually Emma swallowed her pride and called her friend, under the pretext of an upcoming visit to Manhattan. When she asked about the status of the job search and whether she might have a chance, the embarrassment in Laurie's voice had been painful. "I think you would be perfect for this job, Emma, but you've got to understand—there's no way Barnard would ever hire a professor who has killed a student, whether or not the act was justified. Our parents are anxious enough about sending their kids to a big city like New York, with a campus so close to Harlem. Safety is their top concern, and we have to show them that every precaution is being taken; a professor who has any record of violence against students could never get an interview."

Emma had almost dropped the telephone receiver, her shock was so severe. She had envisioned a job at Barnard as a vindication, a step up the academic ladder, from which she could look down and wave at Joe Williams. It had never occurred to her that she would be dismissed as a candidate, but now she understood why none of the colleges she had applied to had asked her for a writing sample or references. It was still early in the search, something might come through, and yet, as

Emma absorbed the impact of Laurie's words, she realized that no matter how lowly the college, she would never get another job as a professor. She was an academic leper.

Laurie seemed anxious to fill the silence. "We are looking for a speaker for women's history month in March. Would you like to do that?" Emma longed to say no, but if she was going to be unemployed within eight months, she would need all the extra money she could get. It seemed ironic that the same colleges that would pay her five thousand dollars to speak at a conference would not let her join their faculties. To them she was a novelty, a short-lived fad on the speakers' tour, not a reliable colleague.

That winter was the worst of Emma's life, as the rejection letters arrived one by one. She felt that she had been reduced to graduate-student status, praying for the unlikely last-minute interview. But she was lower than a grad student, because in those days she had lined up three interviews at the MLA conference. This time, when Joe and two of her colleagues left for the conference to meet the candidates for Emma's job, she stayed behind in reclusive embarrassment. She had been banned from the ivory tower, and the idea of living in Jackson without a job at Holford was the final insult.

The opening at Kelly's House had been an act of God. In March Laurie Copeland called Emma to say that Washington's most famous shelter for women was looking for an associate director who had experience writing grant applications. Laurie knew that Emma had been trained as a hotline volunteer for Jackson's shelter, and had served on their board of directors. "It's not a professorship, but it's important work, and you could probably make director in a couple of years, since you've had plenty of experience with NEH and Fulbright grants."

At Kelly's House, Emma's notoriety had not been a deal breaker—when she interviewed with the shelter's board of trustees, it was clear that they welcomed her background. Here was a woman famous for taking action to protect herself against a violent attack. Not only did they welcome her, they honored her.

"So much of American society is afraid of women's anger," the director had explained when she took Emma out to lunch. "Most people think that women should be sweet and helpful, patient with men's anger while suppressing their own. We want the women who leave our shelter to feel comfortable expressing their outrage and acting upon it in constructive ways. Sometimes women who are abused channel their anger toward their children or themselves, when it should be directed into action toward independence—legal action, economic action, the action of walking away from their abusers. Even violent action in the name of self-defense is sometimes necessary.

"Emma," she had added, "if you want this job, it's yours."

Emma hadn't leaped at the offer. She knew, from her years on the hotline in Jackson, how lonely shelter work could be, learning all the terrible secrets about people in your community. It distanced you from the crowd, to recognize an acquaintance's voice on the phone, then sit through a faculty meeting, listening to a male colleague and thinking: *I know what you did to your wife last night.* But maybe in a large city the work would be less intimate; she wouldn't live among the batterers, wouldn't stand behind them in grocery-store lines, disgusted by their capacity for idle conversation.

Once she decided to take the job, Rob had simply refused to move to Washington. Emma invited him to join her; there would be plenty of work for a computer programmer in D.C. But Rob had never wanted to live in a city, and it seemed a natural ending point to their long-frayed relationship.

Sarah had urged Emma to fight for her marriage. "Rob is a terrific guy. It's only after you lose someone that you appreciate what you had . . . Consider what's best for Maggie."

But even Sarah had to concede that Jackson held no future for Emma. After she moved away, Emma evaluated Rob from her three hours' distance and could see all the goodness in his character and all his love for their daughter, but she knew that he wasn't her soul mate. She doubted whether such things existed.

Yet even as she felt the old grief for her marriage, which surprised her every so often as a dull ache in her chest, the thought of Junot Rodriguez cooking dinner for her on Sunday, waiting with candles and wine and a sympathetic heart, made her smile. The world might still have pockets of love, if she was open to finding them.

CHAPTER 22

AT five o'clock Emma called Sarah to report that she had avoided the worst of the city traffic and would reach Jackson in half an hour. She expected her friend to be waiting in the kitchen, relaxing over her habitual glass of Friday-afternoon chardonnay. Instead, when Emma pulled into the driveway, Sarah was rocking on the front porch swing with Kate and Maggie nearby in wicker chairs, drinking lemonade. *Maggie's told them*, Emma thought. It was just as well.

The watchful trio lent a gravity to Emma's arrival, as if she had come for a risky medical procedure.

Sarah crossed the grass to give Emma a hug. "What happened to your cheek?"

"Karate accident. I'll tell you about it later."

Sarah accepted this as code for "not in front of the girls," who were lingering a few steps back, Kate giving a slight wave and saying, "Hey Mrs. Greene," while Maggie shifted her feet in awkward silence, as she always did at her mother's visits. Lifting her overnight bag to her shoulder, Emma closed her car door and prepared to approach her reluctant daughter, but Maggie moved forward and wrapped her arms around her mom so tightly that Emma stood dumbstruck, her arms slowly rising to hold her daughter's delicate frame. Sarah and Emma exchanged glances over Maggie's shoulder, before Emma stepped back to look into her child's eyes.

"You've grown another inch in the past month."

"I'm taller than you now," Maggie replied.

"Oh no, it must be your shoes."

"It's not hard to be taller than you, Mom."

Inside the house, Kate disappeared into the kitchen to help with dinner, a rare act clearly designed to give Maggie and Emma time alone.

"We're going to meet Mrs. Murdock tomorrow," Maggie explained as Emma carried her bag to the guest bedroom. "Ten o'clock at the coffee shop. I'm sleeping over tonight so you and I can leave together from here."

Emma sat on the edge of the bed. "I can't think of her as Mrs. Murdock. I only know Sandra McCluskey."

Maggie settled down beside her and pulled a folded yellow piece of paper from the front pocket of her jeans.

"This is the note she gave me last week."

Emma read the eight words without comment.

"And today I got something else." Maggie reached over to the bedside table where her math notebook was waiting. "Officer Petty gave me this." She pulled out the letter and handed it to Emma.

"Carver Petty? The black policeman who works at your school?"

"Right." Emma stared at the strange handwriting.

August 10, 2003

Dear Mrs. Stewart,

We met last October, during Parents' Weekend. You took me and Jacob out for a very nice dinner. I heard about Jacob's death and I'm sorry for the pain you must be going through. I also heard that you have brought a wrongful death lawsuit against Professor Greene, and that's why I'm writing.

Although I'm sure you love your son, you need to understand that when Professor Greene says she was defending herself against him, she's telling the truth. I know because last December, when I told Jacob that I wanted to break up with him, he attacked me. Jacob beat me, raped me, and left me with two bruised ribs and a broken wrist. I never went back to Holford, and I didn't bring charges against him, because at the time I just wanted to go home and pretend it didn't happen. Now I regret that.

I realize it must be a shock for you to read this, but what I'm writing is true. The results were witnessed by my housemate, Officer Carver Petty, my parents, and the hospital staff in Jackson. If you continue with this lawsuit against Professor Greene I will testify on her behalf and tell everyone what Jacob did. I'd rather not; it hurts me to even write about this. But what you are doing to Professor Greene is wrong, and it's time for it to stop.

> *Sincerely,*
> *Lauren Cross*

"I don't understand," said Emma. "How did Carver Petty get this?"

"He was the cop who first saw Lauren after the rape. And when he heard that Mrs. Stewart was pressing her wrongful-death lawsuit, he asked Lauren if she would send her a letter, to try to call her off. Lauren sent him this copy."

Maggie expected the revelation to lift some of the burden from her mother's shoulders—to show her that Jacob deserved what he got—but instead Emma looked tired.

"I thought it would make you feel better, to know how bad Jacob was."

Emma sighed. "I always wondered why Mrs. Stewart dropped her suit. I figured Mason Caldwell had stopped paying the bills, or maybe her lawyer convinced her to give it up. But I could never feel glad to hear that Jacob assaulted someone. I see so much rape in my job, it just makes me sad for that girl."

"But it shows that you were justified."

"No." Emma hesitated, wondering how to explain the complexities of guilt to a fifteen-year-old. "What Jacob did in the past, and what I did on that night, are two separate things. I have to live with what was right and wrong in my own actions."

She leaned over and planted a kiss in her daughter's hair. "But thanks for telling me." Pulling back, she saw that Maggie's eyes looked troubled. "What is it?"

Maggie shrugged. "It's just—this girl, Lauren, did more to help you than I ever did."

"You were only five years old. What could you have done?"

"I could have spoken out. I could have told everyone that I heard the students' voices down at the creek, and that Kyle Caldwell came into my room and looked right at me. I could have said that I saw Jacob push his way into our house, and reach for you. If I had said all those things, it would have backed up your story."

Emma shook her head. "The police never really doubted my story, and the fingerprints confirmed it."

"But they had to wait a long time for those fingerprints. I remember you and dad talking about it over dinner. And all that time people were saying terrible things."

"Do you really think the words of a child would have stopped anyone from saying bad things? Kyle and Sandra were going to spread lies no matter what—and once that stuff went viral, there was no way for you to stop it. Nothing you might have said would have made a difference to Mrs. Stewart—she was hell-bent on revenge, and it looks like Lauren Cross was the only person who had the power to stop that train. Any testimony from you wouldn't have mattered."

"Would it have mattered to you?" Maggie asked. "To know that I supported you?"

Emma was silent, wondering what sort of private hell Maggie had endured all these years. She had always sensed the fear behind her daughter's initial silence, but she hadn't guessed that all this guilt was casting another shadow between them.

"You know," she said after a while, "it's easy as a teenager to look back at the situation with twenty-twenty hindsight. But back then, when you were in kindergarten, you wouldn't have understood what was going on around you. Little kids don't really know what college is, or alcohol, or that people are capable of doing terrible things. Most five-year-olds can't even grasp the difference between fantasy and reality. Think of it—when you were five you believed in Santa Claus coming down chimneys and elves making toys at the North Pole. You thought that the tooth fairy brought you silver dollars and that Easter bunnies brought baskets full of candy to children all over the world. Think of what kind of mind a child must have to believe things like that. I doubt you had any clear comprehension of what you witnessed, or what it meant. I think you were trying to help me by staying silent."

Maggie did not contradict her, though in her mind she knew better. The problem was not only her silence at age five, but her fear at age six, her coldness at age eight, and her distance by age twelve. For nine years she had treated her mother as a pariah and she wondered how much time it would take to correct the damage.

Emma propped some pillows against the headboard and scooted back. "Let's talk about something else. I want to hear all about the homecoming dance."

Maggie kicked off her flip-flops, climbed onto the bed, and stretched her long legs beside her mother's shorter ones.

Emma wanted to put her arm around her daughter, but she couldn't gauge whether Maggie would be comfortable with that. Instead she patted her daughter's knee. "Tell me everything."

CHAPTER 23

JACKSON'S coffee shop stood in the center of the town's historic district, where nineteenth-century brick stores with first-floor picture windows were shaded by green-and-blue awnings. When Emma stepped inside, she cringed at the jingle of bells and instinctively turned the right side of her face toward the room, hoping to shield her bruised cheek from the eyes of the middle-aged women who leaned together on the candy-striped sofa to her right.

Normally this room soothed Emma with its warmly bitter smells, but today the place struck her as too bright and exposed. Most people in Jackson still remembered her scandal, and if they recognized Sandra McCluskey sitting with her and Maggie, what new waves of gossip might circulate at the grocery store? And yet, when Maggie announced the location for this meeting, Emma had felt she shouldn't object. This reunion was for the benefit of her daughter, who was now closing the door behind them. Maggie could stage-manage the scene as she wished, choosing the setting, props, and characters, and Emma would play her assigned part. Her sole improvisation was to claim a table at the far end of the front window, in a corner partly hidden by a ficus tree. She hung her sweater on the back of a chair facing away from the other tables, then scanned the room for Sandra, dreading her first glimpse of the woman. Seeing nothing but strangers' faces concentrating on newspapers and companions, she returned to Maggie, who was standing in line at the counter, reading the blackboard specials written in orange and blue and purple chalk.

"What would you like?" Emma asked.

"The house blend."

"You drink coffee?" Emma had always served her daughter hot chocolate.

"No, Mom. I drink Kool-Aid." Maggie flinched at her own reflexive sarcasm. "Sorry."

"No problem." Emma bought a cranberry muffin, hoping to add some padding to her daughter's sharp elbows, and together they moved to the corner, waiting in silence while Maggie picked walnuts from the muffin and chewed them one by one.

Outside the window, Emma saw Sandra coming down the sidewalk, and realized that she shouldn't have worried about gossip. No one would recognize her old student, because Rob had been right about the woman's change—new hair, more pounds, and when she stepped inside, the sleep-deprived expression of a single mother with a young child. Still, Emma knew Sandra immediately—that pale face and weak chin, those eyes without fire—a mature version of the college girl who had answered questions with mumbles. But even as she gritted her teeth, prepared to be contemptuous, Emma recalled something else from that semester, an occasion when Sandra came to her office and briefly felt inspired to write a very good paper. Yes, Emma remembered making a connection with this girl—which had made Sandra's subsequent lies all the more painful.

Sandra did not buy a drink. She walked to their table and stood behind the empty chair, reluctant to sit without an invitation.

"This is Mrs. Murdock," Maggie said.

"We've met," Emma replied. She could feel Sandra's eyes on her swollen cheek, and angled her face away, waving toward the empty seat. "You asked to see me?"

"Maggie requested it," Sandra began as she sat down.

"You didn't want to come?" asked Emma. "Then maybe you should go."

"No—" Sandra paused, all of her prepared words evaporating at the first glimpse of her professor. "I've wanted to speak to you for years, but it's hard . . . I guess I thought that if I apologized to Maggie, she might pass it along, and I'd never have to see you."

"Is that what you would prefer, Sandy? Never to see me?"

"My name isn't Sandy anymore. I go by my middle name, Grace."

Emma flicked her wrist, as if dismissing a fly.

Staring into her fingers, Grace Murdock pondered the white line where her wedding ring had once been. She wished she could convince Professor Greene that nine years might change a woman, especially when those years included marriage, divorce, and motherhood.

Maggie saw her teacher's lowered eyes and her mother's tightened jaw, and she knew that Mrs. Murdock wouldn't have a chance if her mother went on the attack. Maybe her teacher deserved that; maybe she should let her mom rip into this woman, revenge being better than reconciliation. But Maggie hadn't brought them together to witness a fight.

"You should tell my mom the story you told me," she prodded gently. "That's why we're here."

Grace closed her eyes and was silent for over a minute. Was she praying? Maggie wondered. Was she going to get all weird on them? Opening her eyes, the teacher slowly began to offer the facts she knew about Jacob's hypocrisy, Jacob's cruelty, Jacob's heartless murder of a cat. "If he could do that to an animal, I think he could have done it to a person." Grace looked into Emma's face.

Yes, Emma nodded. People who tortured animals were very likely to abuse human beings. The children at the center often shared horror stories of slaughtered puppies, one-eyed cats, and rabbits tossed into dumpsters.

Grace explained how she had come to be at the Greenes' house, and how, after she and Kyle left, they had panicked and concocted a false story. She didn't confess that the story was largely hers; instead she described the lies as a collaboration, letting Professor Greene assign percentages of guilt, like a grade on a group project.

"I'm so sorry," Grace said at the end, "for everything I did to you."

"What is it you think you did to me?" asked Emma.

"I made you lose your job."

Emma looked out the window at a pair of laughing Holford girls, walking with backpacks on their shoulders. Leaving academia had been a hard breakup because she loved the literature and the rambling classroom discussions, the enthusiasm of the brightest students and the long summer months of writing and reading, but she wouldn't admit to Grace that she had any regrets.

"You didn't cause me to lose my job; that change was coming anyway. And the job I took in Washington was a better fit."

"If I didn't make you lose your job," Grace continued, "I made you lose other things—like your house. Wouldn't you have stayed out at Wade's Creek, if it weren't for that night?"

Emma didn't like the direction this conversation was taking—as if this student could exert so much power over her life. Instead she watched Maggie blow ripples across the top of her coffee. "Were you sorry to leave our old house?"

Maggie shrugged. "It's really convenient now, to be living so close to Kate, where we can walk to all the stuff in town. But when I was little, I remember missing the creek and the magnolia that I used to climb. There weren't any good climbing trees at our house."

Emma looked back out the window. The loss of her house, the loss of Rob, the loss of her job at Holford, none of it mattered so much as the one key thing—the most important thing of all—the loss of her daughter's confidence. The image of Maggie's bedroom door slowly closing flashed across Emma's mind, combined with a hundred other visions: Maggie turning her face away on Rob's shoulder, taking a step back when Emma reached for her at a school picnic, looking disappointed when her mother arrived in the afterschool pickup line.

Which was why the hug yesterday had felt so amazing. After nine years of awkward semi-hugs at holiday visits and mechanical kisses on the cheek, without joy, without love, Maggie had finally embraced her mother, and for the first time in her life Emma understood the meaning of the word *embrace*—to be encircled, bolstered, to be upheld. For years Emma had told herself that Maggie would someday understand the past and forgive her, and maybe that hug was the beginning.

She felt a sudden urge for Grace Murdock to be gone. "Is there anything else you have to say?"

Grace hesitated, her eyes falling to her lap. "Yes." She reached into her purse, her right hand emerging in a tightly closed fist, which opened slowly, finger by finger, to reveal Emma's charm bracelet.

Emma stared at the silver owl, the horseshoe, and ballet slippers. She reached out and lifted the bracelet, inspecting the half-inch pewter book that opened to one page engraved with her maiden initials, *EMP*. Emma Margaret Patrick.

"I lied to the police about it," Grace explained. "I told them I was wearing my own charm bracelet that night at your house. I even drove to Charlottesville on the morning of Jacob's death, to buy a silver bracelet and a bunch of charms so I could show them to the police. And they did ask to see it the next day, but they couldn't tell that mine was brand-new. Maybe a female police officer would have noticed how shiny the charms were, but those were male deputies."

"Kyle gave this to you," Emma murmured as she held the charms against her wrist.

"No." Grace blushed. "That's the thing. You were right that Kyle was a thief—he stole stuff every day, including jewelry. But he never took this bracelet from you. I did."

Emma stared at Grace, caught between confusion and shock.

"I went to your office to talk about a paper, and your door was open, and I saw the bracelet. After watching Kyle steal for months, the idea just occurred to me, and I snatched it without thinking."

"So why did you wear it to my house?"

"I had no idea we'd be stopping at your house. I didn't even notice that I had it on, until you grabbed my wrist."

Emma looked at her initials, almost spelling the word EMPTY, and suddenly, without thought or reason she started laughing. Dark laughter, bitter laughter. Laughter at the ridiculous irony of it all. She had threatened to have Kyle expelled because of this bracelet, accusing him of the one theft he didn't commit, and that accusation had sparked her confrontation with Jacob. No wonder Kyle had called her crazy— he probably had no idea why she had grabbed Sandra's wrist and was waving it in the air.

And she had been crazy, after all, to assume that the boys were the guilty ones, and the invisible girl was merely a silent onlooker. How blind of her to ignore the truth—that women could be just as guilty as men, just as devious and violent. In spite of all the crimes that Kyle and Jacob might have committed in the past, on that night nine years ago she and Sandra had been the thief and the killer.

"I don't see what's funny." Grace resented being laughed at. "I've been trying to make up for this, wishing for years there was something I could do."

Emma heard mechanical apologies every day at the shelter. But why not take this woman up on her phony regret?

"There *is* something you can do."

Staring into her former student's eyes, Emma spoke deliberately. "Write down everything you've told me—all the details about Jacob's violence and Kyle's thievery and how you stole my bracelet. Explain every aspect of what happened at my house nine and a half years ago, from the moment you arrived to the stories you told the police. Write it all down, and sign it. Then deliver one copy to the editor of the *Jackson Gazette*, and mail another copy to Janice Lee at the *Chronicle*. The Jackson paper should feature it in their letters to the editor, and Janice will probably use it as the basis for a retrospective article. I bet she'll ask to speak to you, and I want you to accept. In fact, I want you to accept every interview request that comes your way.

"I want vindication," Emma continued. "Maybe then everyone in this town will stop flinching when they see me." She paused. "Do you remember the long poem by Coleridge that our class read? *The Rime of the Ancient Mariner?*"

Grace nodded.

"It's your turn to be the mariner."

Grace stared into her hands again. What was it between this mother and daughter, always asking her to tell her story again and again? From what she remembered of Coleridge, the mariner was a pretty pathetic figure. And yet, he was also a redeemed Christian, lessening his burden with every recitation.

"Okay." She hesitated. "There's just one thing. Let me wait until the spring, maybe in April. Once I send this letter to the Jackson paper, and everyone in town knows who I am and what I've done, I'll lose my job, and I need this job to support my daughter. Give me a chance to finish this school year and line up a job in another place, far from here."

"All right." Emma shrugged. "April. Or better yet, May. May six-teenth. Tell the papers you have a special story to mark the tenth anniversary of Jacob Stewart's death. And here—" Emma reached forward with the bracelet. "Keep this. Show my initials engraved to anyone who asks. It will be a reminder of what you did."

Emma dropped the bracelet onto the table in front of Grace. Grace stared at the chain, not wanting to touch it. She knew it would burn.

Instead she opened her purse and held it open beneath the lip of the table. With one finger, she scooted the bracelet over the edge and let it fall inside.

Grace glanced at Maggie. "I can arrange to have you switched to Mrs. Newel's geometry class, no questions asked."

Maggie nodded.

"Well." Grace scooted her chair back. "I guess I'll leave you two." She stood and lifted her purse to her shoulder before glancing at Emma one last time. "Believe it or not, I really am sorry."

Emma shook her head. She heard so many false apologies in her job, the words sounded mechanical. Still, she lifted her eyes to look at the invisible girl one last time. "If you do these things, you won't need to feel sorry."

CHAPTER 24

HOW typical, Grace Murdock thought as she left the coffee shop. Her English professor had given her a writing assignment with a deadline. Should she do it in MLA format, with footnotes and a bibliography? Maybe she should submit an abstract to Professor Greene, and ask for comments on a rough draft.

But why was she so bitter? This second round at the coffee shop was supposed to have lessened her guilt, throwing another handful of dirt onto her unburied past. Once again the process had been incomplete, and she could feel her conscience weighing on her shoulders, heavy as a winter coat, so that now, as she passed the local artists' cooperative, with its glass ornaments shimmering in the window, its sponge-painted ceramics and watercolor barns, she felt that she was the sole blight on this town's insistent charm, the human stain in a well-scrubbed community.

Confession was not good for the soul. Confession was a trauma, endlessly humiliating, reviving the original pain in all of its acuteness. And how arrogant of Professor Greene to leave her with the bracelet.

How arrogant to instruct her, an adult woman, as if she were still an undergraduate—to tell her what to say and do, what to reveal to strangers. Why should she carry this token of her crime when she was so much changed, so much better? Couldn't Professor Greene see the transformation?

Outside the artists' co-op, a green metal trash can was filled almost to the brim with papers and plastic cups and pound-cake crusts from customers exiting the coffee shop. Grace lifted the bracelet from her purse and held it over the garbage. Screw Professor Greene. Screw the *Jackson Gazette.* Screw this entire, pathetic town. She let go of the bracelet and watched it fall across the lid of a coffee cup, tipping the black dregs over the silver horseshoe and pewter book as the chain settled into the crevices of a crumpled white bag.

Grace continued walking past the bookstore and real estate offices, toward the green car parked at the end of the block. She owed nothing to anyone. Not to Maggie, not to Emma, not to the townspeople around her. And yet, when she reached her car door and took out her keys, she thought of the child waiting for her on the other side of the mountains. To her daughter, she owed everything, would gladly give everything, and how could she face Lily if she did not lay the past to rest? How could she be a good parent if she was not a good person?

The thought of the bracelet lying in that swill of bitter coffee seemed suddenly grotesque, like stories of fetuses tossed into dumpsters. What if Maggie and her mother came out of the coffee shop, walked toward the artists' co-op, and saw, in that trash can, the abandoned bracelet? They would know how quickly she had failed, how shallow was her apology.

Grace turned and was relieved to see no one near the trash can. Hurrying back, she reached in with her thumb and index finger and gingerly removed the dripping bracelet, wiping it with a tissue from her purse and putting it back into her pocket. She would do what had been asked of her. She would write the letters and display the bracelet to anyone who needed proof. But she would sign the letters with the name Sandra McCluskey. Grace Murdock would have nothing to do with it. And when the interviews stopped and the furor died down, and she was established in another city with another job, Sandra McCluskey would mail the bracelet back to Emma Greene with no return address, as proof that she had completed her Herculean labor. That mailing would be the last act of Sandra McCluskey's life, and maybe then Grace Murdock could raise her daughter with a free conscience. Maybe then, Grace could have some hope of becoming amazing.

CHAPTER 25

"Wow, Mom." Maggie took another sip of her coffee. "That was pretty intense. I wouldn't have wanted to be one of your college students."

"I was never that demanding with my students. I probably should have been."

"Things should be pretty interesting around here next May"— Maggie smiled—"once she publishes that letter."

Emma shrugged. "I doubt whether she'll do it."

Maggie's eyes widened. "But she seems so contrite."

"Of course she is. Right now, in our presence, I'm sure she feels very apologetic. But seven months from now, when you and I aren't sitting in front her, and she's gotten on with her life, she won't feel the urgency. She'll have another job lined up, and she won't want to relive the past . . . Besides"—Emma paused—"I don't suppose I really care whether she does it or not. I think it would be good for *her*—she might not realize it now, but it would probably lift a heavy weight off her shoulders. If she lets May sixteenth come and go without saying anything, she'll carry that knowledge with her for the rest of her life."

"So it's like a test?"

"In a way."

"And you didn't mean all that stuff about wanting vindication?"

Emma smiled. *Vindication* was a melodramatic word, straight from her classes on Mary Wollstonecraft.

"You know, Mom," Maggie continued, "all these years I've been a little bit afraid of you."

"I know."

"I'm thinking now that it was stupid."

Emma shook her head. "Not stupid. It was natural. Sometimes I scare myself."

She enjoyed seeing Maggie smile. Maybe she and her daughter would grow to have the same ironic sense of humor. "Can I ask you something?"

"Sure," said Maggie.

"At your high school, is it just Mrs. Murdock that's been bothering you, or is it the whole place?"

Maggie thought for a while. "Mrs. Murdock is the worst part, but the whole place is pretty lame."

Emma looked down into her coffee. "Your dad and I have been talking for the past few months about a private school in Washington, a couple miles from where I live. It's supposed to be really good, with a lot more choices in the curriculum, great teachers and serious students, and terrific facilities. They've got an indoor swimming pool. We were thinking we should all go and visit it."

"Visit it?" Maggie asked. "As in maybe apply there for next year?"

"Only if you like it."

"We could afford a private school?"

"It would be tight. But all the money from my parents' estate has been saved for your education, and it could cover a few years of high school and most of your college. We could manage the rest."

"You think Dad would be okay if I moved away?"

"I think he'd miss you a lot, and you'll have to talk to him about it. But he's the one who brought it up. He thought you might get a better education in D.C., and now that you're becoming a young woman, we both thought it might be time for you to stay with me for a while."

"What about Kate?"

"You could come back to visit her every month, when you visit your dad. And she'd always be welcome in D.C. We were also thinking you could spend your summers in Jackson, since Washington gets miserably hot."

They've got it all worked out, Maggie thought. How much say did she really have in the matter? But when she tried to gauge her feelings, she realized that she didn't mind the idea. She remembered hearing Mike Hodges say that Georgetown was at the top of his college wish list, so maybe this was her chance to get out of this small town, to live somewhere full of choices. It might make sense to go to a better school, in a bigger city with lots of different people, so long as Kate wasn't abandoned.

Maggie noticed that her mom was wringing her hands, and it looked kind of endearing. She wasn't about to jump up and down at the idea of living with her mother, and she would never commit to more than a one-year trial at a new school, but she could see herself spending more time with her mom, now that they were beginning to understand each other.

"Would you like to check out the school's website when we get back to Sarah's?" Emma asked.

"Okay," said Maggie. "Sure."

CHAPTER 26

DRIVING back to Washington on Sunday afternoon, with Jackson growing distant beyond the Blue Ridge, Emma could feel the past growing equally distant. Maggie had made no promises, but Emma thought there was a good chance that a year from now she would no longer be the parent in exile, the woman who commuted back and forth for scraps of time with her child. She would be a mother with a teenage daughter living in the next room—a room Maggie might now decorate, claiming the space that she had thus far treated as a third-rate hotel room.

Emma didn't think Junot would mind the presence of a teenage girl in their lives. He would be happy for her. With his calm manner, he might help Emma to be a better parent.

She had no illusions about the difficulty of raising a teenager, but so much time had already been lost. She resolved to be patient through every adolescent mood, never to say cruel words, never to match rage with rage. When fits of melancholy fell upon her daughter, she would do as Keats advised and hold Maggie's hand and feed deep, deep, upon her peerless eyes. There had been too much anger in her life; she needed much more love.

Let it go, thought Emma as the highway passed beneath her. *Let it all go.*

ACKNOWLEDGMENTS

Many readers have helped to shape this novel. Thanks go to my classmates at the 2011 Taos Summer Writers' Conference—Ro Gunetilleke, Sarah Hedborn, Nancy Best, Nancy Dickeman, and Kathleen Andersen-Wyman—all wonderful writers and expert readers. And special thanks to our teacher, Jonis Agee, from whom I have much more to learn. We are all indebted to Sharon Oard Warner for organizing the conference, and for building a community of writers in Taos for the past twelve years.

I am also grateful to Professor Scott Sundby, from the Washington and Lee University School of Law, for sharing his legal expertise, and to Judy Casteele, director of Project Horizon in Lexington, Virginia, for her knowledge of women's shelters and social services for battered women. The sharp eyes of Beth Pryor Colocci, Susan Ullman, and Arik Levinson saved me from several factual errors, and Barbara Beachler and David Brodie's advice and support have been terrific.

Finally, many thanks go to my editor, Jackie Cantor; my agent, Gail Hochman; my international agent, Marianne Merola; and my wonderful team in Germany, including Kristina Arnold, editor, and Britta Mummler, translator. All of these women have supported my work with unfailing intelligence and enthusiasm.

ALL THE TRUTH

Readers Guide